When the Lonely Walk

When the Lonely Walk

Abi Payton

The Book Guild Ltd

First published in Great Britain in 2023 by
The Book Guild Ltd
Unit E2 Airfield Business Park,
Harrison Road, Market Harborough,
Leicestershire. LE16 7UL
Tel: 0116 2792299
www.bookguild.co.uk
Email: info@bookguild.co.uk
Twitter: @bookguild

Copyright © 2023 Abi Payton

The right of Abi Payton to be identified as the author of this
work has been asserted by them in accordance with the
Copyright, Design and Patents Act 1988.

All rights reserved. No part of this publication may be
reproduced, transmitted, or stored in a retrieval system, in any form or by any means,
without permission in writing from the publisher, nor be otherwise circulated in
any form of binding or cover other than that in which it is published and without
a similar condition being imposed on the subsequent purchaser.

This work is entirely fictitious and bears no resemblance to any persons living or dead.

Typeset in 11pt Minion Pro

Printed on FSC accredited paper
Printed and bound in Great Britain by 4edge Limited

ISBN 978 1915853 158

British Library Cataloguing in Publication Data.
A catalogue record for this book is available from the British Library.

To Hayley,
For always supporting me.

1

I'm running as fast as I can.

This has to be the steepest hill I've ever tried to climb. My breath catches in my throat as I try to gulp in air; I'm not used to running like this. My glasses are slipping down my face from the sweat now covering my nose. I think my fight-or-flight instinct might be kicking in – because I'm sure that adrenaline is the only way that I'm managing to keep running.

But still I don't stop. I can't. I need to get as far away as possible. I'm not a hundred per cent sure that no one saw me climbing over the fence; certainly, it's pitch black, but the streetlights are still on and, though I've chosen a part of the fence that's mostly hidden from the house, I feel paranoid that someone looking out the kitchen window could have seen me. Even if it wasn't when I was climbing over the fence and dropping over the top of it, then I could have been seen scrambling through the undergrowth, onto the quiet village road that the house stands on. Anyone could have seen me. And I'm guessing that if they did, the police are being called already.

I'm not a criminal. I haven't done anything to be locked up in a house with police coming after me if I leave. I'm not a murderer, or a thief, or the illustrious leader of a prominent criminal gang. In some ways, that would be preferable, because at least I would be being kept here for a reason. And you know what? I don't want to have to do this, to have to run away in the night. What right do they have to keep me in that house against my will?

The short story: the Mental Health Act. That's their excuse for locking me up. It's technically legal – but morally questionable, in my eyes at least. I'm only eighteen. I shouldn't be here. No wonder I'm running away.

I reach the top of the hill, and I'm exhausted – my run slows to a jog and then a walk. But I have to keep moving. For all I know, the police could be looking for me already. I don't want to go back to the hospital. I have to keep moving.

I'm rubbing at my chest as I cross the road over to the woodland path. It will be dark in the woods. No one is going to find me there.

2

By the time that I realise we're crashing, the car is rolling down the side of a long grass bank. I scream, but the noise is lost in the screeching of brakes. Hard thumps sound above me as the car bangs into trees and asphalt and the hard grass bank. I'm strapped in – for the first time, glad that my mother is so insistent about wearing seatbelts – and I'm tethered to my seat as the car bashes and rolls.

It's dark and the light of car headlights flashes all around me, from our own car and the cars in the road above. The turmoil feels like it lasts both a lifetime and no time at all. Suddenly, the car stops moving. I scream again, and this time I can hear it. With a final crash, we are wedged up against a few sturdy trees, the car tipped slightly towards one side.

For a second, everything is still.

It takes a second for me to come down to reality. In the front seat, my mum is groaning, and on the driver's side, my dad sounds like he's trying to form words. I can't even understand if they are real words, let alone decipher what it is that he's trying to say. Maybe I'm panicking too powerfully.

I close my eyes and force myself to take a deep breath. I realise that screams are still tumbling out of my mouth and finally I shut them back in. I can hear my dad better now, I'm on the cusp of understanding him...

"Phone," he manages to gurgle, and I finally get it.

Where is my phone? I pat both my pockets, but it isn't there. Slowly, agonisingly, I manage to lift my head from where it's resting on my own chest. I blink hard, once, twice, trying to pay attention to my surroundings. It's dark, and I can't see much, but I can just about see the back seat beside me. I try to calm myself, closing my eyes for a brief second, praying that when I open them, my phone will be within reach. No luck, however. When I open my eyes again, I look back at the seat – but no phone. Nothing.

I breathe out, feeling somewhere between anger and panic. I don't know what to do. My mum is still groaning somewhere nearby. I don't know what to do, I don't know what to do...

Then I see it, and my heart leaps. Resting on the side of the footwell by the other back seat, I can see a vague glint that has to be the screen of my phone.

I can't hear my mum now.

I push that thought out of my mind and, after a brief hesitation, unclip my seatbelt. The car can't roll any more, surely? I push that out of my mind too as I tentatively try and shuffle slightly upwards, over towards the other seat. I can feel on my chest already where the seatbelt has bruised me. Luckily, it doesn't feel like anything's broken. I'm aching, definitely, but not like anything is badly wrong.

Finally I reach the other seat, moving slowly and carefully in order not to unbalance the car. I don't know if that's scientifically possible, but I feel like I would rather be over-cautious than dead.

I lean down, though at this angle I can't quite see the glint of a screen that I thought I saw a moment ago. I pray that it's just the light; if I can't find the phone here, I don't know how we're supposed to get out of this.

But to my intense relief, I only have to rummage for a moment before my hand connects with the cold screen of my phone. I grab *it, forgetting about being slow and careful, and pull it up to my ear. My hand is shaking as I dial 999.*

A calm operator answers me and I feel instantly soothed, instantly a little unburdened, to have a human listening to me as I tell them what's happened. The voice on the other end stays composed, collected, and tells me that people are on their way. I believe her. I trust her.

But I don't tell her the reason that we crashed.

3

I find that I like these woods. When I first arrived and I drove past those woods with my parents, I thought about how fun it would be to have leave from the hospital to come here. I imagined spending my days walking through the trees, exploring. I even heard another patient say once that there's a zip wire in a playground somewhere in the woods. I've never seen it, though. No wonder – I've never actually gotten to go up here before.

Now, though, I'm nowhere near the part of the woods that we drove past. I don't think I'm anywhere near the zip wire either. I'm starting to worry that I'm not near anything. It's pitch black; what I can see is very limited. Not to mention, it's almost 10pm, and there's no one around. Despite the fact that I've been obsessing about running away from the hospital for weeks, I'm starting to worry that I haven't thought this through. Face it, Heather – you're lost.

At least with the light of my phone, I can just about see the path to stay on it. Wandering off the path would not be good. I mean, it's not like I'm headed anywhere specific, so I guess it wouldn't delay me as such, but… well, the idea of wandering off the path kind of brings to mind a whole new degree of lost. At least on the path, I'm 'colouring within the lines', as it were.

It's a nice summer's night, at least. The sun has gone, but the air is warm, a remnant of today's lovely weather. This would be a lot worse if it was winter, I'm sure. At least I'm kind of comfortable.

BANG.

The sudden bang is so loud that I physically step backwards. I freeze, shaken out of my rambling thoughts. Some kind of explosion in the woods – that can't be good. I need to get away from here. Except – where exactly did it come from? If I just blindly stumble on along the path, I could be walking right into something. But if I turn around and walk back – what if it came from that direction?

I need to calm down. I'm vulnerable, and explosions are bad, but I need to calm down. Panicking isn't going to help the situation. I just need to… I just need to pick a direction. And stick with it. Just pick a direction, and keep walking. Casually. Calmly. Collectedly.

I count to ten in my head, slowing my breathing before I start walking. However, I stick to the path even more religiously now. The possibility of actual danger has hit me like a train. I've been thinking so much about getting away, I haven't thought about the dangers of being out alone; there could be a man hidden in the bushes. And there's no one to hear me scream.

My heart starts to race and before I know what I'm doing, my pace has sped up along the path. It looks like there's a clearing up ahead – and a light. That has to be a good thing, right? If nothing else, it calms my heart rate to know that I will at least be able to see my attacker approach me there.

But… what's that?

I'm frozen to the spot. What is that, lying on the path ahead of me? Is it… a *body*? I should be reaching for my phone to call an ambulance, but… it can't be a body. It's… it's glowing, an ethereal blue light that seems to emanate from every one of its cells. It's like one of those glowing aliens, except that it looks… somehow *human*…

Though my first instinct is to run in the opposite direction, I find that my legs are taking tentative steps towards the body. For some reason that I can't explain, I feel oddly unsettled, but I keep walking. Now that I'm a bit closer, I can see that it's a girl, wearing a loose sundress and a pair of open-toed sandals, a zip-up hoodie wrapped around her shoulders. She looks oddly well presented for a girl lying on the floor of the woods at 10pm.

But there's something... there's something that unsettles me about her. It's not the way she's lying; she is stock-still, her head tipped sideways to rest on her cloud of curly blonde hair. It's nothing about her that unsettles me, it's just... the glowing. It's like I can't quite focus on it; it's nothing like anything I've seen before. The light surrounds her – it's not like her phone is just on in her pocket. The light seems to be emanating straight from her.

I'm highly unsettled and I don't know how to react, but I can't deny that I feel quite *drawn* to the girl. She can't be much younger than I am. And she's lying on the floor of the woods. She doesn't look hurt, but... I can't just *leave* her. Can I?

I reach one cautious hand out, where it hovers above hers for several moments. Do I touch her? Do I call the police? And say what – that there's a glowing girl in the woods? That would go down *so* well. Even an ambulance... well, they'd take me instead, wouldn't they?

My hand withdraws. I can't do anything. She's not hurt, she's not in danger. Still, leaving her just lying there in the middle of the woods... who knows who might find her? Who knows what they might do to her?

I stiffen my resolve, reach down to her hand and grasp it. "Hey? Are you alright?"

Silence.

Then her eyes snap open. And she's grinning. "Hey, friend. Where are you headed?"

4

The emergency services take all three of us to A&E.
   I should be relieved, but the rescue is almost as traumatic as the crash itself. My mum lies unconscious as they cut her out of her seatbelt, while my dad just about manages to stay awake to communicate with the paramedics. I feel immensely guilty to be the only one properly awake. Still, the car has gotten so bashed around from when it rolled down the bank that they have to take the roof off to get me out of the back seat.
   I ride alone in the back of the ambulance car. I'm not sure what it's supposed to be called, and at that moment I don't care. The things my mum said about me – she was right. I am bad. This is all my fault.
   There's a paramedic in the front seat who keeps up a steady stream of chitchat that I suspect she doesn't really expect me to follow, let alone reply to. I guess she just wants to keep me as distracted as possible as my whole family travels to the emergency department. I find that I'm shaking even though it's warm in the car and they've wrapped me in one of those tinfoil blankets for shock.
   The paramedic turns to glance at me and her face falls into an expression of sad sympathy. "I know this is scary," she tries to

reassure me. "But you're going to be fine, OK? You were really lucky."

I frown and look down into my lap, unable to think of a response, let alone convey it from my brain to my mouth. The paramedic doesn't look that upset, though. I think she can tell that I'm not being rude; I'm just doing the best I can.

Time seems to be moving weirdly, so I'm not sure how long I'm in the car. In some ways it feels like a long time, but also it is kind of a blur. At some point, I find myself sitting on a bed in the A&E department. There's a doctor looking at the various scrapes and bruises that I've accrued in the crash. Luckily these camouflage the cuts that were there already.

"You've been very lucky," he proclaims at last, frowning at me. "That was a nasty crash. You're lucky to have only broken a few ribs."

Breaking a few ribs doesn't sound so lucky to me, but I allow it. "How are my mum and dad?" I ask, my voice coming out scratchy and urgent.

The doctor looks over to the nurse, who smiles patiently. "Someone will be through to talk to you about them soon, I'm sure," she says calmly. "Try not to worry."

But I am worried. Who wouldn't be worried in this situation? Still, I know that the nurse means well. She's probably not allowed to tell me anything. I mean, they can probably tell my parents stuff about me, but maybe they can't tell me stuff about my parents. I don't know how it works. It's never been relevant before.

The doctor is long gone by this point. The nurse, who is still checking me over, lays a hand on my shoulder in a way that I'm sure is meant to be comforting. Somehow it feels like her touch burns me, but I force myself not to flinch away, to sit quietly and let her touch me if she wants. I'm never keen on being touched, but today I feel so shaken up that I can barely bear it. I don't need questions about that right now, however; I need to sit still, pretend I'm OK and be good.

Still, something clearly shows on my face, because as the nurse pulls away from doing my blood pressure again, she tilts her head to the side, looking at me.

"Is there anything you want to tell me?" she asks. It bites like an accusation despite her gentle but business-like tone. Maybe she's not accusing me, but she's accusing someone.

And though part of me aches to tell her – hell, to tell someone, to tell anyone – I know that it's better to keep quiet. I might be hurting, but I know what I have to lose. Tonight has proved to me what I have to lose. It's too much for me to take the chance.

I shake my head. I keep my eyes lowered, looking at the hospital-room floor, but I feel the nurse's eyes on mine. I hate having to keep a distance from everyone like this. It feels like her eyes are burning into mine, but I don't look up.

She nods silently at last when she seems to realise that I am a pro at shutting myself off. A lot of people think that I don't make a lot of eye contact because I'm shy; and although that's true a lot of the time, sometimes I don't want them to be able to read too much from looking into my eyes. Moreover, that's just on a normal day. Right now, I'm emotional and filled with adrenaline still from the crash. I know that if we make eye contact, this nurse is going to know that there's something not quite right.

So I keep my eyes down, mentally tracing the pattern on the lino. I have to keep myself distracted. With any luck, I can get out of here soon. And everything can go back to normal and everything will be fine.

The nurse looks like she's about to speak when the curtain around my bed is pulled back again. The same doctor comes through the gap, not bothering to ask if that's OK. He doesn't speak immediately, his eyes on what looks like my chart, and the nurse and I wait awkwardly for him to give his pronouncement.

His eyes finally flick up to me and I make eye contact with him. For one, I'm too desperate to know if my parents are hurt or worse; but more, I'm certain that the thought of anything being wrong in my demeanour hasn't even crossed his mind. My vital signs are fine, so he's not worried. He won't notice anything in my eyes.

"Well," he says, in what I suspect is his nice-bedside-manner voice. He gives me a tired and rather robotic-looking smile. "As I say, you've been very lucky. I've just had the rest of our tests back and you seem largely unharmed."

I swallow. "OK," I say, trying to keep my patience. "Yeah, I mean... that's good... but how are my mum and dad?"

His smile remains in place. I try to take comfort from it as I wait for him to speak, but it's so solid that it just looks disingenuous. "Your dad has a few broken bones," he begins. "Getting around might be a bit of a challenge for a few months, but essentially he's fine."

Mostly, I'm relieved, but I don't get a chance to decide exactly how I feel about it before the doctor speaks again. "And your mum – she has a broken arm and quite a bad concussion," he tells me. "It's likely she won't remember any of the crash. There might be other side effects, brain injuries are tricky."

I nod like I understand as the doctor continues on about brain injury. From what I'm getting, they are both alive and will remain so despite the crash. That's all I was hoping for and now that it's come true, I feel giddy and a little light-headed.

Again I feel the nurse's eyes on me but again I ignore them. I'm still nodding when I realise that the doctor has stopped speaking and is looking at me too. "When can I go home?" I ask weakly.

5

Stood in the forest, it's the girl's warm, slightly sweaty hand enclosed around mine that drags me back to reality. I wouldn't call it *clinging*, but I'm in a pretty tight grip. I look down at her as she pulls herself to sitting, her legs crossed. She's still grinning. I feel like she should be more worried; she's just collapsed in a forest in the middle of the night.

The light has gone, as quickly and completely as if a switch has been flipped. The odd part, though, is that I don't remember the switch flipping. Somehow, she is just not glowing anymore. I start – understandably, I think – to doubt that she was ever glowing at all. Maybe it was a trick of the light. Or something.

"What's happened?" I ask cautiously, though I let her keep hold of my hand. I'm not quite sure exactly what to say. I'm very aware that we are in what is essentially a large, empty area of woodland, and it's late. This isn't something that I have a lot of experience with. I hesitate. "What have you been doing?"

To my surprise, her eyes twinkle, like she's exhilarated. "Lying," she replies. "Honest."

I frown as she grins expectantly, waiting for me to crack a smile. She could be waiting a while. It doesn't seem to faze her, though, and I'm slightly wrong-footed by her demeanour. Surely she should be scared, or at least slightly anxious? She can't be more than fourteen, and to be alone this late at night… I'm eighteen and I've been imagining attackers in the bushes. She shouldn't even be allowed out alone at this time. She must have a home. A mum and dad? Or a foster carer, even? Why hasn't someone stopped her leaving the house?

"What's your name?" I try again. Maybe she's in shock. Or using humour to mask her distress. I can't leave her here just because she's making dodgy jokes.

She squirms uncomfortably in a way that makes me narrow my eyes. Still, her grin doesn't falter. "Maeve," she says eventually.

Well, it's not beyond the realms of possibility, but something tells me that she's not being honest with me. I try a different tack. "I'm Heather," I tell her. "I… um… live near here. Shouldn't you be at home? Where do you live?"

I'm trying not to interrogate her, but in a situation like this, it's hard not to. She's biting her lip now as she looks at me, looking like she's wondering how truthful she has to be. I don't know what she's hiding from me, and at any other time I'd walk away – but out here at this time isn't safe for a young girl alone. I can't leave her. I need to ascertain who she is, and what's happened to get her here, unconscious.

"Come on," I say, half-sternly. "Please."

She shakes her head.

I sigh, frustrated as to how much this is making me feel like a bad-tempered teacher. "Look, I'm going to call an ambulance. Something's clearly happened and you were well out of it…"

She shakes her head again, but this time as she turns away from me, I notice something that fills me with alarm. "Are those bruises on your neck?" I blurt out, without even thinking, reaching out instinctively to touch them. Even in the dim light, now that I'm looking, it's clear that they're finger marks. Someone's tried to strangle her.

A lump rises in my throat that I quickly force away. This isn't about me.

The girl – Maeve – jerks away at lightning pace. She adjusts the neck of her hoodie self-consciously and sweeps her hair forward quickly – this isn't something that she wants anyone to see. Well, and why should she? She's scared. Of course she's scared. And it's no great leap to theorise why she won't tell me where she lives.

"Don't call an ambulance," she mutters at the ground, defensive mode firmly on. "I can't take it."

I approach things a bit more gently this time. "You were unconscious, sweet."

Her eyes snap up to meet mine. For the first time, I can see pleading in her gaze. "I'm fine now, though, aren't I?" she bursts out, her voice full of anger that I sense isn't directed at me.

For some reason, the rush of anger doesn't surprise me. Something flickers in me that might be a memory: of being hurt and trying to make it OK by denying everything. The panic, the worry. And the anger that followed.

I hesitate, trying to work out the best way to mollify the girl. I don't need to hear her life story; I don't even need to know who gave her the bruises. In fact, I don't think I want to know. All I need is to persuade her that she needs to let me call someone.

"They could..." I start to say, treading very carefully. "Maybe if things... aren't great... at home... they could find somewhere else for you to live."

She sighs loudly and frustratedly, like my concern is a huge inconvenience for her. "It's fine. I'm just... taking a break," she says quickly and a little touchily. Then she eyes me closely. "Why are you alone here in the middle of the night anyway?"

Ah. There's the question. I suppose all the interrogating that I've done to her tonight kind of warrants her asking questions back. Especially since it's not exactly been small talk that we've been making.

"Well, maybe I'm taking a break too," I defend myself feebly, only realising that with these words, I have legitimised her excuse. I can't call her out on that vagueness now that I'm using the same tack. Damn.

I realise that my eyes have wandered guiltily over to the side, and I force myself look up and meet her eyes again. But to my surprise, her whole face looks like she's won the jackpot. Looking straight at me, she seems to have had an idea.

"Can I come with you?" she asks hopefully.

Double damn. I might even go as far as 'fuck'.

What do I say? I don't know where I'm going. I have no… well, no *concrete* plans – and the vague ones that I do have don't involve taking a fourteen-year-old along with me. And, of course, there's the small fact that I'm under section and legally shouldn't have left the hospital without permission from my doctor.

I'm not mental, I'm not, but legally, I'm on the run. I can't take on a young girl. She'll slow me down, or get us caught – and even if she doesn't, where are we even going to be when the police find me? We could be in the middle of nowhere. What if she gets taken ill again? And what are her parents going to think when they find out I've been absconding with their little daughter? I'm going to come across as a kidnapper.

She smirks slightly at me. "You look panicked."

I bristle, frustrated that my manic thoughts are a joke to her. "Do you wonder why?" I mutter, forcing myself to keep my voice down. "I'm sorry, but I can't take a kid with me."

"And how old are you?" she demands quickly, clearly determined to get her own way.

I sigh. "Eighteen," I admit. "So, yes, I only just became an adult. But I'm definitely one. And you're not."

"I'm fourteen," she protests, sticking her chest out. "I can handle myself."

I can't help but scoff slightly. "Yes, fourteen-year-olds are known for being able to handle themselves."

She rolls her eyes, but even as snappy as my response was, I realise that I've managed to short-circuit my own logic – if I'm saying that she can't handle herself, how can I leave her alone? I need to get the kid somewhere safe, without getting caught myself. This is no easy situation; it's going to be near impossible. If I call an ambulance or the police, she'll run and I'll be left answering questions. What the fuck am I going to do?

As I sigh and look back up at her, I can't help but feel slightly irritated by the little smirk on her face. She knows I'm not just going to leave her.

"Fine," I breathe, giving in. "Fine. You can stick with me."

Maeve's smirk breaks out into a full-on grin. Before I know what's happening, she has grabbed my hand and started to march off, trailing me behind her.

"Let's go, then!" she says determinedly, already going.

"Where are we going?!" I protest, slightly indignant. After all, I'm supposed to be the older one. Shouldn't I be in charge? Or shouldn't I at least know where a fourteen-year-old is leading me to?

She turns to me, still with that grin. "I don't know," she announces cheerfully. "But we can't stay here!"

Well. That's true, I suppose. I'm hoping that she has a plan of where we're going to, because I've got no idea. Where do I take a potentially ill kid? In the middle of the night? This isn't what I planned for, and I'm coming up blank on ideas. What do I do? What do *we* do?

Christ, we've become a unit already. What have I let myself into?

6

A week after the crash, I am back at school.

I don't tell anyone what's happened, though I'm guessing some teachers might have been told. I assume my mum phoned and told them. Though, to be fair, I'm not really sure that there's much to tell them. I'm fully recovered; my 'lucky' broken ribs even feel a little bit better. My dad's on crutches and my mum has no memory of what happened, like the doctor suggested she wouldn't. In any case, it's in the past, now. It has to be.

A few people in my class ask where I've been, and in response, I just stay vague – I tell people that I had a tummy bug but I feel fine now. It's easiest, and I'm used to lying. I don't need the hassle of everyone asking about the big, dramatic car crash.

School has been tricky for a little while. The work itself is fine, I don't have any problems with that; it's more having to be around people. I've always been shy, but now I find myself purposefully avoiding everyone. It's too hard to have to pretend that everything is normal when it hasn't been normal for ages. I try, I do, to stay and concentrate on conversation that I used to enjoy; but, more often than not, I find myself making an excuse and sneaking off. It's just too tiring.

I've found a staircase that only leads to locked doors. I don't think I'm supposed to go up there, but it's quiet, and when I'm up there I don't have to talk to people. The only way I can muster up enough energy to actually go to lessons is by recharging on this staircase, my head resting against the cool stone wall as I relish the total silence.

I wonder, sometimes, where my friends think I am. To be fair, sometimes I wonder if they actually notice. I get the impression that they know that something is wrong, but I haven't told any of them the truth about the various things going on for me. I don't think they could take it. Or on the other hand, I think they would laugh. Or tell someone. Or not believe me.

Maybe I'm not giving them enough credit. Still, I firmly believe that telling them the truth won't lead anywhere good.

In spite of this, though, I know that the situation the way it is isn't sustainable. Eventually, something is going to have to give. In the Harry Potter fanfiction I write, right now would be the point where Remus Lupin would notice that something was wrong with his Fourth-Year Hufflepuff student. And he would take her aside and talk to her and try to help. Or, even better, some inadvertent incident would mean that he would have to rescue her. And she would feel safe.

I don't think there's anywhere I feel truly safe at the moment.

It's lunchtime on a Thursday when I'm sat on the staircase and I hear the bell ring for classes about to begin. It doesn't even make me jump, now; instead, I collect up my folders and my school bag and head to my next lesson. I'm used to this. When I reach the bottom of the staircase, I stop before turning the corner; I listen for footsteps, and only when it's quiet do I slip around back into the normal corridor. I don't think I would get into much trouble for being up that staircase, but I'm paranoid that if a teacher catches me, they'll have questions.

It's ironic; as much as I sneak around and try to be as invisible as possible, I simultaneously feel like I'm screaming that something is wrong. Maybe it's the Remus Lupin thing again – I want someone who has some power to notice how badly things are going wrong for me. I want to be rescued. I'm not strong enough, frankly, to save myself.

It's a depressing thought but it's true. By myself, I am totally powerless. There's nothing I can do except hope that someone realises something is wrong. I'm well aware that maybe the best way for someone to realise would be me telling them – but that, I can't do. How do you even start a conversation like that?

I can feel myself fading away. All the parts of myself that make up me are starting to crumble. I don't feel like myself anymore. I am hiding so much that I am actually starting to blend in with the wallpaper. Is it better this way? I try to convince myself that it is. If I'm invisible, no one will know what's happening at home. If I'm invisible, no one will see the parts of myself that I am trying so desperately to hide.

I trudge from the staircase to our English classroom. I'm about halfway there when I meet a group of my friends. I force a smile in their direction. I'm not mad at them; it's just easier to be invisible when I'm on my own.

"Where have you been?" Amelie asks me lightly.

"I left a book in my locker," I reply quickly, trying to keep my tone light too. It should be an easy question to answer.

She nods, accepting the excuse. "I think we're getting our short story marks back today," she moves on. For a short minute, this seems pretty innocuous news. Then I remember which short stories she is talking about.

They were an assignment that our English teacher set us maybe a fortnight ago. The assignment brief had been wide (even to the point of being frustratingly vague). All we had to do was write a short story, about anything we wanted, so long as it was under two thousand words. While I haven't read anyone else's story, I get the impression that the range of topics that people have chosen have been pretty vast.

Mine, however, has been niggling in my mind ever since I had handed it in. For reasons that at this moment feel ridiculous, I decided to base mine on something that had happened between my mum and me.

It had been somewhat of an impulse decision to actually hand it in. This kind of screaming, I was aware, could lead to complications. I even felt, in a sense, like I was signing my own death warrant. It wasn't explicitly violent, nor was it based on one of the worst events that I've lived through, but I was well aware that it was concerning. This story – well, this story was the kind of thing that would have Remus Lupin right at your side.

Ever since I handed it in, I have been worried about it; about how literally my English teacher would take it. He is the kind of teacher who can go from totally chill to tearing his own hair out in frustration in a matter of moments, but I feel like he is on my wavelength. English has always been my favourite subject. It's literally lessons about books; what's not to like? Most of the time, I get the impression that Mr Cross feels the same way about his subject.

I'm jittery as I mumble a response to Amelie and follow her into the classroom. I'm not sure whether I want him to have read my story yet or not. Maybe I could quickly rush another story and ask him to mark that one, instead. I'm sure that wouldn't seem suspicious or dodgy at all.

Everyone else, though, is keen to get their scores back. Usually, I would be too. Today, though, I feel like a fool. I'm so stupid to have not thought about what repercussions this story could have. What if he realises how true to life what I've written is? What if he shows it to another teacher? I feel like an idiot, doing something so reckless.

I dig my fingernails into my legs under the desk to try and keep my composure. I try to focus on what my friends are gossiping about, but I can't follow the different threads. I'm relieved for a split second when I hear the classroom door open; and then my heart drops. I could put my hand up and say I feel sick. I've got enough of a reputation as an honest hard-worker that Mr Cross will believe me. And even without that reputation, no teacher wants kids puking in their classrooms. He'd let me leave.

But I keep my hand down, trying instead to act natural. Mr Cross seems in a good mood today, and he greets us cheerfully. Luckily, he dives in quickly to the lesson – I don't think my nerves can take too much class discussion today – and pulls out a stack of papers from his bag. "I've got your assignments back," he explains unnecessarily, holding the papers aloft. "They were all very high quality. Really well done to all of you."

There is a buzz of conversation as Mr Cross starts passing the assignments back to each student. My heart is pounding and I feel like my face is heating up. This isn't good – I need to act natural. If he thinks I'm too stressed about this story, it's just going to make things worse...

I'm shaken out of my reverie as I see Mr Cross in front of me, holding out my paper. I try to smile at him as I take it; for a brief second, we make eye contact. His expression is unreadable, though. With any hope, so is mine.

I look down at my paper. The letters don't look like letters anymore. I need to come back down to Earth. Getting myself into a state isn't going to make this any better.

I quickly flip through the few pages to get to Mr Cross' notes at the end. The first thing I see is a large red letter, my grade, an A*. At least I'm doing academically well, even if I'm right and I've made things very difficult for myself. I'm shaking as I force my eyes down to his comment.

A really good piece of work! Well thought out and executed. Keep it up!

Something about the glibness feels like a slap in the face; but what's worse is the sentiment. He thinks I made it up. He thinks it's fictional. He thinks that it's a normal assignment from a normal kid.

Why do I feel oddly let down?

I was so panicked; I thought I had given the game away, for sure. I should be pleased, relieved. The danger is gone. Even as I *panicked waiting for the story back, I thought that things were about to be over. I thought...*

I curtail my thoughts quickly as beside me, Amelie peeks over my shoulder to have a look at my grade. "Hey, go you!" she says cheerfully. "Such an English nerd!"

I laugh and go through the rigmarole of looking at her grade too, before congratulating her. She's got an A* too. It's good, everything is good. Nothing's wrong. The danger has passed.

The rest of the lesson washes over me; I'm barely here. This is unusual in English, but today I just can't think about the book that we're supposed to be discussing. I can't muster up the energy to care about the characters, and the imagery. All I know is that no matter what Mr Cross thinks, I'm still stuck in my own story.

7

As I walk alongside this new acquaintance, I realise that I'm now slightly self-conscious in a way that I wasn't whilst on my own. I'm very aware that the sense of freedom that was coursing through me when I was running up that hill has been dampened slightly. I'm no longer quite free to go wherever.

I notice Maeve give me little glances as we walk in silence. While it's reassuring to see that she doesn't seem to be concussed, or isn't about to have a seizure, the look on her face confuses me. She is looking at me like I'm some kind of miracle that she hasn't quite sussed out yet. I feel mildly unsettled, in a different way than I did whilst watching her ethereal glow; does she think that I've come to save her? That I'm going to – I don't know – punch whoever strangled her in the face? I'm not sure I can be someone's saviour.

It niggles especially because I know that there's someone that I used to look at like that.

I miss Zoe so much that it hurts.

I genuinely don't know what I'm going to do without her; it still hasn't sunk in that I'm never going to see her again. She cared about me. Maybe it was her job, but I firmly believe she cared about me, and there's not many people I can say that about with any conviction. I remember what it felt like when she slipped her arm around me and gave me a little squeeze. I remember her holding my hand. I remember her gently opening my bedroom door and waking me up for therapy group when I felt poorly. She cared about me. I will never believe that she didn't.

And there's no way to explain it. She's my Zoe. She's not my mum, my sister, my friend, my girlfriend, my crush – she's just my Zoe and there's no more I can say about it. How is it that I miss something that most people never have? Why does it feel so essential? I've heard various therapists and even some patients talk about the phenomenon, but I've never been able to *really* explain to myself why I feel about Zoe in the way I do. I don't want to hear from doctors that being this attached to someone is part of my condition. It can't be; it can't feel this real if it's just part of being mentally ill.

I guess it can't help that I have no one else. I'm alone, now. Alone with the memories.

Christ. I hate this.

If I could just hear her voice one more time... But I'm lying, because that wouldn't be enough. I want to hear her voice forever. I want to hear her laugh, see her smile. And I can't. It hurts so much. It actually *hurts*. I just want my Zoe. I just want to feel safe.

She would never not notice how I was feeling. I would never have run away tonight, because she would have noticed how bad I was feeling and talked to me about it. Like I never ended up shoplifting paracetamol and I never walked out into the road and I never drank nail polish. For the first time, when I was with Zoe, talking was enough. I guess the situation I'm in now indicates that it was for the last time too.

No, that's not fair. I don't really talk to the doctors or nurses (unless arguing counts), but I do talk to Katy, the psychologist that they've assigned me at the hospital. And I know that in other circumstances, it might even help, if I wasn't stuck locked up somewhere that I hated. But either way, it doesn't feel like talking to Zoe. It doesn't feel... soothing, I guess. Like it was actually healing me to hear her voice.

I dream about Zoe a lot. They're not always bad, the dreams; but the way that I feel when I wake up from them makes me wish that they had been nightmares instead. I mentioned one of the dreams in a session with Katy the other day. I told her how I dreamt that Zoe had gotten a job on the ward and I'd seen her again; how she had hugged me and told me things were going to be OK.

And to my surprise – Katy had smiled and said how nice that must have been for me.

"Nice?" I'd replied, incredulous. "No. It was horrible."

Because it was. Waking up, being jerked out of her arms, to realise that I would never see her again. That I would never touch her again, or hear her voice again, or be soothed by her again. She's gone and there's nothing I can do. She might as well be dead to me. And I can't even mourn her.

I'm glad she's happy. I know that there's a part of me that wants her to be mourning me too, but I know she's not. And, really, I'm glad about that. I stalk her online presence enough to know that she's got a boyfriend – a big, tall man like I know she wanted. There will probably be a wedding on its way before long. And what have I achieved? Nothing. Months on, I'm still stuck in hospital, barely ever allowed to leave.

Except – well, I'm not actually. For the next few hours at least, I'm (mostly) free!

I can't help but let a small smile creep onto my face.

"At last!" a little voice bursts out from beside me. In truth, I was so lost in my thoughts that I forgot for a moment that I have a companion. And, of course, that I am suddenly the responsible adult.

I give Maeve a sideways look. It's supposed to be stern; but, really, even with the sudden appearance of Maeve, I'm still too wired from escaping to quite manage being tyrannical.

She smiles beside me. "Have you decided where we're going, yet?"

For a second, I feel a little rush of panic. Where am I taking this child? Finally, the start of a solution pops into my head. "There's a late bus service into the centre of town," I tell Maeve, a little tentatively, though I allow my smile to remain in its place on my face. "Into the centre of Weston. I think it's every hour. We should make it; the stop is only five, ten minutes away from here."

Maeve nods and continues to smirk as she looks up at me. It's a friendly smirk, though. "Sounds like a great idea, Captain," she replies cheerfully.

This is exactly what I don't want. "I'm not your captain," I hear myself saying, with a little roll of my eyes – but my voice is softer than I intended, and I realise a moment later that I'm still smiling. Little as I'm about to admit it, there's something hard to not like about this sudden new acquaintance.

Before Maeve can reply, something pops into my head. "Have you got any money on you?" I ask.

Maeve looks slightly put out and pats her pockets in a way that looks almost like an automatic reaction. To give her credit, she looks up at me and answers this time without sarcasm. "No," she says frankly. "Should I?"

I shake my head. "It's fine. My bus pass counts for a companion as well. We'll get you on the bus with that."

It's only when I finish speaking that I realise – I really do seem to have fully adopted Maeve onto my journey now. I'm not sure if it's because she clearly has no one, any more than I do; or if it's because she is undeniably a little bit charming. Mainly, though, I think it's that she has somehow managed to very firmly insert herself into my trip without me having any say. What's more, she knows it.

We walk a little way in silence, with Maeve bouncing along next to my more purposeful stride. The bus stop isn't far –

within five minutes, we are nearly there. We walk briskly out of the wooded area and onto the coastal path.

Out of nowhere, Maeve gives me a little nudge. "By the way," she begins chirpily, "where are we going after the bus?"

Ah. The tricky question.

She raises a good point. When it was just me on this trip, I wasn't even sure where I was going. I just wanted to get as far away as possible. My original intention when I climbed over the fence has stuck in my head, of course – and I still know what that original intention was. An attempt to get away, I suppose, just, maybe… maybe a *different* way of getting away.

But I can't explain the nuances of this to this random kid. Anyway, now that I have a stowaway, I can't go through with anything until I get her somewhere safe. Though, Lord knows where that would be. She has already said no to ambulances and police. Where do I take a vulnerable child when I'm (allegedly) vulnerable myself?

"Where were you thinking of going when you left?" I ask cautiously, tentatively.

Maeve wrinkles her nose and doesn't make eye contact. "I'm not sure. I just had to get away."

I sense that she's not telling the whole truth, but this is the most serious I have seen her since we met. Clearly, Maeve can make jokes about nearly everything, just not this. I have to say, it worries me. Even though she's not letting on about what has actually happened, it worries me.

I choose my next words carefully. "Is there anything I can do to help?"

Before I've even finished my sentence, Maeve is shaking her head furiously. "No," she says determinedly. "No, there's nothing."

"So where *were* you going?" I feel bad for pressing her, but it doesn't sound like she's just going to go home in an hour or two. I wish I had a home I could take her back to. But what will Paige the nurse say if I turn up with a small fourteen-year-old when I eventually go back?

If. If I eventually go back.

For as much as I'm worried about Maeve, it's not like I'm especially safe tonight either. I realise that, as much as I have been insisting to myself that don't have a plan, I know where I'm going – and it's not the path that professionals or friends would advocate me to take. Still, Maeve is totally oblivious, and I'd like to keep it that way. I'll take her somewhere safe, then finish what I left to do.

Beside me, Maeve sighs. "I told you, I don't *know* where. I don't have, like, family or anything that I can go to."

"OK," I say slowly. "So will you let me take you to the police station then?"

Maeve's head snaps round to face me. "Why?" she asks suspiciously, eyes narrowed. Her mood is very much changed. "How would that help?"

I sigh. "Well, because you can tell them about what's happened tonight and they can… I don't know… maybe find you somewhere safe to stay."

"I'm safe with you," Maeve tells me stubbornly. "If you don't want me, I'll go. But I'm not going to any sodding police station."

"OK, OK." I speak quickly, keen to reassure her. Much as I don't need Maeve with me, I can't let a vulnerable teenager storm off into the night on her own. I'll find a way to get her to the police or a hospital or something. For now, we just need to get on the bus.

We walk the rest of the way to the bus stop in silence. For my part, I don't want to anger her any further. For her part, I think she's just pissed off. Maybe a little panicked.

It's still dark at the bus stop, but at least by the road there is a little light from the moon that wasn't visible in the forest. I feel more antsy, stood by the road, even if it's just the quiet coastal path. To my relief, no cars come past. I try to be subtle as I get ready to jump back from the road and hide if any police cars come by.

Still, it's nice to be able to see the moon in the sky, its light reflecting back off the sea past the edge of the cliff. Since I'm on the run, a fugitive even, it makes sense that looking out at a view like that practically epitomises freedom for me. The sea ripples silently in front of us, all the way to the horizon.

We barely wait five minutes at the bus stop before the dilapidated old bus comes trundling down the dark lane towards us. "Here we are," I say, forcing brightness.

Maeve nods, and to my surprise, she has to drag her own eyes away from the sea before she takes a big breath and flashes me a smile. "Excellent," she says, a tiny note of weakness in her voice.

I frown, but for now I just stick my arm out into the road to flag down the bus. In accordance, the vehicle comes to a wheezy stop in front of us. The doors creak open and the elderly bus driver peers through the Perspex screen at the two of us. I step onto the bus and hear Maeve step up behind me.

I dig my card out of my pocket – lucky I decided to bring it – and show it to the bus driver, wordlessly but whilst dredging up a smile for him. I glance back to Maeve and see, in slight relief, that she is beaming at the bus driver too. Possibly slightly too enthusiastically, but still. She sneaks a glance at me, giving me five seconds' warning from the mischievous look in her eye that she's about to say something that she thinks will be hilarious.

She looks straight at the bus driver. "I'm her carer," she half-whispers to him conspiratorially. "She just can't cope without me."

I force myself to keep smiling and not to sigh as the driver waves us on and we sit down. "You're a little shit," I say in an undertone.

Beside me, Maeve is overcome with giggles. I'm glad she's cheered up from how she was before we got on the bus, but I'm a little miffed that it took a joke at my expense to get her there. I see her pocket the bus ticket the driver printed out for her as she flops onto the carpeted seat beside me.

"Why do you have a card like that? *Do* you need a carer?" she asks conversationally, turning to watch me like I'm an interesting specimen – though with something else in her gaze that I can't quite capture.

I sigh. "I've got this far on my own, haven't I?"

"Yeah," she concedes. "But normally? Where did you get the card?"

"Maeve..." I'm tired and not in the mood to explain my entire psychiatric history. "They just get them for us at the hospital. To make time out easier."

For a second I think Maeve is going to laugh, but then she looks at me; and this time, it doesn't seem to be so much that I'm an interesting specimen. Instead, I rather suspect that she is feeling something for me. Not quite pity – I don't think I could take that – but maybe sympathy. I stare at my feet, uncomfortable. There's a short silence.

"I didn't know you were in hospital," she tells me more quietly.

I sigh again. Maeve is turning out to be difficult in a different way than I had expected.

"Yeah, for a while," I answer dully. "And yes, before you ask, I'm supposed to be there now. Can you keep your mouth shut for me?"

Maeve's eyes widen. "You're... you're an *escapee*?" she whispers, and I can't help but let out a short laugh. You forget sometimes that things that seem normal when you've been in an inpatient psychiatric ward are totally alien to the rest of the world.

"Yes, Maeve, OK? I climbed over the back fence," I say, keeping my voice quiet but unable to keep a small smile from my face. Is it bad that I'm slightly proud of what I've done tonight?

For a second, I think Maeve might explode. But, after a minute, seemingly encouraged by my smile, she grins back at me. She seems to have accepted this all much more quickly than I thought she would. Maybe I could have picked a worse kid to have following me around.

The bus trundles on down the coastal path. For a moment, Maeve and I travel in a companionable silence. Finally, Maeve turns to me; but rather than addressing me in her usual manner, with all the subtlety of a hammer, she actually hesitates. It feels as though she's thinking about what she's about to say.

"What's wrong?" I ask her, a little suspiciously.

She looks up at me and then away again. A few times, she tries to speak before stopping herself. Her joking is over now; whatever she's about to say is important to her.

"Maeve?" I ask again.

She struggles. "Is it..." she finally says at last. "Those scars on your arm... did they put you in the hospital for that?"

I flick my gaze down to my arms automatically, and it's my turn to hesitate. I haven't actually known until this moment that Maeve has seen those. I'm wearing long sleeves, as usual. I suppose I must have pulled up my sleeve to scratch or something.

"Right," I say slowly, hesitantly. "I mean... it's a factor, I guess. But there are other things too. I'm just... going through a tough time."

"I get it," says Maeve, and it saddens me because she sounds like she's really feeling it. I don't want to make anyone feel this way. I don't want anyone to feel sad because of me.

We slip into a silence again but this time it's less companionable and I sense that Maeve hasn't dropped the subject. God. I wish she hadn't seen anything. I turn away from her to look out the window, though in the pitch black there's nothing to see. I just can't face looking at her.

Finally, a tiny voice sounds from my left. "Heather?"

I swallow hard. I steel myself and turn around.

I expect to see Maeve ready with more questions; but as I turn to her, I realise that she's trying to tell me something instead. And in the place of speaking, she's holding out her arm to me.

I frown and look down at her exposed forearm. Before I can ask any questions, I see the red lines crowding over her pale skin. She's been self-harming too. Suddenly, I understand the questions about my own scars and it pains me that I might have frightened her by telling her I was in hospital partly because of that.

I can't speak. It's too much.

But Maeve continues to stare at me and I have to respond; I can't just leave her looking at me like that. Slowly, I extend a hand. Not quite able to touch the places where she's hurt herself, I reach for the back of her hand instead. I grip her, not hard but firmly. I don't know how I've ended up with Maeve, but I'm determined I'm going to save her.

8

When I first notice the looks and whispers following me around at school, I try to ignore them.

Following that, I try to convince myself that I'm being paranoid. I remind myself that when I get stressed, I get anxious, and when I get anxious, I spend most of my time thinking that everyone hates me. After the past few weeks, I'm certainly both stressed and anxious. The whispering is probably all in my imagination.

Oddly, though, this time I'm certain that there's something going on. I've even noticed a few side glances from people I thought were friends. My first thought is that maybe someone has found out about the car accident. Or, maybe, the fact that I'm self-harming. But there's something in their looks that makes me sure I haven't worked out what it is that they're saying about me yet.

I don't like it.

One break time, I sit on a table with a few of my friends in our tutor room. There are a few other groups dotted around the classroom, and the room is abuzz with noise. My friends are deep in a discussion about something, and I should be paying attention, but I'm too aware that the group in the far corner keep stealing glances over to us. Every time I look over at them, I'm sure that they are looking straight at me.

I try to focus back on my friends' conversation. Something about homework, or a teacher? I've lost track of what they're talking about. Usually I can orientate myself in these conversations pretty quickly; maybe I'm just too distracted today.

I'm lost in thought when I hear someone call my name. I look up; but to my surprise, it isn't any of my friends. Self-conscious, I quickly snap my gaze to where the voice has come from, fixing my eyes instead on the girl who's said my name. Her name is Paula; I know her pretty well. We've been in the same tutor group for three years, and we get on OK. I've never had any problems with her.

I notice as I wait for her to speak that she looks slightly nervous. What is she approaching me for, that she has to be nervous?

"Can I ask you something?" she says, in a bright tone, though with a definite hint of nervousness still in her voice.

I frown, but I nod. "Yeah..." I say slowly, chancing a glance back at my friends. They look nervous too, and it can't be a good omen that their conversation seems to have very suddenly petered out. Is there something I'm missing?

Paula smiles, but it's not quite right. "Is it true," she begins hesitantly, "that you're gay and you fancy someone in our year?"

For a moment, I'm totally frozen.

How can she... how can she know that? My mind is racing and my face flames as I feel several pairs of eyes on me. I blink a few times, my heart pounding. I feel like I can't connect my brain and my mouth. Everything inside me is screaming, deny it, for fuck's sake deny it!

Finally, after a few seconds, the initial panic settles enough for me to put a fake smile on my face. I shake my head. "Um, no?" I answer, as if it's an odd question. I even add a small laugh. It's a ridiculous question. Of course it's a ridiculous question.

I don't dare to look at my friends' faces, but I feel relief wash over me when Paula smiles back, a small laugh of her own. "So it's not true?" she confirms.

I shake my head again. It's not true, it's not true, it's not true...

Paula retreats to her friendship group and I force myself to turn away too, even though I can feel all of their eyes on me as they discuss in mutters what Paula has just found out. Logically, I know I have dodged a bullet – no one can know yet, I haven't even told my parents yet – but nonetheless I feel a huge wave of anger come over me. I am so weak. I am so useless. I can't even admit the truth.

I feel choked up, but right now I don't want anyone to see. "I'm just popping to the loo before next lesson," I mumble in the direction of my friends, still not meeting anyone's eyes. I don't want their questions either, right now.

I don't give them a chance to say anything in response before I gather up my school bag and some loose folders and walk smartly out of the room. I keep my head down, forcing myself to stay impassive, just someone walking to their next lesson. The last thing I want, at the moment, is more questions. From anyone. Well meaning or not.

I wonder how long it will be before some of my friends won't want to be around me anymore. There are a few people in my friendship group who are religious – will God tell them to drop me? To pretend that all the time we have spent together means nothing? I wish I could say for certain that I'm being silly, that I must mean more to them than that – but, frankly, I know that there's no guarantees. I've seen how uncomfortable they get whenever homosexuality is mentioned. I could be facing cold shoulders very soon, even if I convince them that the rumour isn't true.

And who is this girl that I'm supposed to fancy? That bit is genuinely untrue; there's no one, really, who I would go so far as to say I fancied. Obviously there are girls that I find attractive, but I wouldn't say there was anyone I found special. Even Mrs Fletcher – I joke to myself that I have a crush on her, but really it's just that she's fit. There isn't anyone, yet, who I feel strongly enough about to say that I have romantic feelings for.

No, it feels like that bit has been added; maybe to make the story more salacious, but maybe to start a kind of witch hunt. Everyone will be asking who it is, who the victim is, who has to watch out for me. That's the attitude towards homosexuality that I've encountered so far. The idea that lesbians are predatory is rife in this school.

Even if whoever started this rumour wasn't trying to hurt me, they have almost certainly added this element of the story to make the rumour have more value. A rumour like this will have had a high-ranking social currency. Whoever started it is probably on their way to moving into a more 'popular' friendship group. Good for them.

What makes it worse – there are only three people who could have done this. And I know this because there are only three people that I've told.

Granted, one of them could have mentioned it to one person who then spread it on… but something tells me that it was one of these three people who are responsible for this. I knew I should have stayed quiet. I knew I shouldn't have let anyone know what I was thinking.

I guess it's a lesson moving forward. If I can't even trust my friends to keep something like this *secret, I can't let them know about my self-harm, or the things that've happened that make me need to do it. Ironically, right now, the thing I want to do most is hurt myself. I'm so fucking angry; but already I'm turning it in on myself.*

There's no time, though, now, to do anything. Even though I left a little early from break, my head hasn't been paying attention to where my body has been walking, and I've somehow ended up on the opposite side of the school to where I'm meant to be. The familiar urge to walk out and not come back niggles at me. Today, of course, I would have a reason. Still, I put it to the back of my mind. I don't want to have to explain my sexuality to my parents or teachers yet, or why I'm so upset at a silly rumour.

I arrive at my Italian class at roughly the same time as everyone else. I must be the only one entering the room who is relieved that we have a test today and the teacher has separated the desks out so everyone is sat alone. I fall into a chair silently, taking out a pen and a spare, in case it runs out. I sit near enough to my friends that it doesn't look suspicious, but I don't join in the conversation. Luckily for me, it's barely a few minutes before the teacher arrives and starts the exam.

I thought that having a test to focus on would be the best thing for me right now, but the questions circle around my head. I can't focus. Once again, my mind mulls over what would happen if I just walked out of this classroom, along the hall and down the stairs, until I am in the car park and out the gates. I have this fantasy at least ten times each school day. I never act on it.

But today I can't concentrate back on my work. I have been hoping for such a long time that things are going to get better soon, more manageable; that I'm going to stop feeling depressed and lonely and angry all at the same time. Today just seems to be proving that things are just going to get worse and worse. My friends are going to leave me; I'm going to be even more alone than I am already. I don't know what I'm going to do. I don't want the last few bits of sanity I have left to flow through my fingers.

There's something hard, in my chest, now, that won't go away as I sit in my Italian lesson, staring down at a blank test that I know I'm clever enough to answer. I feel like crying. I don't know what I'm supposed to do.

Finally, I take enough deep breaths that the urge to sob becomes controllable. I don't want to attract the teacher's attention, so I turn the page in my exam, as if I'm having a look at the later questions. I pretend I'm reading, though the words don't even look like words anymore today.

Who was it? That's the main question going around and around in my mind as I sit there silently. Who sold me out? Who decided that being popular was a fair trade for my life being turned upside down? I have no idea how my parents are going to react – but what's really getting me is that the person who spread this rumour had no idea either. My safety was less important than them becoming popular, and that really stings.

I twizzle my pen between my hands agitatedly; I know I need to get cracking on this exam. Everything is falling to shit, but at least I can pride myself on my grades. I'm not sure that should be as depressing as it makes me feel.

But I turn back to the first page of the paper, and I take the lid off my pen. One last deep breath, and then I force myself to actually read the question. All I have to do is answer some questions about the passage given in Italian. I can do that. Come on, I urge myself. You can do this.

Weirdly enough, actually sitting the exam makes me feel calmer. I can answer all the questions without too much difficulty. I feel a little bit more in control. At least this is something in my life that I can do. I get through the Italian lesson, and then another lesson, by focusing on answering the questions put in front of me.

In fact, I am so invigorated by this that when the bell rings for lunch, I head to the quiet corridor where my friends eat lunch every day. My heart is pounding and I'm no end of nervous, but I do it. Where I've got this sudden courage from, I don't know. I haven't been spending lunchtimes with my friends very often even on normal days; I don't know how I've suddenly got the courage to do it today.

When I see my friends, I can tell from their expressions that they've heard. Even the people who weren't there this morning have clearly been filled in. I don't say anything, dropping my gaze to the floor. Still, when I sit down, they don't move away. I sit down on the scratchy school carpet and take out my sandwiches. After an awkward second, I finally meet Amelie's gaze.

"Are you alright?" she asks, uncertainly but not unkindly.

I nod. I'm not sure I'm ready to talk about it, but I appreciate it being asked.

To my relief, Amelie doesn't push it, only nodding herself as the rest of the group continue eating their lunch. For a moment, there is a short silence. But to my relief, it isn't long before conversation starts back up and I can blend quietly in the background whilst I eat my sandwich. Usually being alone recharges me; but today I can't bear the thought of being as alone as I feel.

It's a little later, when everyone has eaten and a few people have dispersed to go elsewhere, that Amelie turns to me again. She knows me well enough to know that even if I didn't want to talk about it with everyone, I'm still probably upset.

"I heard what happened," she tells me, a little awkwardly. "What Paula said to you."

Amelie wasn't there this morning, so clearly it has been talked about in my absence. Not that it will have been a surprise for her; she was one of the three people who I told about this. Maybe the fact that she knows should be a red flag. It doesn't feel like it, though. I trust Amelie. Despite everything I can't tell her, I know that she's not the kind to spread round the things that I have. I don't for a second think that it's Amelie who has told.

I sigh. "I didn't want everyone to know, yet," I admit. I can hear how tired my tone is.

"I know," she says, sadly. "It wasn't me, I swear."

I nod quickly. As I say, I don't for a minute suspect Amelie.

But, I realise, Amelie has a different viewpoint to me in this situation. Though I trust that she hasn't told anyone, I also realise that she may know who has. I look up at her. She holds my gaze; and she seems to very quickly guess what my next question is going to be.

"Do you know who it was?" I ask quietly.

Amelie hesitates. She looks down at the carpet that we're sitting on. I suspect she's deciding the best way to break the news to me. "I think so," she says slowly, eventually. She sighs. "I mean, I know that the story got round on a sports trip," she admits. "So, I guess..."

She doesn't need to finish the sentence. It's just as clear to me who we're talking about.

Charlotte is the only one of the three who is on any sports teams; but more than that, recently, it has started to become obvious that she thinks she can do better than us as friends. Even though I had expected that the motive for someone spreading the rumour was popularity... well, it hurts. It looks like, once again, I have been used as something dispensable.

I rub at my collarbone. Today feels like it is just another blow. I'm not sure how long I can keep doing all of this.

I look over to the other side of the corridor, where Charlotte is sat with a few other friends, out of our earshot. I allow my eyes to rest on her for a moment; and as I do, she looks up and over to me. But she can't meet my eyes. She quickly flicks her gaze away from me and down to the floor. Does she feel guilty? Or does she just want to avoid a confrontation with me? Maybe she just doesn't want me to tell the rest of our friends what she's done.

Maybe, though, she just doesn't care. That's fine, I guess. I know where I stand. I know I'm never going to trust Charlotte with anything else again. At least I didn't trust her with something more serious. At least I didn't tell her about what happened when we crashed—

I cut myself off from even thinking it, too aware that Amelie's eyes are on me. I can't even think about that right now. If today has taught me anything, it's that I need to keep my mouth shut.

9

The bus rattles along through the last few stops before coming to a halt outside the stop in the centre of town. Well, that's what we call it; it's not really a centre. There are a few shops, a pub and a couple of places for food. At the moment, it's lit up with all the 'adult massage' centres in dingy side streets. It's not a great place to be, admittedly.

Maeve and I step off the bus together, thankfully without her making any more jokes about being my carer. Still, she catches my eye, and I manage a small smile back.

As the bus makes its quiet way along, I look around aimlessly. I'm not sure what I had intended to do once we got here. Part of me still wants to take Maeve to the nearest police station, where she can talk to someone about why she's run away. She's not safe wandering around a dodgy town like this one. Is she even safe with me here?

But before I can make any decisions, I spot a police car coming down the coastal road that the bus has just driven down. There are no sirens, but I panic. Instinctively, I grab Maeve and pull her down with me as I duck quickly behind a low wall. We stay frozen there as the car drives on and gradually goes off into the distance.

Breathing a sigh of relief, I finally let go of Maeve and pull myself up to sit on the low wall. I rub the bridge of my nose. Taking a young girl to a police station where she can be looked after and I can then leave is one thing; I may want the safety of the police for Maeve, but not for me.

Of course, she is looking at me slightly uneasily. "What was that about?" she asks, a little tentative.

I sigh as she cautiously sits next to me on the wall. "I'm sectioned," I tell her tiredly. "For my mental health. The hospital will call the police when they realise I'm missing and then the police have the power to take me back." I pause. "I'm not ready to go back," I add, and I can hear the strain in my voice.

Maeve gives me a scared look. "Is it horrible, there?" she asks, her eyes wide.

Shaking my head, I pick at a piece of fluff on my jeans. "No," I tell her weakly. Am I reassuring her, or myself? "No, it's not horrible. It's just... a hard place to be. And I just want it to end."

I regret that last sentence as soon as it's out of my mouth. I can't help but notice the shift in Maeve's expression. She understands what I mean. Of course she understands what I mean. We've only met each other tonight but I feel oddly strongly that Maeve understands me.

"Do you want a drink?" I ask suddenly, trying to change the subject. "I mean, I know you're a bit young – shit, you are young – but we could have one? From the dodgy newsagent across the road?"

To my relief, Maeve's concerned expression mellows a little. I can tell she's pleased I want to keep her nearby. "Yeah," she answers me, more cheerfully.

"Great," I say, trying to match her tone. "Look, I've got ID, and I'm guessing you don't. So I'll nip in by myself if you wait here. What do you want?"

Maeve's eyes look caught in the headlights for a split second, and it hits me hard just how young she actually is. Should I be buying her alcohol? Probably not. Oh well. One drink can't hurt.

"Smirnoff Ice," she says, looking slightly proud that she's managed to name an alcoholic drink off the top of her head. I can tell she's not an experienced drinker. That being said, neither am I; but even I know what a shit drink she's picked.

"OK," I say, resisting the urge to laugh. "I'll see if they've got one."

I check my pockets: change, a few bank notes, my room key from the hospital, my ID and my phone (turned off, of course). All set.

"See you in a minute," I tell Maeve, and she beams. For some reason, this makes my heart ache a little bit.

I half-walk, half-jog over the road to the dodgy newsagent opposite. It's the kind of newsagent that smells ever so slightly of damp and more strongly of incense, and rather than selling the crisps and chocolate that all normal newsagents sell, they instead sell the most obscure flavours and brands that you don't find elsewhere. I'm always surprised it doesn't shut down, but somehow it manages to keep going.

They do have a good selection of alcopops though; I easily find a Smirnoff Ice for Maeve, and I barely have to venture further into the shop to find a little bottle of cider for me. Keeping my expression neutral, I approach the counter where a man sits, watching me.

"ID?" he asks immediately, clocking my slight frame and baby face.

I dig in my pocket and pull out my ID to show him, praying that the name doesn't stick in his mind. I'm probably being paranoid, but I don't want to leave a trace for the police.

I'm just handing over the cash for the drinks when I hear a bottle smashing outside. It should be a commonplace noise, in town, at night, but I feel panic rise up. It's silly, it's probably just someone too drunk to hold on to their beer bottle – but what if it's not? I force myself to keep calm as the man hands over my change. I stuff it into my pocket quickly as I flash him a quick smile in thanks. Breathe, breathe, breathe…

Just as I'm coming out of the shop, though, I hear another smash. What shakes me even more is that – once again – this is louder and more violent a sound than someone just dropping their drink. This is the sound of a bottle being hurled with considerable force.

And my worst fear is realised as I spin to face the direction the noise came from. Cowering, crouching, squeezing herself down to be as small a target as possible, is Maeve.

My fight-or-flight instinct kicks in instantly. I run towards the fracas at full speed, barely aware of what I'm doing as I shout at the men cornering Maeve: "Hey! What the fuck do you think you're doing?"

Maeve doesn't surface from her ball, but the men turn to look at me. To my surprise, the expressions on their faces aren't jubilant, as if it's fun for them to throw bottles at a young girl. Nor do they seem to be getting off at frightening someone who can't fight back. Instead, they turn to me looking uneasy, or even, maybe, frightened. I'm confused. What could *Maeve* have done to scare four fully grown men?

"What's going on?" I ask harshly, slightly impressed by the authority in my normally quiet and timid voice. "What are you doing to her?"

"Her?!" shouts one of the men. "It's not a 'her', it's an 'it'!"

And the other men are nodding in agreement, squaring their shoulders as if they are fighting an important fight, a crusade. They glare at me and I force myself to glare back, but really, I'm confused. What on Earth is he talking about? For the first time since I ran over, I take a proper look at Maeve. She is crouched down in front of a low wall, her knees to her chest and her face buried in her hands. I want to go to her, but the four burly men block the way.

I decide quickly to ignore his comment, because, frankly, I don't understand. "I'll call the police!" I shout at him instead, puffing out my own chest like a pigeon. "I will! Do you want to get done for assault?"

There's a tiny pause as the men exchange glances and I take the opportunity to go in for the kill. "She's with me, and she's underage," I tell them, my voice dangerous now. "Leave us alone or I swear to God we will both be giving statements."

"It needs to be dealt with!" shouts one of the men back at me. "I ain't leaving this… this—"

"*She is a kid,*" I reply angrily. "There's nothing to be 'dealt with'. Leave us the fuck alone."

The smallest of the men finally pipes up. "What if it hurts someone?"

It bristles that once again, he is referring to my friend as 'it'. But what really astonishes me is that there's a clear note of fear in his voice. What on Earth has Maeve done to scare a man twice her size? Once again, I'm confused – but I'm not leaving her.

"She's with me," I finally say stubbornly.

One of the men snorts, but another one is looking right at me. "You know what, babe," he says, a little blearily. "If you want it, yeah? It's yours."

I still don't have a clue what he's on about, but, narrowing my eyes, I nod fiercely. Regardless of what he's on about, I do want Maeve. Maeve is, indeed, mine.

The man looks ever so slightly relieved – and to my relief, he beckons to his friends and starts to make off. The other men exchange looks but really, they all seem to be quite thankful to have an excuse to leave. Whether it's me and my threats, or the fear that Maeve has somehow instilled in them, they are moving away and I'm seriously, seriously relieved.

I let them get ten or fifteen metres away before I rush over to where Maeve is still huddled against the wall. "Are you OK?"

I ask urgently, crouching down next to her. Without looking up, she shakes her head fervently.

"I'm scared," she tells me in a cracked whisper. "They scared me."

Oh, Maeve.

I move from my crouched pose to sit down next to her, and after a minute, I tentatively take her hand. I can't quite bring myself to be surprised when she grips my hand back, hard. It's clear that this kid has been through some stuff. I wonder if anyone has ever bothered to stand up for her before.

"It's OK," I say, keeping my voice gentle. "I know they scared you. They scared me too. But they're gone now, OK? It's just me here. Just me."

Maeve squeezes my hand harder but nods, and there's a pause. "I know," she finally says, the faintness of her voice in sharp contrast to the buoyant kid who was grilling me on the bus. It only makes me sadder when she adds, "Thank you for saving me, Heather."

I let myself give out a tiny sigh, mostly to try and keep my own tears back. "I didn't, really," I tell her. "But it's OK."

Maeve nods again, and it's only a second before she is leaning her head on my shoulder. This kid is definitely getting attached – but somehow it doesn't worry me as much as it did earlier. I think I'm getting attached to her too.

I let the silence continue for a minute, but even as scared as I can tell Maeve is, I have a niggling desperation to understand what has just happened; I'm itching to know what made the men so frightened. "Why were they scared of you?" I ask, my question direct but my tone gentle. I'm confused, yes – but mostly concerned. Is this something that's going to happen again? Is this something that's going to get Maeve hurt?

There's another short pause, but, finally, Maeve raises her head. "I don't know," she says tiredly, her voice still quiet, and her face pale and drawn like she's recovering from illness. "They just started shouting and I didn't know what to do, and then they started throwing things, and they were so much bigger than me—"

She's babbling now, and I squeeze her hand tight to try and calm her down. Finally, she breaks off and turns to look me right in the eye. "Is there something wrong with me, Heather?"

Immediately, in almost a knee-jerk reaction, I'm about to start shaking my head and giving the answer that I know I should be giving. But then – is there something weird about Maeve? I mean, I found her in the middle of the forest, alone, in the middle of the night, when she's only fourteen... and, of course, there's the fact that I'm trying to put out of my mind – she was *glowing*. Can I explain that away? And even if we ignore that, there's still something about Maeve that makes me feel slightly uneasy. I can't put my finger on what it is – but there's just something not quite right.

"Of course not," I say quietly, soothingly. "Of course not."

Maeve closes her eyes but nods gently, mollified and reassured. Even as she calms down this little bit, I find myself less worried. I don't think there's something *wrong* with Maeve. I think maybe she is scared, and damaged, and adrift.

I don't quite know what to say when Maeve next speaks. "Where to now?" she asks, the ghost of a tiny smile returning to her face.

10

A few weeks after the rumour starts, I'm heading to a PE lesson with a few friends when we reach the noticeboard by the changing rooms. I'm all ready to walk right by it – I am most definitely not on any sports teams – before Amelie catches onto my arm.

"They've swapped around the sports for PE today," she says, without much interest. "We're on rounders now, not rugby."

I look at the notice, and Amelie is right. In itself, this is not particularly interesting. As a group of people who are forced into PE, my friends and I don't try too hard at it. We just turn up where we're supposed to and try to avoid actually doing anything. This is the same whether we're on rounders or rugby.

But then I remember something – we're supposed to wear our short-sleeved tops to rounders.

This is going to be a problem. I haven't yet worked out how I am going to hide the cuts on my arms in summer when I know I will have to wear a short-sleeved top for PE; and I certainly haven't banked on having to do it this soon. Nothing has healed yet. In fact, the cuts from last night might still be bleeding a little bit.

I feel panic rise in me but I can't show it. My friends don't know about the self-harming – even if they have suspicions, they haven't mentioned it to me – so I can't ask them how to hide it.

After Charlotte's indiscretion, I have felt even less than trusting any of my friends with the information. Besides, I don't know how you're supposed to bring up something like that.

I scroll through some solutions in my mind, some reasons that I would need to keep wearing my long-sleeved rugby jersey for rounders. I consider an embarrassing birthmark, a dangerous tendency towards sunburn... but I can't think of anything that seems reasonable. Finally, I have to go with the only excuse I can think of – that I've left my short-sleeved top at home. I didn't think I would need it, after all, before this last-minute schedule change.

I don't know what I'm going to do next week. At the moment, that is a problem for future-me.

Amelie gives me a look when she sees that I'm wearing my white rugby jersey. "We're supposed to be in our polo shirts," she reminds me.

I try to keep calm. "I know," I answer, trying not to answer too quickly. Stay casual, stay casual. "I just left mine at home. We thought we were on rugby, didn't we?"

To my immense relief, this seems to satisfy her. Whether it satisfies Mrs Fletcher and Mr Stuart or not, is another matter.

I try to stay inconspicuous as I sit with my friends on the floor of the sports hall, waiting for the teachers to come in and take the register. So far, no one else has mentioned the rugby jersey. Maybe it's just not that much of a big deal. I'm overthinking it. I hope hope hope that I'm overthinking it.

Finally I see the door swing open, and the two PE teachers come in, the register in Mrs Fletcher's hand. She is relatively well liked, so the class quietens for her quickly. I can feel my face flush and my heart beat as she starts to call out names. All I want, today, is to blend into the background enough that I don't have to use my excuse. I'm invisible most of the time anyway; all I want is for that to continue for roughly the next forty-five minutes.

My name comes in the register and I answer quickly. Mrs

Fletcher's eyes flick over to me, but a second later, she is reading out the next name. Is it that simple? Have I gotten away with it?

My class is filing out onto the rounders pitch, however, when Mrs Fletcher's hand lightly touches my shoulder to get my attention. In any normal situation, I would enjoy Mrs Fletcher's attention being on me. Today, however, I just feel panicked. For once, I actually want her to ignore me.

I force my gaze up from the floor to meet her eyes, trying to act as if I have no idea what she could want. But she jerks her head to the side, a clear gesture for me to leave the line and wait. Unfortunately, I have no option but to go along with this request.

I wait at Mrs Fletcher's other side as the rest of my class finish spilling out onto the field. Mr Stuart is already out there, yelling warm-up instructions. I try to force myself to take deep breaths, to act casual, to act like everything is fine. The last thing that I want is to betray to Mrs Fletcher that there's actually something wrong.

It seems to take an age for Mrs Fletcher and me to be left alone. At last, she turns to me with a frown. "Why aren't you in your proper kit?" she asks me directly.

I try to look normal. "Sorry," I say quickly. "I didn't know we were doing rounders today. I thought it was still rugby. This is the only kit I've got."

Mrs Fletcher continues to frown at me. "You know you're supposed to bring all your kit. To avoid this."

Finally, I have an excuse to look at the floor. "Sorry," I repeat.

I hear her sigh. My heart leaps; have I gotten away with this? I can't think about next week right now. If I have a reprieve for now, I can think of something for next week, I'm sure.

But then Mrs Fletcher speaks again. "Well, there are a few polo shirts in lost property," she says firmly. "You'll have to borrow one of them. I want to see you on the pitch in five minutes."

I don't have time to think of an excuse before Mrs Fletcher gives me a look and walks out onto the pitch herself. For a minute,

I freeze. I have literally no idea how I'm going to get out of this. What reason could I have for not being able to wear lost property?

I have to collect myself; I can't just stand here. Letting anyone realise what an issue this is for me is tantamount to going out onto that rounders field with my arms cut to ribbons. I shake myself out of my panicked thoughts and walk quickly back into the changing rooms.

As soon as I get there, though, I collapse down onto one of the changing benches, rubbing the bridge of my nose. I have no idea what I'm going to do. I'm not ready for everyone to know that I'm screwed up. I'm definitely not ready for everyone to know why. And this is the thing in my school – once one person knows, everyone knows. The incident with Paula a few weeks ago proves that.

I try to force myself to breathe but I can't. I'm shaking. I've messed up everything. I shouldn't have self-harmed. Or rather, I should have hidden the self-harm better. It's depressing that it's the second thought that I instantly cling to. I don't care that I've hurt myself. I just don't want anyone else to know.

I'm not sure how long it is that I sit there, motionless except for some panicky tears. For the first time, I'm glad that Mr Stuart is notoriously strict on letting people go to the loo during his classes because the changing rooms remain mercifully empty. I go over and over my thoughts as I look at the linoleum floor; is there the tiniest possibility that Mrs Fletcher might forget about me? That she might just think she missed seeing me on the field?

But I know there isn't. I'm in the fucking deepest of holes and there's no way out.

Suddenly I'm filled with a huge burst of adrenaline. I leap up from the bench and half-fly across the room to my school bag. I rummage in it, my hands still shaking. It doesn't take me long to find the blade; I always leave it in the same place. I pull it out of my bag and sit down shakily on the bench again.

I try to convince myself that no one is going to come in, but I barely need persuading. I don't fucking care! I hate that I'm in this situation. I shove my sleeve up to the elbow roughly, not caring about if it hurts. One of the cuts from yesterday catches on my sleeve and a tiny bead of blood blossoms on my arm, but I need more than that. I grip the blade tight and press down hard...

I'm still buzzing with adrenaline when I hear the door to the changing room creak open slightly. For a brief moment, the sound is like tinnitus: annoying but not quite real. Then I remember where I am. I quickly pull my sleeve down over my hand, slotting the blade into my pocket. I need to look OK. I suddenly realise that I have tears all over my face, and I'm trying to blot them when a voice calls out.

"Is everyone decent in here?"

I wildly consider staying silent – but I'm guessing that if I do, Mrs Fletcher will just go and get another teacher to accompany her in here. My first try at speaking comes out as barely more than a croak; I clear my throat and try again. My voice sounds pathetic even to me.

Mrs Fletcher pushes the door open the rest of the way. A huge wave of anxiety washes over me and I feel frozen once again, staring down at the changing-room floor. But I know that I have to act natural. It feels like a physical effort to wrench my head upwards to meet her eyes. I can't quite muster a smile, but from the look on her face, she doesn't expect one.

Her face is more cross, though, than anything else. She thinks I'm messing around, that I just don't want to do PE. "What are you doing?" she asks, a note of impatience clear in her voice. "Why aren't you changed?"

I clear my throat again, more to give myself a bit more time than anything else. I don't know what I'm going to say. "I just..." I manage to choke out, my voice wobbly, before I realise that Mrs Fletcher isn't actually listening. Her eyes are fixed on my forearm. Everything seems to move slowly as I follow her gaze. I can see now what she's staring at.

On the sleeve of my white rugby shirt, there is a scarlet stain blooming.

I move quickly again, pulling my arm into my stomach, trying to hide the stain. But all this achieves is to smear the blood over my stomach too. She's seen it now, and there's no way that she's going to let this go.

I'm frozen in silence and Mrs Fletcher is silent herself, approaching me cautiously. I clench my fist, trying to steel myself for what's coming. I have to lie; I have to think of a lie.

But when Mrs Fletcher speaks again, her voice is softer. "What's happened here?" she asks, much more gently. Though she's clearly trying to be calming, I can hear the worry in her voice. This isn't what she expected when she came in here.

I swallow. "I scratched myself on the wall," I manage to squeak out, my voice defensive. "I was just cleaning it up."

She sighs ever so slightly. It sounds sad. And her eyes, fixed on mine again, are sad too. Maybe she really doesn't want me to be hurt.

"Can I see, please?" she asks, polite and kind, but firm. When I don't move, she tries again. "I'm a first aider," she offers. "However this has happened… well, let me bandage you up. Then we can talk."

There is no way out of this. Lying about my kit, not turning up to the lesson, being found covered in blood… none of this exactly screams that I'm OK. Mrs Fletcher knows that something is going on. Any fool would. I have no excuse that would even slightly make sense here.

So, finally, I nod. I haven't got a choice. Mrs Fletcher lays a cautious hand on my shoulder, touching it lightly. "Come on," she murmurs. "Let's go to my office."

I allow her to touch my shoulder and steer me out of the changing room, hoping that no one is hanging around to see anything. I don't usually like being touched, but I feel like flinching away would just make all of this seem worse. When I chance a glance down at my arm, the blood stain is still just as obvious; in fact, it's probably growing. I feel a little light-headed, but I'm not dramatic enough to claim it's from blood loss. It's probably more anxiety. Still, it doesn't help. I feel like I'm floating.

Numbly, I follow Mrs Fletcher out of the changing rooms, into the office block across the car park and then finally into her office. I've never been in here before; I'm well-behaved, and I don't participate enough in PE lessons to manage to get injured. I feel slightly exposed. The office has a large window looking out onto the sports pitches, and the wall that divides us from the rest of the building is glass too. I hope it's soundproof.

I hover awkwardly while Mrs Fletcher reaches up to take down her first aid kit from the top shelf. She turns around and lays it on the desk before looking up at me. "Take a seat," she says, her voice still calm and soft. Silently, I obey, and sink into the plastic chair on the student side of her desk. She doesn't comment but brings round her office chair so that she's right next to me. She unzips the first aid kit, before turning to look up at me, her head tilted sympathetically.

"Can I see, please?" she repeats. I wonder, briefly, what she would do if I just ran. If I jumped up from this chair and burst out of the door and through the car park and out of the gates and into traffic...

I force myself back to reality. There's nothing I can do but roll up my sleeve.

Mrs Fletcher takes a little breath in when she sees the wound – involuntarily, I suspect. But she quickly regains her composure, nodding, as she has a look at what I've done.

"This doesn't look like a scratch from the wall," she comments, still calm as she takes out an antiseptic wipe and tries to wipe away some of the smeared blood on my arm. I have an urge to snatch my arm away, to shout or snap at her. But she's being nice. Well, she's trying to be nice. I should be compliant.

Still, I stay silent. I don't know what the correct response to her statement is. It's not exactly a question, and I don't feel like chatting. I swallow hard but don't say anything.

I can tell that she is considering her words very carefully when she speaks again. "Can you tell me what really happened?" she asks, very, very gently. She doesn't look up at me, maybe to try and make me feel less like she's interrogating me.

I take a deep breath, once again stalling for time. But I can't think of any reasonable explanation for the gash on my arm. It's blatantly obvious that I've done this to myself. I know it, and Mrs Fletcher knows it. Why am I prolonging this?

"I did it to myself," I say, very quietly. My voice is wobbly, and croaky, but I've told the truth.

Mrs Fletcher gives me a small, sad smile. "I thought so," she admits softly. "I'm glad you were able to tell me the truth." She pauses for a moment. "And that's why you didn't want to wear short sleeves? This, and... all the older cuts?"

I nod wordlessly. I feel like I should be panicking, but I'm still numb.

"Alright," says Mrs Fletcher quietly. "I understand now."

There's a brief silence, as Mrs Fletcher takes out a packet of paper stitches and starts to close up the wound with them. There's something heavy in her demeanour now. I wonder if she is feeling guilty that she didn't pick up on it sooner. Still, I'm sure there's another question on her tongue that she's deciding how to word; and finally, she spits it out.

"Why do you do this?" she asks hesitantly.

I have to close my eyes. I don't want to have to answer this. Though I can't deny that I've been fantasising about telling someone about the self-harm ever since the first time I did it, somehow now that the moment is here, I don't know what the fuck I'm supposed to say.

"Is it something at school?" she asks when I don't answer. I get the impression that she is trying to make this easier for me, that she's trying to give me a starting point to explain why I'm slicing up my arms.

I shake my head. I may not enjoy school at the moment, but I'm guessing she's talking about bullying, and that's not happening to me at least. I could tell her about the rumours going around about me – and how everyone seems to know I'm gay long before I wanted them to – but I'm not sure what she can do about that. She can't stop people laughing, giving me looks. Maybe if I told her the truth, she would be laughing at me too. I don't know Mrs Fletcher well enough to know what her reaction would be.

Her eyes are still on me. To my relief, she nods and seems to accept that she was barking up the wrong tree. But that doesn't mean she is done trying. "Is something going on at home?" she pushes, though her voice is still gentle.

Of course, I can't answer that. Nothing good would come of answering that. But I hear myself breathe out raggedly – and I kick myself internally. I need to act like she's way off the mark, again.

My face is flushing as I look up at her; I feel overwhelmed and I start to jiggle my leg anxiously, almost as an automatic reaction. For a second – a brief, brief second – I consider telling her the truth. But that's almost laughable. I can't tell her that, and you know what? I refuse to. She won't understand.

Finally, I shake my head. "No," I answer quietly. I don't know what else to say. Maybe the briefer I am here, the better.

Mrs Fletcher frowns, but I think she's more concerned than anything else. "Alright," she says slowly, but the frown doesn't leave her face. "You know, whatever it is, whatever the problem is, you can always talk to me. Or another teacher."

I look back down at my knees. She's being kind, I know she is. But she just doesn't get it. There's so much – and I wouldn't know how to start. Even if I wanted to tell her, I wouldn't know where to start.

I draw my uninjured arm around my belly protectively. I just want to disappear. Everything has gotten so complicated – too complicated. Maybe I should have started self-harming years ago, when I would have actually been able to tell Mrs Fletcher about what was going on. Now? Now, it's all pushed down too deep down. Maybe it's not that I should have started self-harming; maybe it's just that I should have tried to speak to someone earlier on.

Of course, I know why I didn't, and never would have. But that is neither here nor there now.

I don't look up at Mrs Fletcher as I nod listlessly, deciding that it's easier to just play along than to admit to her that I'm never going to approach a teacher with all the things bothering me. Unless Remus Lupin starts teaching at this school, I'm not going to be able to tell any teachers anything.

Mrs Fletcher sighs. "Alright," she says again. I feel her eyes on me as she continues. "Just remember, my office door is always open," she tells me, and I'm surprised how gentle she sounds. Tears prick in my eyes; I'm kind of touched, but I push them back. I can't afford to start talking just because people have been nice to me.

11

It takes us until the seafront is absolutely quiet again, the men long gone, before we finally climb back up to our feet. Before I have a chance to speak, Maeve grabs her drink from me and starts gulping it. Admittedly, after such an incident as we've just had, I'm not sure if giving Maeve alcohol is the best thing to do, but there's not a lot I can do about it now.

"Just… slowly, yeah?" I say weakly.

Maeve nods, before taking another big gulp. I hope there's not too much alcohol in a Smirnoff Ice.

We walk quietly along the seafront. Resignedly, I open my own bottle and take a long draught. It's soothing, though I don't know if it's the alcohol kicking in or just relief to be moving away from the obviously dodgy spot we've just been in.

"I'm hungry," announces Maeve suddenly. "Are you hungry? I'm hungry."

I look over to her; she looks a little manic, swinging her arms at her side with her fingers constantly twiddling, wrapping around each other. Somehow, the combination doesn't look quite right.

"Alright…" I say slowly, frowning slightly. "Well, what are you hungry for? I guess some shops and stuff will still be open—"

"McDonald's!" Maeve exclaims loudly, beaming, barely letting me finish. "Chips! My mum never let—"

But Maeve's manic determination wavers at this. For a minute, the silence is heavy and awkward. For a moment, I dither – but then I remember that the best way to get information from Maeve is to ask questions. If I don't ask, I don't think I'll ever know.

"Is that what…?" I begin, determinedly keeping my voice wheedling and gentle. "Is your mum… really strict?"

I realise that the question comes out a little lame, and Maeve sighs. "No," she says flatly, but stubbornly. Though the brightness she was exhibiting when we first met seems to be gone for the moment, the determination that went alongside it is resolutely back. "She just… nothing."

I frown but I don't know what to say. I don't know how to help. It's quite clear to me by now that I don't want Maeve to have to go back to her family home. Something has obviously happened there. If nothing else, those bruises, the ones she's trying to hide from me with her hair… how can I just let that go?

Unfortunately, I can see only one way to try to get her to open up.

"Things were hard at home for me too," I say carefully. I know that I have to be careful about how much I reveal to her – not because I don't trust her but because I don't want her to have to carry it around with her.

"Who says things are hard at home for me?" Maeve asks – but at least the flatness is gone and she sounds a little warmer.

I shrug, watching her closely. "No one," I say, keeping my tone casual. "But I'm not going to tell anyone if things are tricky for you right now." As soon as I say it, I wonder if I'm telling the truth. Is it wrong to make a promises like this, that I know I can't keep?

Maeve sighs. "Look, it's not… it's not *great* but it's fine, OK? My parents are just really stressed."

"Yeah, so were mine," I mutter darkly before I can stop myself. Somehow, I don't expect Maeve to reply, and she doesn't.

We walk in silence for a while, the atmosphere a little tenser than before. Maeve stares straight ahead as if she is determinedly not making conversation. For my part, I just don't know what to say.

Finally, I speak. "What's your favourite subject at school, then?" I ask, a little feebly.

Maeve turns to me, a slight stroke of incredulity on her face – but she humours me. "English," she tells me. A little glint appears in her eyes before she speaks again. "But also PE because the teacher's fit."

I let out a chuckle, surprising myself. "Yeah, I had a fit PE teacher too. I guess they're the only teachers walking around in tiny shorts."

Suddenly my mind fills with an image of Mrs Fletcher – an image of sitting outside her office – but I push it aside. She was fit, focus on that. In any case, something about our shared embarrassment seems to make Maeve smile too. Then she laughs. And before I know it, we are walking and laughing and everything feels a little bit more OK.

*

When we enter McDonald's, it's largely as I expected it would be. It's the nearest food place to all the pubs and bars in town, so during the night it tends to be mostly full of people wanting a drunken snack. That being said, it's too early for it to be massively busy just yet. There's a couple of teenagers with red-rimmed eyes who look like they have the munchies, but apart from them, we pretty much have the place to ourselves.

"What do you want?" I ask Maeve, with a little smile. I'm the one with the money, but I don't want her to feel awkward about it.

Maeve looks up at the menu. To my surprise, she suddenly looks a little bit overwhelmed.

"Um…" She falters for a minute. "Chips?" she says uncertainly. "And Coke?"

Something clicks from what she half told me earlier. "Maeve?" I ask. "Have you ever been in here before?"

For a second, Maeve looks slightly mutinously at me; but then she hangs her head. "I know it's weird," she half-mumbles, before finally admitting, "My mum doesn't let me."

I sigh slightly; my mum didn't let me have McDonald's as a kid either. I understand feeling out of place somewhere that's supposed to be familiar to everyone. "Don't worry," I tell her reassuringly. "I only came in here for the first time a year or two ago. Only since I came into hospital."

"Silver lining of being incarcerated?" Maeve mutters and I have to smile.

Still, I can tell she's anxious about the whole thing. "Look, I'll get us both chips and drinks, and you go and find a table," I tell her, hoping to make things a little bit easier. Though, I'm sure Katy the psychologist wouldn't agree with me. She always tells me that 'avoidance maintains anxiety' and all that.

It doesn't take long for me to buy and pay for the food. Now that I'm seeing it and smelling it, I realise that I'm really hungry too. I spot Maeve in the corner, fiddling with her fingers again as she looks around at the tables. She's picked a big table in the corner, by the window and far from the counter; I suspect that she wanted to be in as quiet an area as possible. I make my way over to the table with the food, and I can see the relief on Maeve's face as I come closer.

"Thank you," she says, and dives in.

I'm about to do the same when the door to the restaurant swings open again. I look over automatically – and quickly drop down under the table in panic.

"Er…" says Maeve, somewhere between confusion and amusement. "What are you doing, exactly?"

But this is no time for jokes. I crawl frantically to the far side of the table, so that I'm pressed right against the wall. "Shut up!" I hiss urgently. "The police!"

I can see just enough of Maeve to see her look over to the door, clock the police officers and turn a delicate shade of white. "Oh shit," she breathes. "Are they going to arrest you?"

I have to stop myself rolling my eyes, even as panic is rising in me. "They'll be looking for me," I explain, as quickly but tolerantly as I can. "They'll take me back to the hospital."

But as soon as I say this, something hits me. "Maeve," I say directly. "Will your parents have reported you missing?"

It hurts in my chest a little bit, despite the panic, as I look up at Maeve and she has a rueful little smile on her face. "No," she answers, a little pained. "They won't have reported me missing."

What is going *on* in Maeve's house? But right now, I have to force myself to put it out of my mind and not ask any more questions. If the police catch me, then they'll take Maeve too and she'll be taken back to that house. For both our sakes, I have to stay hidden.

Fortunately, Maeve seems to understand this without me having to tell her. She keeps her eyes on the table and, with a furtive glance over at the tills, she quietly dumps one plastic cup out of sight on the floor, and rearranges the food so it looks more like she's just having a really big meal by herself.

(In the middle of the night?! But there's nothing I can do about it now.)

"I told you I was hungry," she breathes without looking at me, as she starts on one portion of chips.

I don't laugh; the situation is too serious. But I have to trust her. Where I'm hidden under the table, I can't see the queue, the till, the door – or the two police officers. All I can see is Maeve, and a few table legs.

I alternate between crossing my fingers tight and clenching my fists as I sit there in an agony of panic. What's going on? Have they spotted Maeve? It flashes into my mind just how suspicious it might look for someone so obviously young to be out alone at this time. Granted, it's unlikely that they'll leap to the conclusion that she's with an escaped psychiatric patient who is currently hidden under the table, but it still wouldn't be ideal if they started questioning her.

Suddenly, I feel a swift kick to my shoulder and I freeze even stiller, now totally motionless. My heart contracts and I hold my breath. Have they seen Maeve? Have they caught sight of me? What's happening? I'm so frustrated that I can't see what the danger is.

And then, to my horror – heavy footsteps indicate that large boots are approaching. Police boots? I flatten myself further against the wall. This is it. I'm going to get sent back to hospital and Maeve – well, Maeve might get hurt even more. And there will be nothing I can do to stop it.

The footsteps come nearer and nearer before finally coming to a stop. I wait for a deep, authoritarian voice to tell me to get up, but instead, I hear the sound of chairs scraping back. Chancing a glance to where the sound is coming from, I see two sets of clumpy police boots sat at the table directly next to us.

I don't dare to shift from the exact position that I'm in – it seems to have kept me hidden so far and I'm not in a position to start trying out anything else. The downside is that where I'm now flattened against the wall, I can't see Maeve anymore. I hope furiously that if she's panicking, they can't tell. Actually, no, I hope they're paying no attention to her whatsoever. Just a young girl having McDonald's alone. Nothing to see here.

I can't quite order my thoughts enough to tune into what the police officers are saying, but I hear the general buzz of their voices. All I can do is hope that their break time is short. How long are police breaks? Five minutes? Or could I be sat here for fifteen minutes, thirty minutes, an hour? I groan internally.

But then something happens that very nearly stops my heart

– a small container of ketchup falls off the edge of the police officers' table and rolls towards me.

Before I know what's happening, above the table Maeve's reflexes (which I admit are lightning-fast) kick in and suddenly she throws herself down between the tables, hiding me from view while under the guise of retrieving the ketchup. She grabs the container and sits up slightly awkwardly, holding the ketchup aloft – nothing to see down there, the ketchup is here!

"Here you go," I hear Maeve proclaim brightly, sat back up. "Don't want to lose your ketchup!"

Christ, I hope this is more convincing to them than it is to me.

There's a pause, but to my relief, neither police officer looks under the table. Still, I don't relax. "Cheers," says an uncertain voice that I don't recognise. "Everything alright, here, my love?"

This is exactly the kind of question that we don't need. Somehow, though, I don't panic quite as much as I should. Maeve is handling things remarkably well.

"Yeah, all good," comes Maeve's breezy voice. "I'm just waiting for my friend."

Which, to be fair to Maeve, is kind of true. She is indeed waiting for her friend – to come out from under the table. I cringe, still frozen.

"Alright," says the unfamiliar voice slowly, but sounding – maybe, just maybe – a little less concerned. "Go carefully, yeah? It's late to be out alone." There's a short pause, and I hear a small rustling before the police officer speaks again. "This is my card. Call me if… if you need."

I don't hear any response from Maeve – but I see her sleeve move, taking the card. I assume she's smiling or nodding or something acceptable to the police officers because I hear them go back to their own conversation. All we need now is for them to finish their food and *leave*.

However, as things happen, I'm sat scrunched up under the table, frozen, for a good while longer. With my phone still lying on the table, I don't know what the time is, but it feels like an eternity before I hear boots moving again, and Maeve finally pokes her head under the table. "They're gone," she tells me, sounding highly, *highly* relieved.

She's not the only one. Finally, I'm able to stretch out and clamber out from under the table. I feel stiff and achy as I flop down into my chair again and stretch my legs under the table. Mostly, though, I'm euphoric that they've left, and we've gotten away with it.

I turn to Maeve, beaming. "Thank you," I say sincerely. "You were amazing."

Maeve grins. "I know! I nearly died when they dropped the ketchup!"

And to my own surprise, I find that I'm actually giggling. I don't giggle! But right now, I'm buzzing so excitably from our close escape that I can't remember how to be as withdrawn as I usually tend to be.

"Did you leave me any chips?" I ask Maeve, raising one eyebrow playfully.

"I had to pretend it was all mine!" replies Maeve indignantly, but still with a huge grin on her face. She pushes one portion of chips towards me and gives me a cheeky smile before asking, "Ketchup?"

She falls about laughing at her own joke, and though I roll my eyes, I laugh too. Suddenly everything feels hilarious.

"I'm starving." I grin, starting to shovel cold chips into my mouth. "It must be the adrenaline, I could eat a horse!"

It's nice to feel relaxed, now that we've escaped danger for the moment; it's nice to feel that being with Maeve and talking with Maeve is just so *easy*. We get each other! Even though we're on the run, I feel safe. They'll never catch us. And, if they do, then at least we've had a good adventure.

And if they do, if they do – I will protect Maeve. I won't let her get hurt again. I won't let her get hurt like I did.

12

Even though Mrs Fletcher manages to bandage me up very well, I still get sent home for the rest of the day.

For a while, I sit in a chair outside Mrs Fletcher's office, still in my rugby kit. I get the impression that Mrs Fletcher doesn't want to let me get changed, because that would involve leaving me alone for too long. I kind of don't blame her, but I feel very self-conscious sitting here like this.

She phones several people while I sit outside the office. On the bright side, it would seem that her office is soundproof after all, though she is clearly keeping an eye on me through that glass wall. I don't know who any of the people she phones are, and after a while, I stop being able to keep track of how many calls she places. When she put me out here, all she said was that she had to speak to a few people. She didn't tell me who, though she did say it wasn't her place to call my parents.

This was definitely ominous – saying that it wasn't her place implied to me that it was someone else's. Presumably my head of year, or the school nurse. I know I have no choice in the matter. Even if I had a legitimate reason for not wanting my parents to know, they probably have safeguarding shit to think about. And, of course, I can't tell the teachers the real reason why I don't want my parents to know.

I've been avoiding this situation for months, but now it's here, I feel oddly calm. Well, part of me feels like crying, and part of me feels like throwing something... but it's all detached. My main body – if that's a thing – feels numb. Even after everything that's happened in the last hour... I feel nothing. I'm an empty vessel, frankly.

I'm watching out the window as I see the rest of the class coming back into the changing rooms from the rounders pitch. If they hadn't changed the sports schedule today then I would be out there with my friends, not tired in the slightest from an hour of dodging the rugby ball. Luckily, no one seems to see me sat outside Mrs Fletcher's office as they go past.

Then the door to the block of offices swings open, and Mr Stuart walks into the room. He already has a little frown on his face, but when he sees me, he looks all the more confused. "Why are you here?" he asks sharply.

I see his gaze go down to my bandaged arm, and once again I try to hold the arm close to my stomach. I stare down at my shoes. "Mrs Fletcher told me to sit here," I say at last, my voice oddly hoarse.

"Hmm," is the only response that I get from him. Still, his gaze leaves me and I relax slightly in relief. As he looks up, I see him catch Mrs Fletcher's eye. I can't see her response as I face straight ahead, but she must wave him away, because with a final frown at me, he turns and leaves the block.

He's going to come back, though, I know. Even if it's after I leave. Eventually, he's going to have to know. How many more of my teachers are going to have to be told? How many of my teachers has Mrs Fletcher already phoned while I sit awkwardly in this waiting room, tracing patterns on the carpet with my foot?

It's not long after Mr Stuart leaves that Mrs Fletcher finally comes out of her office. I look up immediately, realising as I do that I must seem jumpy. Mrs Fletcher gives me a kind smile.

"I've just spoken to the school nurse," she tells me, her voice still gentle. "She's called your mum. She'll be along to collect you soon."

I drop my eyes back down to my lap. I feel tears coming and I know I have to hold them back. Nodding quickly at Mrs Fletcher, I blink hard. I'm not sure exactly why I'm about to cry; I don't feel sad, or even panicky. I just feel... drained. Today has been too much.

"I'm sorry," I breathe, without looking up.

There's a little pause as I suspect Mrs Fletcher is frowning down at me again. "You have nothing to be sorry for," she says, sounding a little surprised. "No one's angry at you."

(This is patently untrue; but in Mrs Fletcher's defence, she probably thinks she is telling the truth.)

I bite my lip hard, and somehow I still can't look up. For a second, Mrs Fletcher hovers next to me; but then she sits down on the chair next to me and reaches over to touch my shoulder again. "You're going to be alright," she says kindly.

I nod automatically. I don't know what other response to that there is.

Mrs Fletcher sighs quietly. "Are you sure there isn't anything...?" She trails off, her head tilted sympathetically at me.

This feels absurd; for so long I've wanted to talk to someone, for someone to notice how much pain I'm in. Why am I not telling Mrs Fletcher anything? Shouldn't I be jumping at the chance? For a crazy second, I consider blurting out everything. But I can't. I shake my head firmly. I wish there was something easy that I could confess, something that Mrs Fletcher could actually help with.

I can tell that she's not satisfied, but she squeezes my shoulder lightly before giving it a pat. "Your mum will be here soon," she tells me again. "Shall I walk you to the main office? You can wait for her there."

I swallow. "What did they tell her?" I ask at last.

Mrs Fletcher hesitates. "That you hurt yourself today, I think," she tells me cautiously. "And – I expect – that you've done it before." Head still tilted, Mrs Fletcher sighs again. "To be fair... you haven't told us very much. There isn't much to pass on."

I guess she has a point. Though, that being said, I know she means it as a bad thing. As if the more I share, the more they will be able to help me. But really, right now, I'm just glad that I've managed to dodge almost every question that Mrs Fletcher could have thought to throw my way.

Maybe that's obvious on my face, because Mrs Fletcher looks a little sad. "You'll get there," she says heavily. The statement in itself is somewhat ambiguous, but I kind of know what she means. And I know that she means it kindly. Whether I will get there, or not...

"Come on," she says. "Let me walk you to the main office."

She doesn't trust me to get there safely on my own is the implication, but I nod and stand up. For a moment I dither as to whether to cover my bandaged arm with my sleeve; but actually, I think the massive blood stain is going to displease my mum more than the bandage. At least the bandage is still white. Unspoiled. Less aggravating.

Mrs Fletcher and I walk to the main office in silence, stopping only at the changing rooms to grab my school bag. Luckily, everyone has finished changing back into their school uniforms by now. When we reach reception, Mrs Fletcher gives a quick but significant look at the ancient receptionist, presumably to tell her to make sure I don't go anywhere, and turns to me.

"You're going to be OK," she says gently, and, touching my shoulder again, she leaves me alone to wait for my mum. I wonder, briefly, what she will tell her husband about her day. If I will feature or if she will gloss over it. If she knows that there is a lot that I'm not telling her.

This train of thought ends abruptly when the door to reception buzzes, and my mother steps into the long room. The look on her face is enough to tell me that it's not going to be a fun ride home.

She says a few words to the receptionist as I grab my school bag. Of course, to the receptionist, she is polite and friendly; but the fact that she won't even meet my eye isn't a great sign. When I have collected up all my things, my mum turns without a word and walks out the door she came in through, out to the car park. I don't say anything either, even as we reach the car and get inside. It's only when my mum is starting the engine that the silence is finally broken.

"Whatever's wrong," my mum says tersely, "this isn't the way to deal with it."

I sigh. I don't know what I'm supposed to say here; all I know is that I am determined not to apologise. For one thing, it's none of her business. What I do to my body is up to me. Besides, really – does she have a leg to stand on when it comes to this issue?

I stay stonily silent. For a minute, so does my mum. I'm not sure if she's just concentrating on driving as she backs out of the parking space and joins the road.

But before too long, she speaks again. "This shouldn't be your way of dealing with... stress," she says snappily, sharply.

I speak before my mind has time to remind my mouth to shut up. "Stress," I repeat, and my voice surprises me in how harshly it comes out. "Stress?!"

She shakes her head dismissively. "Well, whatever," she says with a condescending little sigh. "Acting out like this – what is it supposed to achieve? What if it hadn't been your teacher who found you today? What if it had been one of your friends?"

I resent the implication that my friends wouldn't stand by me, that their knowing about my self-harm would cause problems for me. Obviously I can't guarantee how they would respond, but I'm fairly sure that they wouldn't have a go at me like she is now. I don't trust most of my friends very much at the moment, but in a fight between them and my mother, I automatically take their side.

"I didn't mean for Mrs Fletcher to catch me," I snap.

She sighs again, impatient. "You wanted to make a scene," she corrects me. "Why, I don't know, but—"

I'm tempted to swear at her but I'm well aware that that would make things worse. "And what about all the other cuts?" I interrupt. "All the ones in secret?"

"You're the one doing it," she reminds me harshly, almost sarcastically. "You tell me."

"Like I would," I retort before I can stop myself.

That's the truth, though. I can hazard a guess as to why I'm doing it, I suppose, but she would be the last person that I would tell the truth about it to. Firstly, I hardly need to – if she would get her head out of her arse, she would know why. And even if she doesn't know right now, well – treating me like I'm just a problem to solve isn't exactly the best way to get me to open up.

And more so – I know once her initial anger at this has abated, she is going to start asking questions like it's her birthright to know. Like I don't have a choice but to confide in her. And I know that an attitude like that is going to make me even angrier. She doesn't get to abandon me, to forget about me, and then demand that I tell her about my life. She's abdicated the right to act like that, in my view.

We drive home without another word. For my part, I'm frustrated and upset and stressed. I don't need her making it worse. For her part? I think she just knows that this is a battle that she can't win.

I slip my shoes off at the door and leave them by the foot of the stairs before I walk up the stairs to my bedroom and shut the door. I dump my school bag by my desk and for a second, I stand, lost. I can hear my mum downstairs, clattering around as she makes a cup of tea. In all honesty, I hope she just leaves me alone.

I lie down on my bed, facing away from the door so as to have time to pretend to be asleep if my mum does come in. I look down at the arm that two hours ago, Mrs Fletcher was carefully bandaging. Sometimes I wonder – Mrs Fletcher is fit, and I know I have a little thing for her, but today, I wasn't thinking about that. I was thinking that she made me feel safe.

The arm is wrapped up tightly in several layers of bandage, and though I have a brief urge to rip it all off, I leave it alone. It feels like it's nicer to leave it intact. Ironically, it's the only part of me *that feels intact right now. I draw my arm towards me protectively, and now I'm curled up in a ball, almost in the foetal position.*

Suddenly, I'm exhausted. Today has been exhausting. To be fair, I'm tired a lot of the time at the moment anyway. But today has been something else, frankly.

I manage to roll over to the edge of my bed to grab my blanket from where I've left it lying on the floor. I grasp the soft fabric and pull it up onto the bed with me. It's not cold in here, but I feel like I need something covering me. Somehow, I feel the tiniest bit safer now I'm cocooned. My little teddy bear, who I left lying on the pillow this morning, is nestled in by my neck, doing her duty to protect me.

I didn't lie down to sleep, but now I'm warm and I'm lying on something soft, my eyes are starting to close themselves. Maybe a nap isn't a bad idea. To move now, to shake off this tiredness and try to force myself to do something... No, it isn't going to happen. I'm going to drift off...

It feels like an age later when I start to wake at the sound of my bedroom door creaking open. My automatic reaction is to stretch, but instead I stiffen, forcing myself to keep completely still. I'm not sure why. Maybe I just want to keep my mum from coming in.

I hear the door creak open the full way and then footsteps come into my room. I stay still, but I can't stop her from approaching my bed and then sitting on the edge. With all the criticising I do of my mum for not knowing me, I know that she can tell I'm awake. There's just something in my pride that means I can't turn over and face her.

She smooths my hair out of my face and for some reason this makes my chest hurt a little bit. It's odd that most of the time, I don't get on with my mum; because when she wants to, she knows how to mother me. She has barely touched me, and already I can feel myself forgiving her.

"Are you cold?" she asks softly as she takes the edge of the blanket and gently pulls it over the place where it's fallen off my shoulder while I was asleep. She sighs, but this time it isn't irritable or impatient. It's soft and I feel cared about.

"Look at me," she says, and finally, reluctantly, I turn over on the bed so that I'm looking into her eyes.

I don't get a chance to talk before she continues – not, admittedly, that I would know what to say anyway. "Your dad gets so angry at me when you're like this," she says, very quietly. I feel guilt rise up; I hear them shouting at each other. Not even just when they think I'm asleep, like the cliché. Though they don't outright go for each other when I'm there, they don't exactly have qualms about getting shots in at each other.

This is not the first time that my mum has told me that the problems in their relationship are my fault. I guess she has a point. In any case, I don't argue.

"What did you tell that teacher?" she asks. Her voice is still quiet but the softness has somehow become a little menacing. I try to return myself to the feeling of warm safety, but it won't quite come.

I shake my head. "Nothing," I reply, my voice coming out hoarse. "Just that I've done it before."

Ashamed, I look away, and suddenly my mum is motherly again, stroking my shoulder. "That's good," she tells me, quiet but definitely praising me. "You know if you start telling them… these things… they're just going to think you're ridiculous, don't you? Or they'll overreact and you'll end up in a foster home. You'll have to change schools and leave all your friends…"

She trails off, her fingers playing with my hair, as I shake my head again. I can't quite speak right now, but she knows what the gesture means. She knows I won't tell. I don't want my life destroyed when all I have to do is keep my stupid mouth shut.

"Shall I get you a drink and a biscuit?" she asks, like I'm a child. Still, it works, and slowly I sit up, nodding this time. As much as I fight with my mum, I know that it always ends up here. I'm her baby. I'm too stupid to think for myself.

13

We sit in McDonald's for a while. Maeve, who for some reason is absolutely ravenous, devours chips, burgers, mozzarella sticks and then ice cream. I do my best, but I can't keep up with her. It only when I awkwardly point out that my funds are becoming depleted that she eventually stops.

She sits back against the plastic seats, her hands resting on her belly. This is the calmest I've ever seen her and I make a mental note to feed her next time she needs calming down.

Maeve looks at me. "Do you have a boyfriend, Heather?" she asks, her tone more cautious than usual.

I let my gaze rest tentatively on Maeve. "That's personal," I point out, but I'm not really offended. "No," I answer. "No boyfriend."

Maeve fixes her gaze on me but doesn't say anything straight away. It looks like she trying to work out how to phrase her next thought – or whether to say it out loud at all. Still, she doesn't seem agitated. Just thoughtful.

"What about a girlfriend?" she asks, still watching me carefully.

Ah. That's more tricky. It usually takes people longer than this to work out that I'm gay; and it's always a bit tense revealing it to someone new.

"No," I say slowly, a bit hesitantly. "Not right now."

Her eyes don't leave my face. "But you'd like one? At some point?"

Her gaze is penetrating and unwavering, and it occurs to me that it kind of seems like Maeve can read me like a book. It would be impressive if it wasn't so wrong-footing.

Finally, I nod. "Yeah," I admit. "I would like that. Being in hospital and stuff, I haven't had many chances, but… yeah."

Something flashes across Maeve's face that I can't quite read. But before long, her face is back to that gaze. She's looking right into my head, I'm sure of it.

"You're out, though?" she asks directly.

I feel a small smile play around the edges of my lips. "Yes," I confirm. "I'm out. Everyone knows."

I expect Maeve to smile, to make a joke or to laugh; instead, I see tears bead at the corner of her eyes. She drops her penetrating gaze down to look at a patch of spilled salt on the table. Before I know what's happening, tears are dripping fast onto the brightly coloured plastic.

"What's wrong?" I ask, totally wrong-footed again.

Before I can say anything else, Maeve shakes her head violently. She clears her throat, hard, as if to hold back another wave of tears, while her sleeve against her face quickly wipes away the tears that have already fallen. She takes a deep, deep breath. And then I see that she's smiling through the tears.

"It's just nice to hear," she chokes out, albeit with the smile still sticking to her face. "You know, love and that." She rubs her eyes once again with the palm of her hands.

"Right," I reply cautiously. "Well, yeah… it's OK…"

She nods hard. To my relief, she seems to just about have a handle on her tears now. Even so, she doesn't meet my eyes like she did before. Instead, she rests her chin on her hand and shifts around to look out of the window at the car park.

One thing niggles at me and I have to remind myself that it

has to be better to be direct.

"Maeve?" I ask, a little tentative but trying to keep my voice gentle. My PE teacher pops into mind but I push that thought away. This isn't the same; I'm a friend. I'm not going to follow a procedure and make things worse for her.

Maeve doesn't look at me and continues to look out of the window. Her forehead is rested on the cool glass now, but I suspect that she isn't paying attention to which cars are going into the drive-thru. Finally, though, she gives me a little nod.

I take this as an invitation to carry on talking, and I decide to just outright ask. "Maeve, are *you* gay?" I ask bluntly, even as I lower my voice to keep the conversation private.

She doesn't turn to look at me, choosing instead to keep staring out at the dark car park. "I don't want to talk about that," she finally says evenly.

I hesitate for a minute, tempted to ask more questions – and I quickly decide not to push it. I know when I was Maeve's age, I wouldn't have wanted someone asking me questions about my sexuality. Besides, not wanting to talk about it, coupled with tears, kind of suggests that she's questioning at the very least. And when you're questioning, I suppose you don't want to be pushed for an answer.

But there's one thing I feel compelled to ask. "Is that why your parents are… stressed?" I ask, my voice still low, intentionally using Maeve's own word. "Your sexuality?"

Finally, she turns her head to look at me, a little frown on her face. "No," she says dismissively, but her eyes are fixed on me again now. "They're just stressed. Will you drop it?"

I hold up my hands in surrender. "I'm sorry," I say quickly. "I don't mean to pry. I just want to make sure you're safe." I pause, then finally voice my biggest worry. "Maeve, we can't run forever. We need to work out where you're going to stay."

"I don't know that I am," she replies in a tiny, sad voice.

For a moment, there's silence.

I blink. "What?" I ask hesitantly. "What do you mean?"

I can hear the sharp note in my voice and my heart is thumping. Has Maeve come out tonight for the same reason that I have?

"Maeve," I prompt. "Come on, talk to me."

But she doesn't speak, instead just shaking her head. I don't know what to do. I feel panic rising. I can't let her; I've been thinking all this time about keeping her safe from her parents – should I be keeping her safe from herself?

"I'm not talking about suicide," she says at last, her voice surprisingly level and calm, though still with that sadness running through it.

I physically feel the relief in my chest as I allow myself to believe her. Maybe I'm being a hypocrite – but I don't want Maeve to go.

"OK..." I say, trying to be in control but my voice comes out hoarse. "What... well... what did you mean, then?"

She sighs. "It doesn't matter."

I find myself leaning across the table, as if being physically closer to her will get her to listen. "But it does," I press. "Look, it's obvious something's wrong."

But she's shaking her head. "I'll work it out, I'll work it out," she insists, back to not meeting my eyes. She clasps her hands tightly. "I don't want to talk about it anymore."

My instinct is to press harder, to keep asking questions, to find out what's wrong and persuade her to let me help her. But it's starting to dawn on me that the more I push her, the more she shuts down. No matter whether I choose to be gentle or pushy, it just isn't working. I need to try something else. Even if I don't know what that is quite yet.

"Anyway," she says suddenly, shaking me out of my thoughts. "What about you? What are you going to do when *you* get caught?"

I sigh, the prospect depressing. "Go back to the hospital," I say gloomily. "I don't have a choice."

"Well, yes," she says impatiently. "But I mean, are you going to get better?"

I furrow my brow as I look up at her. That question is a surprise. I haven't been expecting that.

Finally, I nod. "I suppose so," I say hesitantly. I don't really know what else to say. There isn't really much else you can say to that question, no matter how you really feel about it.

How *do* I really feel about it? When I first got taken in hospital, I thought it would fix me. But several years in, it clearly isn't doing that. Admittedly, I've had periods of doing better, of being kind of happy – but how does it always seem to come back to this?

Now more than ever, I just want it over. Everything, over. Coming out tonight… I know exactly what I was coming out to do. I'm wondering if tonight is the night at all; but I desperately want it to be.

I'm sure that there's no way, however, of verbalising any of this to Maeve. But I haven't banked on Maeve's dogged determination.

"I know you're just saying that. That you'll get better," she tells me bluntly. Of course she does. How does she read me so successfully?

I shift uncomfortably. "I don't know what you want me to say," I tell her, and it saddens me to hear the weary note in my own voice. The fact that it's come so far – that it's come to this.

But if my voice sounds sad, it's nothing compared to the look on Maeve's face. I notice with a pang that tears are welling up in her eyes again. "I just don't want you to kill yourself," she manages to choke out as more tears start to fall.

I'm not equipped for this. Because I can't say what Maeve needs to hear from me – I can't say that I won't do it, because if not tonight then it will be next week, or next month. All I'm doing by not doing it tonight is postponing the inevitable – and how can I say that to a fourteen-year-old who has obviously grown fond of me?

I have to rest my forehead on the sticky plastic table for a minute to compose myself. When I finally look back up, Maeve has stopped crying, but her expression is one that I can't look at for long.

"What are we going to do, Heather?" she asks in a small voice.

I can't answer her. I have no idea.

14

It's a Tuesday when I empty my books into my locker, as well as anything else in my bag that I deem to be superfluous. I'm left with my phone, my purse and my diary. They are the only things that I can think I might need for where I'm going this afternoon.

With whispered laughter following me everywhere, with the impossible situation at home, with teachers looking at me like I wasn't the kid they thought I was… I can't pinpoint the exact thing that tips me over the edge. It's just too much. I'm not sleeping and I can't concentrate. Whatever I'm doing, there is a gnawing pain in the centre of my chest.

It's time. I don't know how I know this, but I do.

There is a tiny bit of relief that my bag is now so light. Maybe it's the thought of never having to go back to studying from those textbooks. Soon, this will be over. I think that's what is really causing the sense of relief. Because I know that I can't keep doing this.

The advantage of going to an independent school is that the school doesn't really have any measures to prevent truanting; I guess if your parents are paying, you're less likely to peg it. It's not hard to get out of the school building, and the main gates, front and back, are always open. Today, I walk out of the back gate purposefully. I don't think anyone sees me, but if they do, I doubt they think anything is amiss. They probably think I'm just going to the dentist or something.

It's another slight relief just leaving the gates. This place has felt like a prison the last few months – if not the last few years. I know that now that I've walked out, there's no going back. How many times have I pictured doing this? And in every version, I know I can only do it once. This is it.

I haven't decided, exactly, how I'm going to do it. I've thought of a few options. I have money on me – not a large amount but enough to get a train somewhere to throw anyone who might care off the scent. Or I could use the money for pills, over-the-counter ones. Paracetamol, or cough mixture, maybe. Something that's toxic in large quantities. Or I'm sure I can find somewhere that will sell me a thick cord. Thick enough to hold my weight.

You can guess, now, what it is that I'm planning to do this afternoon.

I know that I have a few hours before anyone notices that I've gone missing. Five years of being a goody-two-shoes in my lessons have earned me the kind of reputation with teachers that means they won't question my absence. Even though I suspect most of them know about the self-harm by now, I don't think they will put two and two together. The truth of what I'm going to do this afternoon has probably not even occurred to them.

I haven't told my friends where I'm going, but they won't wonder where I am either; I have been spending even more of my time on my own recently. I do feel a pang of guilt, though, when I think about them. I know that what I'm about to do is going to hurt them. And that they might feel guilty that they couldn't stop me – but it'll be better in the long run. They won't have to deal with me anymore. They won't have to think about me anymore. I'll fade quickly into a memory. And that will be better for everyone.

I walk down the hill leading from my school into the town centre. It's a long way, and I feel slightly sweaty on this hot day. It would have been better if I could have changed out of my school uniform, but I don't have any other clothes with me. Dressed in my uniform, I feel a little conspicuous. I could be imagining it, I suppose, but I'm sure I'm getting looks from people I pass. In any case, I keep walking purposefully.

I don't know the way very well; usually the only place I walk to from school is the train station to get the train home, in the opposite direction to the town centre. Something keeps me going, though. It's easier to just keep walking than to think too hard about which way I'm going.

I find myself in a park. It's not the park that I've spent time with my friends in, at least; it's on the other side of town to where we usually hang out. I'm not sure I could face being in the usual park, where I first told Amelie, Charlotte and Lydia that I was gay. More than that, though, I have good memories of that park. I don't want my friends to know that I died somewhere where we were happy.

I'm starting to shake, now. I haven't taken this decision lightly – how many times have I wanted to do this but I've held myself back? It was always going to end like this, and I genuinely feel like I've held on as long as I can.

Still, in the park, I take a seat on a bench. I'm sweating, and almost without thinking, I roll up my jumper sleeves. Since Mrs Fletcher caught me, and both the teachers and my parents found out about the self-harm, I have been much less careful about which parts of my body I cut. Frankly, I no longer feel the need to hide it. Consequently, my forearms are now covered in fresh cuts to an extent which they weren't before.

I close my eyes. My body is in fight-or-flight mode, but I feel oddly calm.

I start guiltily, however, when I sense someone sit down beside me on the bench. My eyes snap open and I swivel to face whoever it is. It takes a few seconds for my eyes to focus and register that the person next to me is a kindly looking older woman.

For a second, I hope that she just needs a seat, but I quickly realise that she's looking right at me. Self-conscious, I roll my sleeves down hurriedly, edging away from the woman. The damage is done, though. She's seen the cuts. The expression on her face tells me that with no doubt whatsoever.

"Can I give you a hug?" she asks gently.

I feel slightly frozen and my mouth is dry. I don't feel like I can speak. Is she being genuine? Should I be suspicious? She is a stranger, after all, but... I get a strong sense that this woman's intentions are good. I nod, and she pulls me quickly into a tight embrace.

"Oh, my dear. You're really suffering, aren't you?" she murmurs into my hair.

Tears spring to my eyes but I still feel frozen. Is this a sign from the universe? Or just a weirdly timed coincidence? I didn't think anyone would care. But this woman cares, and she doesn't even know me.

I suddenly feel panic rise up in me, and I automatically jump up, wrenching myself away from the woman. Any calm is now gone; I can feel the terror that my eyes must be showing. For a brief moment, the woman looks slightly put out, but then I can see her register the look in my eyes.

"It's alright," she says quickly, her voice still gentle. "Look, I'm not going to... do you want to help me walk my dog?"

I can tell she's grasping at straws for a way to keep me nearby, to stop me from hurting myself anymore today. She must be able to tell that I'm in danger somehow. Why else would I be alone in a park in the middle of the day, covered in cuts, still in my school uniform?

I'm shaking my head, though, backing away. "I have to go," I choke out.

The woman's eyes are big. "Come on, love—" she begins, but I'm already running. I'm so stupid. I shouldn't have sat down; I shouldn't have relaxed. I chance a glance behind me as I run, and

I can see the woman has her mobile phone to her ear. She's calling someone. Probably the police.

Suddenly the hours that I thought I had have depleted down to barely any time at all. And I have to do this today. I've walked out of school. I've run. I have to do this today.

My many options are slipping away through my fingers like sand. I haven't got time to get to the station, even if I'm not caught on CCTV; I haven't got time to buy a rope, or wait for pills to take effect. I only have one option left that I can think of. It was the last one on my list, but now it's looking like it's the only way.

I run across the grass and out the gates. The river runs parallel to the park, and as soon as I'm out of the gates, I'm on the river path. It's quieter there, with fewer dogwalkers and little kids, and I slow to a purposeful stride, because now at least I know where I'm going.

Sweat drips down my back as I walk so fast that I'm essentially running. The sun beats down on my head; where half an hour ago, it was pleasant, now it's forceful. I feel like it's pressing down on me, crushing me.

To my relief, I don't see any police; I can't think of any reason why they would need to be patrolling around here in the daytime anyway. The river is in a nice area of town, and it's quiet at this time. It feels so odd to be looking out for police when I haven't done anything wrong. This is a very new feeling for me. I'm not a criminal and I never have been.

I keep walking and try to focus on looking normal. Not much longer, not much further. I'm buzzing now, with adrenaline and anxiety. I've never really been out on my own much. Especially not in such an intense situation as this.

I can't decide how I feel when I finally see the bridge loom in my eyeline. It's a big bridge, high above the river, but not big enough to be covered in fencing like some of the main ones. There isn't even a plaque advising people to phone Samaritans. As this flashes into my mind, I briefly debate calling them. Calling anyone.

But I can't think of anything they would be able to say to make any of this feel less terrible.

I stop on the pavement, as I reach the bridge. There's something daunting about this – but of course there is. This isn't just life-changing; this is life-ending. I don't believe in the afterlife. I know that I'm never going to see any of the people I love again. I'm never going to have a job or a husband or a baby. Any of the things that people have planned out for me.

Tears bud in my eyes and I don't feel strong enough to hold them back. I stand for a minute, tears dripping down my face. I try to shake myself out of it; I'm only wearing the minimal amount of makeup that I can get away with in school, but that includes mascara, and I'm going to have black all down my face soon. I use the corner of my jumper sleeve to try and wipe some of the mess on my face away.

But if I'm honest – I don't care. I just want this over. I just want to stop feeling like this. I've got to steel myself. I've got to be brave. I don't want to be sobbing when I die. I want to walk into this bravely.

I force myself to start to walk; there's a pavement on either side of the bridge, with the road running through the centre. There aren't many cars driving over at this time. This is a good thing, I'm sure; fewer people to see what I'm doing. Fewer people to try and stop me.

I reach the apex of the bridge in seconds. I'm shaking. I grip the edge of the wall. Something tells me that looking over isn't going to help anything. I know it's going to hurt. I know it's a long way down. Obsessing over it isn't going to help.

I have to keep urging myself, keep forcing myself on, before I am finally able to push down firmly on the wall and haul myself up to sit on the edge of it. I hear a car beep its horn at me, but it doesn't stop. Of course it doesn't.

This is it. I'm going to keep edging over until I fall…

15

As the night goes on, and the pubs start to close nearby, McDonald's starts to fill up and feel less like a safe place. Not only am I worried that the police will turn up again to round up those who are drunk and disorderly, but the whole environment is really starting to make me feel anxious. I'm not good with big crowds – and I'm sensing Maeve isn't either. I open my mouth to suggest that we leave; and right on cue, we hear the sounds of an angry yell coming from the women's toilets, followed by a smash.

I don't have time to react before a large woman comes crashing through the toilet door. She doesn't stumble out; she flies out. I don't even have time to react to this before another, smaller woman follows her, marching out of the door and jumping on her without any hesitation.

I lurch back automatically, and beside me, I vaguely register Maeve freezing. I don't know what to do. This is no play fight; the smaller woman seems determined at the very least to rip the other woman's hair out. The larger woman shrieks in pain as the smaller woman yanks handfuls of her hair, her arms flailing, trying to land a blow to get the other woman off. Finally, purely as a strike of luck, her fist connects with the side of the other woman's face and knocks her sideways, hard.

I'm shaking as the smaller woman cries out in pain; but, luckily, security has clocked the both of them, and soon two burly men are rushing towards the women, each grabbing one and pulling them away from each other. Now, all they can do is shout abuse at each other; still, this doesn't seem to deter them, as they start to yell two tirades that soon merge into one.

I turn around sharply to suggest that it's time to go; but as I look around, Maeve has already bolted. I catch sight of her at the entrance, rushing through the door like something out of a cartoon. I'm suddenly reminded of myself at fourteen, when my English teacher put on a film one morning (probably at the end of term) and let it play over the lunch hour so we could see the ending. But I never saw the end of the film – there was a graphic domestic abuse scene and I bolted, like Maeve has just done. The teacher had buggered off by that point, so no adult ever got to see my sudden exit. Sometimes when I look back, I wish they had. It would have made things much easier, in some ways, for someone to even have suspected that something was wrong.

But I have to push that out of my mind, and I quickly grab all of my things from the table. Then I hurry out of the door that Maeve has just flown through, winding my way through a throng of drunken club-leavers. I look around; which direction has Maeve gone in?

Luckily, I spot her quickly, not too far from the entrance. I grimace; Maeve is bent over at the waist, vomiting onto the pavement as she hugs her stomach. Maybe it was all the junk food. It's not a situation I'm desperate to deal with; but it's Maeve. I guess I have to. I quickly make my way over.

I lay my hand on her back, rubbing gently. To my relief, she seems to know that it's me, and she doesn't flinch away from my touch. I'm not sure I would go so far as to say that my touch is comforting her, but she doesn't flinch, and that's something.

"You're alright," I say grimly. "That's it. Breathe, Maeve."

She does so, and it seems to help. Retching a few more times, her body seems to be satisfied that it has gotten rid of absolutely everything from her stomach. She takes a few more deep breaths before finally spitting out the remnants of bile from her mouth. Grimacing, she wipes her mouth with the back of her hand. Luckily, I have a few napkins from McDonald's stashed in my pocket; I pull out one and hand it to her.

"You're such a mama bear," she grumbles, but she takes the napkin with something like gratitude. She wipes her mouth before dropping the napkin into the nearby bin. She blinks. "Probably should have hurled into the bin, shouldn't I?"

I smile; it's not the strongest of jokes, but I sense that Maeve wants to keep the atmosphere light. I take my hand off her back, and for a second I think I see something like loss in her face. Like she didn't want me to let go.

"How are you feeling?" I ask gently.

Maeve sighs. "Sorry. I know it's grim. I just puke when I get scared. And I was pretty full of ice cream."

"This is true," I agree. "I guess I know in future that a second McFlurry would be a mistake."

"Yep." She sighs again but manages to pull a smile onto her face.

It doesn't fool me. Maeve's right: I'm a bit of a mama bear in certain situations. Granted, I'm not always the best at showing that I care about people – for some reason, the thought of it tends to make me anxious – but one on one with people, I can usually manage it a little bit more easily. And for some reason, I feel comfortable with Maeve.

"Sit down, sweet," I say, a little hesitantly but keeping my voice gentle. I look around and see a bench not too far down the street, so, putting my arm around Maeve, I lead her over to it. I feel like a teacher. Or a nurse. But most unusually, I feel like an adult.

Maeve wobbles a bit as I get her over to the bench, and as she stumbles back to sit down, her legs nearly give way. Luckily, my arm is still around her, and I grip her tightly as I help her to collapse backwards onto the bench a little bit more slowly than her wobbly legs clearly want to.

"I'm sorry," she says weakly.

I smile ruefully and shrug, mostly glad she's seated now. I don't let go of her just yet, though. "Nothing to be sorry for," I say evenly. "Just take a minute. When you're ready, we can get out of here."

She nods, taking another deep breath. To my relief, she seems to be regaining a bit of colour in her face. I don't want to try and walk her through the streets of Weston while she's still feeling dodgy, that's for sure. But then, to my surprise, Maeve lays her head on my shoulder. My arm is still around her, so I guess it isn't totally out of the blue – but I'm not sure that anyone has ever done that to me before. Finding it hard to show affection for people tends to mean that they don't show much affection towards me either. Hesitantly, I squeeze her shoulder and rest my head lightly against hers.

There's a moment of silence, with the two of us sat still, before Maeve finally speaks again. "Let's go," she says, trying to sound upbeat. "So that no one associates that puddle of vomit with us," she adds, but she doesn't fool me. I can tell that she's still afraid of the noise and the violence we witnessed.

Still, I nod. She has a point. "Yeah, let's go," I concur. "Probably best that we don't get arrested for fouling the street."

We start to walk, not really heading in any direction. I can sense Maeve's readiness to be far away from the restaurant, and far away from the fight. Me, I'm unsure what to say. How do I make her feel safe when I can't guarantee that she *will* be safe?

It's cold out now – it's summer, and the moon shines easily through the clear night, but it's cold. I find I'm curling my hands up into my sleeves. I didn't really plan my outfit for my escape attempt. What I was wearing wasn't something that I thought about when I was preparing to leave; so much so, that it's probably quite lucky I wasn't wearing pyjamas when I scaled the fence. In any case, I'm in jeans and a thin cardigan, and it's starting to get cold. But there's very little I can do about this now.

I turn my attention to Maeve again and for the first time I think properly about what she's wearing. She's in a strappy sundress and a zip-up hoodie; her legs are bare and her feet are only covered with open-toed sandals. "Are you cold?" I ask, a little tentatively. "Should we find somewhere else inside to go?"

Maeve shakes her head. "Nah," she says, in a clear attempt at breeziness. "I'm not cold. Let's walk for a bit. Ooh, we could start a bonfire!"

A laugh escapes my lips. "Like I'm letting you mix with fire," I point out, a smile on my face in spite of myself.

Maeve grins. "Yeah, that's true," she admits, though she doesn't seem put out at all. "Then we should keep walking. Is the beach near here?"

I nod. "It's not far. It's definitely walking distance."

"Brilliant!" says Maeve loudly. I'm not surprised somehow when she tries to stride ahead – and quickly realises she doesn't know where she's going. She turns back to me. By this point, I'm smiling. "Show me, then!" demands Maeve indignantly, a grin all over her face too.

We walk in companionable silence for several minutes as we pass the joyful landmarks that make up Weston-super-Mare: past big discount shops, supermarkets and streets that are entirely taken up by shit-looking takeaways. As we start to approach the middle of town again, the sounds of a drunken fight blare out from a street or two away. Next to me, I feel Maeve stiffen; and I'm not surprised when she reaches out and grips the fabric of my cardigan.

"It's OK," I say bracingly. "We'll avoid them. We don't need to go down there."

Maeve blinks at the floor, and the bravado that has characterised most of her interactions tonight is starting to slip a little. "You can't always avoid them," she says softly. She's right, of course; and I know, sadly, that it's not something Maeve will forget in a few years' time.

But Maeve's attitude to this when's she so young… well, it worries me. It can't just be what happened earlier, the men throwing bottles. That was bad – and, in all honesty, I still don't understand it – but something in Maeve's demeanour makes me think that there's not just one bad memory that she's drawing on.

"Please tell me," I say gently. "Please tell me who hurt you."

She sighs and for a moment she doesn't respond. "You can guess," she says at last. "You've been asking all the right questions."

Somehow, I'm not surprised. Maybe it's spending the last two years in hospitals with people who have been hurt too much, but I feel like I've got a pretty good instinct as to when something is wrong. What really cemented it, though, was Maeve's admission that they won't even have reported her missing.

"Then let's go to the police," I say earnestly. "You're only fourteen, right? They can get you into foster care. You'll be safe, there."

Yet even as I say that, I remember a younger kid that I knew when I was living in an adolescent hospital, who ended up in a children's home for a night. She said it was horrible. In fact, every younger kid that I knew in the hospital should be popping into my mind right now. It wasn't fun being stuck in those places at sixteen, but being in an institution at fourteen must have been even worse. I can't promise Maeve that she will get a nice foster family living in a friendly, comfortable home.

More than that, though, I can't promise that the police will help. I can't promise that whatever it is that she tells them will be believed. I know too many people who have disclosed things to professionals only to not be believed. I mean, that's half the reason that I haven't told anyone much about what's happened to me. I can't guarantee that it's going to be well received.

Maeve seems to be thinking along the same lines. "I can't tell anyone," she says hollowly. "It's too... messy."

I frown. "Too *messy*?"

But clearly she is already regretting her words and she shakes her head like she's ridding her ears of water. "Don't worry," she says quietly, before putting a bright, painted smile back on her face. It looks like it takes a large effort, and, honestly, it's not that convincing, but I know that she has closed the door on that conversation. I can knock, but she isn't going to answer.

"You know what?" she says almost forcefully, dragging me out of my thoughts. "We should do something." She doesn't give me time to protest. "Like really *do* something. Something we'll remember."

I feel my face frowning before I've quite caught up with what she's saying. "I thought we were going to the beach?"

She shakes her head. "Changed my mind," she says quickly, though she isn't meeting my eye. "I mean, you have to go back to the hospital at some point, fair enough, but they haven't found you yet. We could have *hours*. To do *anything*. Especially if we go somewhere... exciting. Important."

My head is reeling slightly. "Right," I say slowly. "Where exactly did you have in mind?"

Maeve chews on her lip, clearly deep in thought. "I'm not sure," she says ponderingly. "There must be something. What about the sea?"

I frown more deeply. "Well, yeah, the sea isn't far," I answer hesitantly. "But I think it would be pretty dangerous to try and swim in it while it's dark. And the beach down at the coastline is basically just sinking mud, you have to be careful even during the day..."

"You've definitely got an adventurous spirit," says Maeve with a roll of her eyes. "Jesus. Scared of sand."

Maeve's eyes twinkle at me and I know that she doesn't mean it maliciously. "You can literally die from getting stuck in it," I protest, but I'm forced to smile. She's right. I'm not the adventurous kind anymore.

But Maeve's train of thought has already left the station, puffing on to another idea. "So the beach is out… and I'm guessing that the cliffs are going to be too dangerous for Health and Safety Champion over here…" She raises her eyebrows and I roll my eyes almost dutifully, though I'm still smiling. "What about the pier?"

"It'll be all locked up," I point out. "Otherwise it would get robbed."

"True," concedes Maeve. "But what about the old pier? The one that burnt down?"

I hesitate. On the one hand, trying to get down the old pier sounds like a horrendously dangerous idea; on the other hand, it sounds like the kind of horrendously dangerous idea that Maeve will insist upon and drag me along with. I'm not sure how to protest against this idea without just sounding like a buzzkill and making her all the more insistent. And there is something in her tone… something desperate, like this is some kind of last-ditch attempt. I'm just not sure what it is that she's attempting to do.

It pops into my mind briefly that I'm the adult and Maeve is literally a fourteen-year-old child. But this thought doesn't last long.

"Birnbeck Pier?" I ask cautiously. "Just outside of town?"

Maeve nods excitedly. "Yeah!" she says with fervour. "The derelict one!"

"It's derelict," I point out. "I don't think you can get onto it."

This only seems to excite her further. "There must be a way!" she insists enthusiastically. "It's, like, a Heritage site, isn't it? So they must be trying to preserve it or something?"

There is some logic to this, but it feels pretty specious to me. "That doesn't mean you can get all the way down it. In fact, that doesn't mean you can get onto it at all. If anything, that means that they will have it all locked up. They probably don't want people getting onto it."

Maeve's eyes twinkle. "Why wouldn't they want an escaped psychiatric patient and a runaway teenager getting onto a derelict pier?"

I roll my eyes again. "You think you're mocking me, but really that's my point," I say, though I have to laugh. "I think it would be pretty bad press if we fell off it in the middle of the night."

Fell *through* it, actually, I note, and my blood runs slightly cold.

Maeve, though, is all pumped up now. "I think it would be bad press if the police failed to notice a missing person hiding under the table at McDonald's," she counters, obviously finding this whole thing hilarious in a slightly hysterical way. "Come on!" she insists. "Nothing about tonight is going to be sensible. Take a risk, Heather!"

I'm about to protest further when something Katy has said pops into my mind. She says that I 'catastrophise' – in other words, that I always think the worse. In this case, I'm having visions of Maeve slipping on a loose board and crashing into the sea below, where her unconscious body will be swallowed by a huge pile of quicksand. Normally, Katy would be asking me not to focus on this outcome, but actually in this case, I think that it's perfectly logical to imagine that. Considering that it could quite easily happen.

But maybe Maeve is right. Where has cautiousness got me? Stuck in a ward that I hate, with no one to talk to because I'm too scared to make friends. I've tried to put energy into the things that I should – exams, uni, career – but it's all collapsed around me. All my friends are getting drunk at freshers right now, excited to be off at uni. And I have nothing.

I stick my chin out slightly, trying to get my expression resembling decisiveness and determination. "I guess we could try," I concede, and, frankly, the smile I get from Maeve is enough of a reward.

"Let's go," she says mischievously.

16

Is it illegal to try and jump off a bridge? Either way, I'm sat crying in a police car and I don't know what's going to happen to me.

Snot is dribbling from my nostrils down over my chin. I'm too anxious and upset to wipe it away. Effusive tears trickle down the same path. I can't catch my breath. As I give a particularly wheezy sob, the police officer in the passenger seat turns around and gives me a sympathetic smile before handing me a tissue. I want to thank him, but the words don't come out.

"Try and take some deep breaths," he says kindly. "Eh? Things will seem better when you've calmed down."

I try. I do. But I can't see how things will feel better. I'm broken, shattered, spoiled. I'm tainted. I need to die.

"I need to leave," I manage to sob out to the police officer. "I can't... I can't..."

While I'm speaking, I barely realise that I'm yanking at the car door handle furiously. But it won't give. They've locked me in.

"Hey, hey," says the policeman. "I'm afraid we can't let you out just yet. Deep breaths, OK?"

But I can't do that. Why won't the bloody door handle work? I need to get out, I need to get away. I need to... I don't know... take an overdose, or find another bridge...

"Hey," the policeman repeats. "Don't cry. We're going to take you somewhere safe."

It's clear he's a little out of his depth and I don't blame him. Taking a huge deep breath, I just about manage a coherent question. "Where?" I choke out.

The question surprises him. He hesitates for a moment. "I... well, there are a few places nearby..."

He doesn't know what's going on, it's clear. There was another police officer, somewhere, I remember, but I can't see where she's gone; she disappeared just after she grabbed me. To pull me back from...

No, no, no, no – don't think about that, don't think about what nearly happened. I need to die, I can't go getting scared. Don't think about it, just think about how to get away. This policeman, he's clueless – there must be a way around him.

"I need some air," I tell him, my voice still choked and panicky. "I'm going to puke."

Christ, it's such an obvious ploy that I might as well have told him I was on my period. Somehow I still expect him to react quickly to this, letting me out before I sully the nice clean car – but he does seem to have some kind of sense in him, as he opens the glove compartment instead and passes me a paper bag. Fuck. There's no way that he's going to let me out of this car, is there?

I take the paper bag reluctantly, and, abandoning all pretence, I discard it on the seat next to me. When I look up, I see the policeman has the faintest glimmer of a sad smile on his face. I'm not going to puke, and we both know it. The second of connection calms me down, ever so slightly.

My voice is still shaky, but the panic has definitely abated a little bit. "Where are you going to take me?" I ask again.

He sighs. "Somewhere that we call a 'place of safety'," he tells me, sounding a little calmer himself. "Probably a psychiatric ward."

I look up at him. "But I'm not..." I blurt out. I can't finish the sentence. I take a deep breath. "I'm not mentally ill," I tell him firmly.

"I'm not saying you are," he says cautiously. "We just need to make sure you're... safe."

"So I don't die," I mutter, my voice biting, even as I don't fully intend the words to come out. I know that this is exactly what he means.

To my surprise, he smiles slightly. A little weakly, a little ruefully, but he smiles nonetheless. "Exactly," he confirms bluntly. This is the most direct I've heard him. He breathes out deeply. "Look, they'll assess you, and maybe they'll keep you in, or maybe they'll let you go. You've just got to trust them. OK?"

I nod listlessly. What else can I do?

It's a while before the police officers outside of the car decide among themselves where we're actually going. The same police officer sits in the front of the car while the other officers that have congregated have the discussion. I see them make phone calls, too. How much, really, is there for them to talk about? What can they possibly be saying about me? I notice that the officer who pulled me back from the bridge seems to have a lot to say; every time I see her, she's deep in conversation with another officer or talking to someone on her phone.

By the time she moves back to the car and opens the driver's side door, I have cried myself into silence. I feel drained, spent, empty. There are no tears now, because I really cannot see the point. My head is rested against the car window, and I wish I could sleep. I need to not have to think anymore.

I should be furious with myself that I've messed this all up, but I just feel numb. Right up until I was pulled back, I was thinking that this time can be the only time I try to kill myself. Now I know that I was wrong about that. I will do it tomorrow, if I get the chance, or the next day. Next time, I just have to be quicker.

As the police officer from the bridge gets into the car, I sit up wearily. She glances sideways at her partner.

"I've told her that we're taking her to a place of safety," he tells her, in a kind of staged voice that knows I'm listening.

She nods but doesn't smile, as she looks over to me. "We've found somewhere to assess you," she tells me, her voice serious and heavy. "It's been a bit difficult because you're so young, but we've found somewhere safe."

They exchange another glance, whilst I nod without really caring. I'm too exhausted to ask questions.

*

The assessment takes place in a room with all the charm of a GP practice waiting room. What's more, time seems to be passing excruciatingly slowly, whilst the scene also manages to be hazy like a dream. There are two groups of plastic chairs, is all I can be sure of – one for me, and one for the professionals who get to ask the questions.

I don't have the energy for this. Sometimes I manage a sentence in reply to the questions they ask; sometimes I don't even manage a word. It's too much. I can't do it. It's too much.

They ask straightforward questions, like, "Do you still feel suicidal?" And I can answer those ones. But they also ask questions like, "Why do you feel suicidal?" These questions are more difficult. Although I've longed to talk to someone for months, I don't have the energy to explain how I'm feeling to these strangers. It doesn't feel important anymore. Besides, doctors asking questions from a clipboard doesn't exactly feel like the conversation I've been craving.

I want to curl up and sleep.

It doesn't take them long to decide what they're going to do. They tell me, starkly, that they're going to have to detain me. This means putting me under section. I don't entirely blame them. I can barely manage a sentence in reply.

"Where are you sending me?" I ask, only able to manage a faint, exhausted voice.

The two doctors exchange a glance. "It's a little way away," one of them tells me. "But you'll be looked after, there."

Somehow, I doubt this, but there's very little I can do. "When am I going?"

The doctor looks past me, out at the car park that I was frogmarched across by police to end up in this waiting room. "You're going via secure transport," she tells me, with maybe the tiniest hint of sympathy, but not really answering my question. "I think they'll be here soon."

I find that I don't actually care. I don't know what secure transport means, and I really don't care.

Still, I almost laugh when the doorbell eventually rings, and I turn in my chair to see the secure transport car. It's a huge black van, and there's four burly looking individuals ready to escort me. Isn't this a bit of overkill? I feel like I pose the risk equivalent to a stray crisp packet at the moment. Why am I being treated like I'm dangerous?

They pack me into the back of the van, one guard on either side of me, with another driving and another sat in the front. The fuck do they think I'm going to do? In my normal state, I'm sure that I would be trying to cook up ways to escape, maybe playing the 'I'm about to vomit' card, like I did with the police officer. But somehow, I think it will be even less effective with these security guards. I don't bother.

And while I assumed that 'a little way away' meant half an hour, instead I feel like it must be at least four times this that I sit in the car, squashed in the middle seat. Not, of course, that I have any way of telling the time. But the time sitting there feels like treacle, sluggishly stretching on and on between my fingers.

I'm afraid, when we finally pull into the car park and I see the sign. It's for a psychiatric facility. The building itself terrifies me; I assumed I was being paranoid when I thought that it would look like something straight out of a horror film. Instead, we're pulling up to a huge concrete structure, surrounded by fence after fence. It's too dark to see anything but its immensity and total lack of charm, or even warmth. Fear pricks at me uncomfortably. I can't deny it. I don't want to live here, for any stretch of time.

As they open the car doors, I once again think of making a run for it, but there's no point. Even if I did get away, it's pitch black and I don't even slightly know the area. I would have no idea where to head. No, I have no choice but to comply as the four security guards form a tight quadrilateral around me, those on either side of me holding on to me firmly. I move with them through the car park, making no attempt to escape their literal clutches.

There is a cluster of people who must be nurses waiting for me on the other side of the glass doors. I catch a brief glance of my reflection as the guards pass me over to them. I look like a zombie. I genuinely look like a corpse, pale and blank and my eyes set deeply in their sockets.

The nurses don't speak to me. I feel like a delivery of goods that they have to transport, as they speak to each other briefly, a little tersely. I don't feel like a person anymore.

They lead me through a warren of corridors, at such a brisk pace that I quickly lose track of how many corners we've turned. For some reason, I'm surrounded by an escort of six nurses, even though I heard both doors lock firmly behind us. There's no way I'm escaping from this place tonight.

My feet drag along the floor as I try to keep walking through my exhaustion. I'm unsure if any of the six nurses notice how tired I am because, either way, none of them seem too bothered or even try to offer sympathy. In fact, they all seem so calm that they are barely even present. They are thinking about what they're going to have for tea tomorrow. I think vaguely that they must do this a lot. Maybe they're so calm because I'm not kicking off like people usually do. Maybe I'm just small fry, to them.

We pass through locked door after locked door before I finally get led into a small room. There are windows but it's the middle of the night by now; I can't see anything outside, and I can't see much inside either. There's a light on the ceiling that leaves the room dimly lit. Without a word, the nurses leave and I hear the lock click as the last one shuts the door behind them. Maybe I'm not small fry, if I need locking up. Maybe they just really don't care.

The room is empty, half-heartedly furnished with beanbags and a few plastic dining chairs that remind me of primary school. The brightness of their colours jar with the dinginess of the rest of the room, with its faded paintwork and dated curtains. I bring my knees up to my chest, curled so tight that my feet are resting on the seat of the chair too. I run my fingers over the side edges of the chair. I can feel where parts have been cracked off, probably from the chair being thrown. What have I let myself into?

I'm not sure how long I spend in the room, curled up in the chair. None of the other residents seem to be awake; I can hear nurses moving around and opening and shutting the locked doors, but I can't hear voices or anyone interacting. I'm exhausted, but I can't sleep in here. Not just because it's uncomfortable; truth be told, I can't settle until I at least know what kind of place this is.

Finally the door, heavy and creaking, opens again and my head snaps up, pulling me out of drowsiness. There's a nurse in the doorway, watching me.

"Do you want some breakfast?" she asks me.

I look around the room for a clock but there isn't one. "What time is it?" I ask blearily, hollowly.

"Er..." She looks back into the room she's come from. "About half three, I think."

This has been a weird night. Thankfully it's almost over.

I nod, though food is the last thing on my mind at the moment really. When did I last even eat? Did I have dinner last night? I can't remember. I don't think I did. I really should be hungry.

"Come on, then," the nurse says – without a smile, but not unkindly. I heave myself up from the plastic chair and stumble after her into the next room. She shuts the door behind me and locks it. I'm not sure whose safety she's trying to ensure by locking a room empty of anything except plastic chairs and wipe-clean beanbags.

I stand awkwardly in the lounge that she has let me into. Once in, I can see that it looks depressingly, and possibly a little scarily, sparse; there are two sofas pointed at a television behind a thick Perspex screen, and a dining table surrounded by the same colourful plastic chairs. That is pretty much the end of it.

I spin around when I hear the nurse speak to me. "Toast or cereal?" she asks. She's moved out of the lounge now, into a little room with a stable door. The bottom of the door is closed, and she leans through the gap left by the open top half of the door to peer at me. Behind her, I can just about see kitchen cupboards and a toaster sat on a worktop. What I end up focusing on, however, is her direct gaze. I'm not used to this level of scrutiny.

"Toast," I decide tiredly, less because I actually want toast and more because it's an easier decision than picking between cereals. "Please," I add. I'm exhausted, but I still have my manners.

The nurse stays silent, giving me only a curt nod. Well, I'm sure she's exhausted too. Or maybe she's an abrupt kind of person. Either way, I can't say I mind. I'd rather she be abrupt than chatty at the moment. I don't have the energy for small talk.

I stand awkwardly motionless in the middle of the room while the nurse drops bread into the toaster. She doesn't turn back to me, instead choosing to stand with her back to me while it toasts. Again, I'm not overly bothered about her choice to do this either. I'm happy to stand and limply wait.

After a moment, the nurse turns around, and as I look back over, she is handing me a plate. I take it automatically. "Thank you," I say numbly, but I finally feel something as my stomach grumbles slightly at the sight of food. Maybe I am hungry. Still, I'm less than impressed with the food itself. The toast is what I think people call anaemic, and the nurse has helpfully covered it in a greasy butter substitute. Note to self: next time, say cereal.

I take my disappointing toast to the table and sit in one of the brightly covered plastic chairs to eat it. I was vaguely convinced that my mouth might not even be able to remember how to eat;

but now that the food is in front of me, I remember the steps. I bring it to my mouth, bite, chew. As it turns out, I manage to finish the toast without taking too long about it. It's not as bad as it looks, and I feel vague relief.

Once again, I don't realise the scrutiny I'm under until I turn around and see the nurse still staring at me. I feel awkward as I stand and return the empty plate to her. "Thank you," I say again, but she only nods. Not the friendliest.

I rub my eyes. I'm so, so tired.

I'm digging my nails into my arm to try and keep myself awake when I glance over to the nurse; once again, she's watching me. I try and soften my gaze a little; I don't want to look like I'm glaring at her when really I'm just trying to force myself to stay awake. But the nurse doesn't look offended or angry. Instead, she's tilted her head to one side. She looks inquisitive.

"You're really tired, aren't you?" she asks, almost sounding sympathetic. Maybe I've judged her wrong.

For a moment I try to dispute this with my expression, try to keep looking like I could stay awake all day – but it doesn't last. My shoulders slump, I look to the floor and I nod ashamedly.

She nods too and I finally get a small smile from her. "Last I heard, they're making up a bedroom for you," she tells me. "I can check for you. And then you can get some sleep."

I feel almost a physical response, I'm so relieved. I want to sleep so badly.

But as the nurse lets herself out of the kitchen and locks the door behind her, I'm starting to worry. I want to sleep – I so want to sleep – but is it safe? Even as I'm exhausted, I can't help but still feel keyed up. Though the last hour has been totally calm and unremarkable, everyone is still asleep. What's it going to be like when all the patients wake up? Who am I here with? And what are the doctors going to do to me?

The nurse unlocks another door and lets herself in. I'm not sure at first if I'm meant to follow, but as I peek around her as she opens the door, I can see desks and computers and what looks like a huge day planner on the wall. It's an office, clearly. I can hear a conversation, though the voices are too hushed for me to make out any of the conversation. Trying not to wake anyone up, I suppose – but for me, standing alone in this empty room with only the sound of whispers in the air, it's eerie.

Luckily it's not long before the nurse re-emerges. "Come on through," she says, but instead of opening the office door, this time she unlocks another door beside it. I will never know my way around this rabbit warren. Still, I follow her silently through another two locked doors before she shows me into a bedroom.

And I know I should be worried – I am, actually, worried – but as soon as I see the neatly made-up bed, I realise I have no chance of staying vigilant. I curl up, still fully dressed, on top of the covers, and fall sound asleep.

17

We walk for nearly an hour before we find ourselves in the middle of an empty shopping complex.

In truth, I'm surprised that we manage to end up near civilisation at all. There's Wi-Fi at the hospital and I never leave my bedroom there, so I haven't bothered to sort out any data for my mobile phone – Google Maps is out, as is any kind of GPS map I might be to access. I don't go out, except with my mum and dad, who both have fully functional phones of their own.

I don't bother to ask Maeve if she has a phone; I haven't seen her carrying one, and in her thin dress and hoodie, there aren't even any pockets big enough to hide a phone away. The mystery of how she ended up unconscious (and glowing, I remind myself) in the forest still niggles in my mind. Aged fourteen, no money, no phone – and she ends up alone in a forest on the outskirts of Weston-super-Mare.

To be fair, it's not like she's timid; Maeve knows her own mind and I can't deny this. If any fourteen-year-old could end up in this situation, I suppose it would be her every time.

And the next half an hour proves this; because after spending this amount of time out in the cold, trying to navigate through a district of large supermarkets, most people might be starting to get tired of the idea of finding Birnbeck Pier. But, for some reason, Maeve's fervour about this knows no bounds. She marches purposefully, slightly in front of me, while I try and navigate based mostly on having driven through these streets in my dad's car. I think we turn back on ourselves eight times in total.

Clearly, she has never been here before; I have to call her back several times as she marches on down a blatant dead end. Even I know, from my very few trips out of the hospital, that we need to get out of the industrial district to get back to Birnbeck. But Maeve? Maeve either has the worst sense of direction I've ever seen, or she's not used to being out on her own.

I think back to when I was fourteen; I don't think I was used to being out anywhere unfamiliar either. I would go out with my friends from school, but as I recall it, we stayed in the centre of town or went to one of the parks about ten minutes' walk from the high street in the summer. I didn't have to do much navigating.

Of course, I'm talking like I'm such an adult now – I'm not allowed out unsupervised, and I barely take the supervised time out of the hospital that I'm entitled to because I'm so bad at asking the nurses for it. Leave-wise, it's mostly Costa with my mum and dad. Which is a little depressing when I think about it.

I've been asking for unescorted leave every week since I got transferred to the adult hospital. The nurses and therapists that worked at the adolescent ward I was on before, they all told me that everyone gets unescorted leave on adult wards. So I turned up expecting it after a week. I knew that they would have to know that I was safe out alone before they gave me the leave, of course – but I haven't even been self-harming (that they know about), and the powers-that-be here still haven't deigned to grant me any. It's frustrating, because I know that the breathing space would make things a little bit easier for me. But I'm powerless and there's nothing I can do.

It's possible that feeling like that might have contributed to my decision to hop the fence at 9pm on a Wednesday night. I feel powerful for getting out, on a fucking high because – for now, at least – they don't own me anymore. Only one thing troubles me as I think about it: that, according to the rules, the nursing staff should have locked the door that I got out from when it got dark. They never do – they don't bother most of the time so they don't have to keep locking and unlocking it every time someone wants to go out for a fag. But the point is, they're going to be in deep shit from the manager when she realises that they haven't bothered to lock it tonight.

It's hard to feel sorry for them, when I can literally think of one staff member that I get along with. There are even a couple of them who have been pretty unpleasant to me at times. And I can count the number of staff members who have actually tried to understand how I feel on one hand. I know that, what with my age and my diagnosis, I'm not from their usual demographic of patients; but I don't think I would feel as adrift as I do if I thought that any of them would care if I didn't come back tonight.

Should I feel bad that they're going to get bollocked for not doing something that they are supposed to do? Especially since it's not just bureaucracy; it's literally a rule that's there to keep people safe. As much as I'm on a high that I was able to get away, I also feel… kind of vulnerable. That the hospital weren't doing what they were meant to do to keep me safe.

Being free tonight has come with an odd aftertaste of fear. I can go where I want; but I can also do what I want. And if I'm honest with myself, I know what I came out to do tonight.

For the minute, though, I have Maeve to look out for, marching ahead of me, down a road which clearly leads to a Sainsbury's warehouse. I roll my eyes and call after her. This is my task for right now.

"I know where we're going!" she announces, though it is quite clear in my mind that she doesn't.

Finally, though, we find a road that actually leads somewhere, and ten minutes later, we are finally out of the big retail park. Now, for the first time, I think we are actually close to getting to Birnbeck Pier. I wish I was easy-going enough to just enjoy this ridiculous journey for what it is; though, having said that, if I am anxious about getting there, then what the hell is Maeve? Her fervour makes me even more nervous. Why does the sudden idea matter enough to her that she is marching on ahead of me so purposefully? I wish I could blame her determination on her being young and innocent; but she has clearly been through too much for it to just be that.

What is she hiding, right now? Somehow I can tell, just from looking in her eyes, that she isn't the happy-go-lucky teenager that she's acting like she is. Someone, or something, has hurt her. And I can't believe that she deserved it. What's happened to her? And why?

I am suddenly aware that I used to hide my pain like she does.

I don't want to feel like this anymore.

I stop, suddenly. The weight of emotion hits me with full force. "Maeve," I manage to choke out as I stumble backwards, my hands looking for a surface to rest on, any surface. A few steps back, my fingers make contact with a wall, some kind of building, and I slide down into a heap, my knees pulled up to my chest.

Maeve turns around; I'm not sure whether she heard me speak or simply sensed that I was no longer right behind her. Her face furrows into a frown, looking unsure.

"Are you OK?" she asks, sounding more uncertain than I've ever heard her be. I think I'm scaring her.

I shake my head, trying to gulp in air that just isn't coming. I rest my forehead on my knees, trying to block out everything going on around me. Of course, I know this is a panic attack – keep reminding yourself, this is just a panic attack – but there is a part of me that thinks I'm going to die here in the Tesco Extra car park.

There is a moment of silence that feels like an age as I try to focus on taking deep breaths, before finally I feel Maeve touch my knee, her hand resting there lightly. It's an indecisive touch, and I'm not sure if she's still uncertain, if she doesn't know what to do. To be fair, I only have any idea of what to do when someone is panicking because I've seen so many staff members in hospital deal with it happening. Before that? I would have been in a total blank.

I guess she is being brave, reaching out and touching me when my response to it could so easily be to flinch backwards, away from the gentle weight of her fingertips on my knee. I feel guilty, somehow, that Maeve has to deal with me like this. She's too young. Too fragile herself.

I'm hyperventilating, now, though I try and force myself to keep calm. "Heather?" I hear from somewhere in front of me. It's Maeve, just Maeve. How can I be scared of such a kind-sounding voice? How can I be panicking when all around, there is just the dark? Empty roads leading to empty car parks for empty shops. I'm alone, so who is going to hurt me?

The gentle rubbing sensation is still present and I try to focus myself on that. I don't need to panic. I'm *not* alone. I have Maeve. And even though I haven't even known her a day, I know that she doesn't want to hurt me.

I'm not sure why, but my mind decides to dredge up a memory of having a panic attack in hospital. I can picture the support worker standing in front of me, trying to get me to keep eye contact with her – her hands gripping gently on the tops of my arms – and telling me to think of the alphabet, to recite it with her. Don't think about the fear – don't think of all the things that are going to hurt you – don't think about the fact that you cannot seem to get *any* air into your lungs – just go through the letters. A, B, C…

So that's what I do now. I feel the weight of Maeve's fingers and I feel the cold night air and I feel the tension in my stomach, but I don't think about these things. I recite the alphabet. A, B, C... that's all I need to think about. Just the alphabet.

By the time I'm at Z, my breathing feels more normal. And if I'm honest, it's nothing short of a fucking miracle.

"Heather?" I hear Maeve try again. This time, I'm able to weakly lift my head and look at her. My glasses have steamed up; I can't quite see her properly. I pull them from my face and wipe them on the sleeve of my cardigan before putting them back on.

Now I can see Maeve clearly, kneeling down in front of me, her fingers still on my knee. For a brief moment I think she's relaxed, but then I look up at her face. She isn't even nervous, or concerned – Maeve is scared.

I immediately feel a wave of guilt – I've hardly done this on purpose, but as the older one, I'm the one that should be keeping it together. I guess I'm just not very used to being the grown-up. After all, my eighteenth birthday was only a few months ago, I only moved to the adult ward a few weeks ago. And in the adolescent ward, like in school, the hierarchy of patients being minors and staff being adults was laid on thick.

I feel... I feel *adrift*. I'm not old enough for this. I'm not strong enough for this. I can't manage this.

"I need Zoe," I burst out, and press my forehead back onto my knees again.

Even just saying her name sends my thoughts reeling back to when I knew her. I feel a genuine, physical pain when I think about the fact that she's not here. She's off, probably with a fancy new psychology job by now... She might get married, or have a baby soon. Not only will I never see it, but I'll never even know. I think back to afternoons spent on the ward, with Google in front of me, trying to work out how to find her online. Unfortunately, she's tech-savvy enough that there were very few things of interest that I could find.

I miss her so much.

If she was here now, she would be talking me round; she would be persuading me to come with her, back to the hospital. She would grasp my hand or touch my shoulder. She would know exactly what to say, what to do. She would care. Of everything, that's what I'm most sure about. She would care.

I hold on to the fact that, right before I left, Zoe hugged me tight. A proper hug, not even a half-hearted one. And I held on to her back. I don't think I've ever felt so safe. Why did I feel so safe when I knew it was about to end?

I knew leaving her was going to be unspeakably hard. But actually, I'm finding the hardest part is existing now that she's well and truly gone. I thought I would find someone else that I could trust. So far, that hasn't happened and somehow I don't see it happening anytime soon. I'm alone, now. I know the best thing to do. For everyone.

Tears are forcing themselves onto the back of my eyes, but I keep my face pressed down on my knees, physically pressing back the tears as if I'm stopping a leaky tap dripping. I don't want Maeve to see me crying right now.

"Who's Zoe?" I hear a quiet voice ask at last.

Of course it's the obvious question; of course it would be the first question that she asks. Already, though, I am regretting bringing Zoe up. How do I explain it to Maeve?

I take a deep breath, but without lifting up my face. "She worked at the last hospital I was in," I say, my voice low and a little hoarse. "She was a therapy assistant."

I can't see Maeve's face, but I feel like she's frowning. "Right…" she says slowly. "And you… trusted her?"

There's a short silence. Eventually I nod, even though 'trust' doesn't begin to cover it. I don't know how to explain these things to a fourteen-year-old.

"And now you've moved… you can't see her anymore," Maeve continues, sounding almost like she's talking to herself.

"And you miss her."

I nod again, and finally I find my voice again. "She used to make me feel better," I choke out. "So few people…"

I feel tears coming but once again I push them back. It takes physical strength and for a moment it's all I can focus on. Luckily, I'm good at hiding how I feel. It drives Katy crazy, I think.

I lift my head again – not to look at Maeve this time, I can't quite face that – but I tip my head back and rest it on the rough stone wall behind me. This is messed up. I have almost forgotten that Maeve is sat there with me when she speaks.

"Not to be… um… insensitive," she begins, and I brace myself. She's probably going to be insensitive. "But there are therapy workers where you are now, right?" she presses on. "Maybe one of them can help, when you go back."

I sigh. I can't be angry at Maeve exactly, because she is so young, and this situation is so complicated. I don't think I could explain it to her if I had a month of Sundays. And I don't want to get into it in a Tesco car park in the middle of the night when the police could come and catch me at any minute.

My arms snake around myself and for a moment I just sit. I don't know how to explain what I'm feeling, but I don't like feeling in danger like this. I know Maeve and I need to get moving, but I feel almost paralysed.

"It means more than that, doesn't it?" she says, and this time I can hear the sadness in her voice. She may not understand but I can see that she wants to.

Finally I look back at her. "Yeah," I say simply. It's all I can manage at the moment. Maybe later I will try and explain my condition to Maeve, but right now I can barely get my breath. I don't have the energy to start trying to explain things.

The air is heavy and I don't know what to say. After a moment, Maeve sticks her other hand out and takes mine. "Don't be sad," she says, softly.

I take a deep breath. "I'm trying," I reply, as I always do to questions like this. I'm not sure if it's true – am I trying hard enough? There's little I can do to try. I mean, if I could choose not to be sad, surely I would. If I could take away all the things that make me sad, surely I would. Isn't that the case for everyone?

Maybe Maeve is too young to understand this. I may only have a few years on her, but my last few years have been so intense that in some ways I feel like I've aged about twenty. That's why the impulsivity that I have had tonight takes me so much by surprise. I spend most of my time feeling like I'm about forty, but would a forty-year-old jump over their back fence and go on an ill-thought-out adventure?

I don't move and I wonder if Maeve is despairing. When she speaks again, her voice is more urgent. "Let's keep going," she says, an odd intensity in her voice. "Come on, Heather. We might only have a few more hours before you get taken back. Let's *do* something."

I close my eyes for a moment. "Why does it matter?" I ask, my voice heavy now.

"*Please*, Heather," she says quickly. It isn't lost on me that she has totally ignored my question. Maeve doesn't know why. Because there's no reason to do anything.

My mood has dipped badly and, try as I might, I can't draw up any more enthusiasm from anywhere. The adrenaline that has been in me all evening might have been flushed out, now. The idea of standing up even feels too much.

"We both know that I'm not going back to the hospital, Maeve," I say quietly.

For a moment, there is complete silence. I haven't got the energy to say anything else, and I don't think Maeve knows what to say. But now that I've worded that thought, it occurs to me that it has been hanging over both of us all night. It's too true. We both know that tonight is the night that I stop breathing.

If I had my way, I would fade out. Not even as dramatic as a star dying millions of miles away. More like one of those glow-in-the-dark stars that kids stick to their ceilings. After twenty minutes, their light just starts to go. If you're still awake after thirty minutes, you're back in the dark. A cheap imitation that you might once have thought was a star. But really they're just flimsy plastic, sucking in a tiny bit of life from a day in the sun.

But I know that I can't hope for anything peaceful. I've spent too much time around suicidal people; I've heard of too many suicide attempts to know that if you really want to die, you have to do something serious. The kind of thing that you can't get away with in hospital, with their lists of contraband and their room searches and their escorted leaves. This is my time. Tonight is my time. I don't think I'm going to get another chance.

Maeve and I sit in silence for what feels like a long time.

"What about me?" she asks, painfully vulnerable.

Part of me wishes that I hadn't told her – she's so young and even if she wasn't, I've spent enough time in hospital to know what it feels like to learn that someone you care about wants to hurt themselves. Wants to leave you. But the other part of me, well… she had to know. I only have a few hours. I need to get her somewhere safe – because I'm not letting her watch me die.

"I'm going to take you to the police station," I say, still quiet but more steadily. "I'm going to stand outside and watch you to make sure you go inside, and then I'm going to run and you won't need to hear about me ever again."

I look up at Maeve just in time to see her face crumple like I've physically hit her. Tears start to roll down her face. "I don't want… this to end," she says in a tiny voice. "I don't want *you* to end."

I manage to muster up a small, sad smile as I shake my head. "You don't need me, Maeve," I say, more gently. "I'm too… too fucked up. You've got a chance. You can get away from your parents and have an education, a career."

To my surprise, Maeve glares at me. "So can you," she says insistently. "You've got help, now—"

I shake my head again. "It's too late," I tell her, though I feel my heart ache as I say it. Aching for poor Maeve, caring about me – aching for the few people who care about me – but I am too tired. I can't do this, anymore. I haven't got the energy.

Maeve's hand is still gripping mine, becoming ever sweatier and hotter as she refuses to let me go. Tears are running down her face thick and fast, now, and she is starting to sob. "I won't let you," she wails. "There has to be something… something I can do… something to make life worth it—"

"There's isn't," I say, but my voice cracks.

Maeve picks up on the crack immediately. "See? *You're* not even sure! Th-there's a chance!"

I rest my forehead on my knees, briefly this time as I try to keep things together. "You're going to be fine," I tell her firmly. "The police are going to listen to you and find you a nice foster home."

I see something flicker across Maeve's face that I can't quite read. Before I can ask about it, she bursts out at me. "I'm not letting you!" she half-shouts. "You're not taking me to any police station—"

I bite my tongue to try and keep all emotion out of my voice. "A hospital, then. A&E."

"Like you're going to put me through that," she says fiercely.

I sigh, forcing myself to pull my hand away from Maeve's. I see fresh tears coming to her eyes. I don't want to hurt her but I have to stop all of this – all of this crazy journey that we've taken together. It isn't right and she's just a kid. I will call 999 if I have to; I can't let her come with me. Running my hand through my hair, I look back at her.

"I can't look after you, Maeve," I say, my voice quiet but heavy. "I will take you somewhere safe and I will make sure you're alright there, but after this we're never going to see each other again. I'm going to be somewhere safe, too."

She stares at me furiously. "Don't give me that bullshit," she says, her voice harder than I've heard it all night. "You're not going to be looking down at me like an angel. You're going to be decaying in the earth."

She's not wrong, and that probably should worry me, but it doesn't. I swallow hard and force myself to shrug. "I'm sorry," I say lifelessly. "But we've got to go, now."

I finally get to my feet, my head spinning a little bit. I look around; the car park we're sat in looks just as nondescript as it did before I started to panic. There are a few supermarkets, some car parks and a road with no name or signs. I swallow. How am I going to find the police station from here? It strikes me that I don't even know where it is. I have absolutely no idea which direction to head off in.

But across from me, Maeve jumps to her feet as well. She's still staring at me with that intense, fierce look in her eyes. "You can't make me come with you," she says stubbornly, folding her arms.

I sigh. "I thought you wanted to come with me?"

"If I can actually stay with you, yeah!" she says passionately, edging towards shrieking now. "Not if you're going to leave me behind!"

I dig my fingers into my temples in frustration. "Maeve, I can't..." I trail off. I'm finding it hard to collect my thoughts. "I can't just decide to not do something I've thought about for ages, because of a kid that I've known for, what – three hours? I wish you the best, but... it's too late. It's not up for debate. I'm sorry."

I can hear how harsh I'm being and I hate myself for it, but I need to get her to listen. Maybe it will hurt her in the short term to hear me imply that I don't care much about her, but in the long term, taking her somewhere safe – and leaving her – has to be for the best.

Maeve stares at me, and I hate the way she's looking at me. I wish it didn't have to be like this.

Then her gaze drops. She stares at my feet, then up at the sky. I think she's trying to get a hold of herself and her emotions. Surely that has to be a good thing?

But then she's staring at me again, and I realise that what she's searching for is an idea; because when she gets one, it's readable all over her face.

"So you'll make sure I'm safe first?" she says, and though it feels like a trick, I'm relieved that she seems to be giving in.

I nod. "Of course I will. I'm not going to just leave you."

"Good." She nods firmly, her eyes on me. "Then you'll have to catch me first. You know where I'm going."

And before I can say anything else, Maeve turns away from me and runs full pelt down the road, heading for Birnbeck Pier.

18

I first meet Zoe two weeks after I arrive at the hospital.

At this point, I am still terrified of my surroundings. I haven't gotten used to the constant noise yet, nor the unpredictable kicking-off that happens a couple of times a day. I can't relax; every time that I think that things have slightly calmed down, someone finds something sharp or tries to strangle a member of staff, and it all ends in them being restrained to their bed and injected in the arse with sedative.

I am still on the admission ward, where they put people who have just arrived (or people who are too 'unsettled' to stay upstairs). This means that – apparently, I am going totally on the word of the staff about this – it is much quieter upstairs. All I have to do is be good for a while, and I can go upstairs. I hope they let me do this soon. I can't take all of this noise.

I'm off one-to-one observations now, though, at least. For the first week I was here, I was followed around twenty-four seven by a nurse or a support worker. Including in the bathroom and while getting changed. Frankly, it scared me. But I had enough sense to do what they wanted from me, guessing that if I did, that they would take me off it.

Now I am just being checked on every fifteen minutes, I have been self-harming in secret. I don't think they have worked this out yet.

One morning, they let me through to the communal room to do some activities. There is so little to do here that they have even been able to persuade me to join in on shit like origami. I hate it, but at least it is something to do. It keeps my hands busy, if nothing else. But that morning, the redhead who usually does activities with us is off sick. Instead, we get Zoe.

The noise makes me turn around as she opens the door with her key fob and comes bouncing in, holding boxes full of coloured threads (thin thread, of course – nothing thick enough to hang yourself with). She dumps the boxes, straightens up – and, by chance, catches my eye, giving me a smile.

The first thing I notice is how pretty she is. Because she is – absolutely. I'm not sure that anyone here knows that I'm gay yet, so with any luck, no one will notice that I'm ogling one of the activity coordinators. The second thing that I notice, though, is how kind her smile is.

I don't get much time to think, to plan how I'm going to talk to this girl – because as soon as we make eye contact, she comes cheerfully bobbing over to where I'm sat. I feel my face flush slightly before she even speaks. So much for keeping things under wraps. I scratch at my arm anxiously, and I can't hold her gaze. I don't like eye contact at the best of times.

"Hi," she says, kindly, warmly, gently. She knows how to build rapport with patients, clearly, and she's doing it on me. "I'm Zoe," she continues, not seeming to mind too much that she's looking at me but my eyes are trained on the floor. "I'm one of the activity coordinators."

I know this to be true, so I nod. I know the response that I'm supposed to give, but I can't get any words out.

She smiles nonetheless. "We're going to be braiding bracelets this morning," she tries again. "Would you like to come and have a go?"

Her gentle tone soothes me somewhat; and so, though I don't speak or look up at her, I nod again. I would want to join in whether this lady was running the group or not. Bracelet-making is definitely above origami. Besides, maybe I can make one for Amelie, for when I next see her. I think she'd rather that than a wonky paper swan.

Zoe tilts her head at me, still smiling. "Come over when you're ready," she tells me gently.

A few minutes later, I do. I have to screw up my courage to get there; but there is something within me that is desperate to spend time with this girl. I'm drawn to her, and I can't help it.

The second time I meet Zoe, I'm crying.

I've been moved to the 'settled' ward by this stage, the mystical place known as 'upstairs'; because, although they catch me self-harming occasionally, they still don't realise just how much I'm hurting myself in secret. They also don't realise – or don't want to address – that I'm not eating, and I'm losing weight fast.

I suppose I thought – well, I suppose I thought that this was all going to make me better, quickly. That I was going to come out cured. Right now, I don't feel better, and what's more, I don't know why I should. I get interrogated by doctors every week or so, but otherwise I feel like I'm being 'managed' – by which I mean, medicated up to my eyeballs and restrained when they catch me self-harming. I don't know how this is meant to make me better.

I still want to kill myself. I can't seem to get that particular thought out of my mind, no matter what drugs they pump into me. I'm broken; I'm damaged goods. It would be better for everyone, I'm sure, for me to fade out of existence. I'm low all of the time; I haven't got the energy for anything. Sometimes it feels like I'm sleepwalking. Watching everyone around me interact while I am a silent doll in the corner.

Things are still tough, and to be fair to the doctors and nurses, they do acknowledge this. I'm not quite sure what they think I'm thinking, though. I can't talk to them. I can't trust them. I'm stuck *in my little bubble of hating myself and, though I sometimes feel them knocking, no one has managed to get into the bubble.*

At lunch I pretend to eat a cheese wrap whilst hiding as many scraps of tortilla up my sleeves as I can. What I leave on the plate, I surreptitiously try to make look as small as possible. No one asks any questions.

It's only when I return to my bedroom after lunch to get rid of the scraps that I suddenly feel totally adrift. I'm alone here; I push the staff away and interact only very cautiously with the other patients. Everyone at school has forgotten about me. I feel stuck in limbo; like I'm just being held here for no reason. How is this going to help? How is this supposed to help? I feel penned in, like cattle. None of this is making me feel any better. All it's doing is stopping me killing myself. And even on that front, I'm starting to think of some ideas.

Usually in my room, I sit on the floor and read, but today I find myself almost sleepwalking over to the bed. I don't want to sleep; I just want to lie. I lie on my side, on top of the blankets, facing away from the door. My knees draw up to my chest and I hold them to me like I'm afraid of losing them. I try to make myself feel solid; I try to make myself feel like I exist – but it isn't working.

I haven't cried for a while, I realise hazily; even when I'm self-harming, I feel slightly numb. The thoughts that go around and around my head are very rarely pleasant, but I put up with them. I hate them and I'm hurting, but all I can do is tolerate it. I don't know what else I'm supposed to do.

Now, though... the numbness is gone and the thoughts that rush through my head feel like they've been amplified. I can't tolerate this. I can't even cut it away, this time. I don't know what to do. I don't know what else I'm supposed to do.

A sob catches in my throat and surprises me, as a rush of tears comes through and starts to pour down my face before I have time to stop it. I blink hard, yet tears continue to come. Somewhere in the back of my mind, I remind myself to stay quiet, to not alert any nurses. In this state, though, I'm not sure how much I care.

The sobs keep coming, and I'm covered in snot and tears when I hear a quiet knock on my door. I stiffen, my breathing raggedy, and start to push myself to sitting; but I'm nowhere near composed when the door is tentatively pushed a little way open.

I can't meet the person's eyes, almost clawing at my face as I try to quickly wipe away any evidence of tears. I leap up from the bed away from her and stare down at the floor. I feel like I'm bracing myself for a blow. I chance a small glance in her direction; though I can't look up at her face, I know from the black dolly shoes and patterned trousers that she always wears that it's Zoe. She's good at making friendship bracelets from thread, but how is she with people crying?

"Hey," she says, sounding genuinely concerned. "What's happened, sweet?"

I shake my head, wrapping my arms around myself protectively, gripping the tops of my own arms. I stay staring at the floor. I've wiped a lot of the snot and tears from my face with my cardigan sleeve, but more of both just keep coming. I see mascara smeared all over my sleeve; I must be covered in makeup. I feel scared and I can't quite get a hold of myself.

Tentatively, Zoe takes a few steps towards me. To my surprise, I don't back away. The blanket is still wrapped around my shoulders, almost protectively. Zoe won't hurt me, surely Zoe won't hurt me... I try to talk myself down from the peak of anxiety I'm in, but I just can't do it.

By this point, Zoe is standing close enough to touch me. She doesn't, though. I think she can sense that it's not the right time for that. I wonder if she knows that I oscillate between hating being touched and craving any physical contact that I'm offered. I'm not sure why. Maybe it's because I oscillate between knowing I can only rely on myself and being desperate for someone to help me.

Although, maybe, actually, physical contact is supposed to feel nice. Maybe when I desperately want a hug, I'm finally harnessing a part of me that is actually supposed to be there.

But I have to put this out of my mind, because Zoe's right – it wouldn't be a good idea to try and touch me right now. I'm shaking and I can't stop crying. "Hey," repeats Zoe, even gentler. I can see that I've worried her. Not only has she never seen me like this, I don't think anyone else here has. I'm not sure that anyone ever has, full stop.

"What's happened?" she asks again. She seems remarkably in control; she must have done this before. For a second, that makes it worse. Am I just the latest kid in a line that Zoe is nice to? Somehow, though, I don't feel like that. I feel – bizarrely – like she cares.

I swallow hard. I feel a little queasy, probably from all the tears and the panic. I don't want to vomit on the floor, so it's only when I'm sure I'm not going to do that that I force myself to finally open my mouth.

"I feel lost," I whisper.

I expect to regret speaking as soon as the words are out of my mouth, but Zoe doesn't look angry. Instead, she frowns in concern. "Oh no," she says, and it sounds sincere. "Is there… is there something making you feel like that?"

I'm almost surprised; she seems to believe me. What I said sounded ludicrous – 'lost' isn't a feeling – but she seems to understand. Or if she doesn't understand, at least she's listening. I actually believe that she wants to talk to me, that she wants to know why I'm crying in my room. She doesn't have to do this – she could palm me off on a nurse to give me more medication – but she's taking the time to stay here and listen.

I feel a rush of emotion that I can't quite define, and suddenly, words are tumbling out of my mouth. The tears are still coming and my voice is broken with sobs, but I'm talking.

"I'm all on my own – I feel all on my own – and most of the

time I don't feel anything, I just feel numb, like I'm sleepwalking… I can't cope and I'm… I want to die…"

I can hear myself continuing in this vein for a while. To my surprise, Zoe isn't trying to butt in or get me to stop talking – she's actually listening. It crosses my mind that I might not be making much sense to someone who really doesn't know me that well. But Zoe continues to listen.

After a minute, I finally run out of steam and the stream of emotional words peters out. I am still looking at the floor, wiping tears off my face with my sleeve. Zoe looks at me for a moment, her head tilted to one side. I can tell that she's trying to decide how best to approach this. Finally, she walks quietly into my bathroom and comes out with a few tissues and a packet of makeup wipes.

When she comes back into my bedroom, she lays a hand firmly on my shoulder. "Come on, let's sit on the bed," she says softly, gently, steering me round. I surprise myself that I don't even stiffen when she touches me. For some reason, her touch doesn't feel wrong like so many people's do. I let her move me across the room and I let her sit on the bed beside me.

For a moment, she doesn't say anything, just handing over the tissues to me. I take them gladly; it's much easier to clean my face with tissue than with a woollen cardigan. When my face is dry, she smiles slightly and pulls out a makeup wipe from the packet, once again quietly handing it over. Though I don't usually let people see me without makeup, I'm sure that I will look a damned sight better without makeup than with these mascara tracks all down my face. I suddenly feel very young.

There's a moment of silence. I'm still getting on top of my tears, but the sobbing has stopped, and I feel a lot calmer than I did. Now, more than anything, I feel embarrassed. Embarrassed that Zoe has seen me like that; embarrassed that I've let myself get into this state. I'm almost cringing, expecting to be reprimanded.

"Tell me why you feel like you're on your own," says Zoe, softly. I'm not sure how long we talk for; on the one hand, it could be minutes, but we cover so much that it feels like hours. I surprise myself that I tell Zoe the truth. That isn't what I usually do. Why do I trust this young woman so much?

Finally, she looks at me with that small, sad smile. "Thank you for talking to me," she says. Her voice is always quiet, but I feel like it is extra soft as she looks at me now. I know she is trying not to spook me. There is something especially nice, in the fact that she cares how her voice affects me. She wants me to feel better. It shouldn't be making my heart glow. Somehow it is.

"It sounds like you've been bottling all of that up for a while," she continues, still gentle. "It's good that you've spoken to me."

I look back down to my lap, trying to believe her. Talking has never done great things for my life. I've heard the whole spiel about it so many times; it just has never worked for me so far. I should be kicking myself, right now, for telling Zoe everything I've told her today. Why am I not kicking myself?

I don't understand why I trust her. I barely know her. How do I know she isn't going to break my trust? How do I know that she even gives a shit about any of this? I guess I don't. My mind is going a mile a minute, my thoughts are still racing; but I feel calm. I feel... I don't know the word. I feel like my heart is glowing. I feel warm.

"I think you'll feel better if you come out of here," she tells me, more firmly. "Group is about to start. We're baking this afternoon."

She smiles at me encouragingly. For once, the encouragement isn't even necessary; I like baking. Though, in fairness, I would do anything that Zoe wants me to do right now. I would sit through another hour of origami in a heartbeat.

"Alright," I say, my voice still shaky; I hope that no one will notice that I've been crying.

"You can put your makeup back on before you come in, if you want," Zoe says, seeming to read my mind. She hesitates. "You know I need to let the nurses know what we've spoken about?"

I bite my lip, but I nod. I do know that she has no choice but to do that. Usually it would put my back up, but right now I'm struggling to care.

Zoe smiles at me. "Come through in a minute," she says warmly. "Alright?"

I nod again, trying to find a smile myself. This task is ten times easier than it would have been an hour ago. As Zoe stands up from my bed, I think of the one thing that's been niggling at me. "Zoe?" I ask quietly.

She turns as she's leaving the room. "Yeah?" Her smile is still on her face.

"How did you know I was…?" I say tentatively, uncertainly.

Zoe blinks, and her smile takes on a bit of a rueful feel. "I heard you," she says sadly. "As I was walking past. And I just thought… that you needed someone."

I feel another rush of emotion. She's right. I really, really needed someone.

19

As I watch Maeve run away from me, my first instinct is to yell her name after her; but I stop myself at the last moment. I don't need to draw attention to myself right now, and anyway, I feel bitterly sure that she isn't going to stop and come back. For some reason – for whatever reason – she wants to take me to Birnbeck Pier, and she isn't going to give up. This I know for certain.

I have no option but to follow her. I'm exhausted, and I'm frustrated, but I can't just let her go. I'm not letting her go back to her parents and I can't let her run around Weston-super-Mare alone. It's not the safest of places and I can't run the risk that some drunk guy will grab her. And she's naïve too. She's too trusting. If I leave her, now, and do what I planned, then she will probably get hurt. I can't have that on my conscience. I can't let that be my legacy.

And even more… there's a part of me that can't quite just abandon her yet. Maeve maybe trusts too easily, but the only other thing I'm sure of is that she trusts me. I can't just leave her like Zoe left me.

I sigh deeply, gritting my teeth. It's probably best that I don't let her get too much of a head start. At least I know where she's headed to – but it isn't lost on me that she doesn't have a clue how to get there. I don't know which roads she's going to take. What's more, I don't know if she's ever going to get to Birnbeck Pier. It's not guaranteed that she'll find it when all she's really doing is running through streets vaguely near it.

So, with only a minimal noise of frustration, I follow her. Truth be told, I'm furious that she's able to control me like this. What does it matter to her if I hurt myself? She isn't going to see me after tonight anyway. And I was going to see her to safety first. Things were going to be fine for her.

What did happen to her neck?

I shake that thought away, focusing instead on following her. As pretty a girl as Maeve is, she's on the bigger side – I hate to think it, but surely she can't run that fast. I'm slimmer, quite possibly slightly fitter – I must be able to catch her up without too much of a fight?

But half an hour later, I realise that I've been over-optimistic – which isn't something that happens often for me (as Katy loves to remind me). As it turns out, it has been quite easy for Maeve to lose me completely. To be honest, I'm not sure exactly what I'm going to do about this. I try for a few minutes more to work out which way she has gone, but it quickly becomes apparent that there's not much I can do. I have to find her. I'm going to have to just head for Birnbeck Pier.

I'm out of breath but I decide to keep walking rather than taking a break. The quicker I can find Maeve, the better. I can see the sea in the distance, in the gaps between the buildings. If I keep going towards the sea, then I can follow the coast round to where Birnbeck Pier is. Admittedly, I don't know why I'm only thinking of this plan of action now. This is the kind of thinking that would have been extremely useful an hour ago.

Still, it's with me now, and I'm striding down a dodgy-looking side street, in the vague direction of the coast, when I hear a woman scream. I freeze. It's not a jokey drunk scream or a sound of frustration. Whoever is screaming like that is genuinely agonised. I don't know what to do.

Part of me wants to run in the opposite direction; if someone's screaming like that, that means someone else is doing something terrifying. If it's a large man, there's nothing I can do to help the woman. And if someone's getting attacked, then it isn't unreasonable to think that the police might be there pretty soon. I can't see the police. They'll recognise me straight away and that will be that.

But if I was the woman screaming – and, to be fair, I have been the woman screaming – I would want someone to come and help me. I can't just leave someone, even if there's nothing I can do. I have to try.

And besides – what if the woman screaming is Maeve?

I swear under my breath at the thought, but it's this that really gets me moving. I turn sharply right, towards the source of the sound. The paranoid part of myself feels like I'm moving towards a trap. I try to push that thought out of my mind. Why would anyone want to trap me?

But even at the end of the road, I feel quickly that something isn't right. When the scream finishes, there is eerie quiet. I glance around; I can't see anything amiss. It's only when I turn the next corner onto another side street that I even come into contact with anyone else.

The woman isn't screaming, now, but she's in tears – and she's sat in a heap on the edge of the pavement, clutching her ankle. I hear her swear under her breath, and I can tell she's in pain. Has she fallen?

"Hello?" I say cautiously. "Are you… are you OK?"

I walk closer to the woman, tentatively, trying not to spook her. This late at night, I know that she can't assume that I have good attentions, even if I'm female and frankly not the strongest-looking. She looks like she's been on a night out; she's wearing a tight dress and heels, and her hair looks like it was straightened a few hours ago. Her makeup is smudgy, though I'm probably the last person who can cast a stone about that at the moment. I'm sure that my face is covered in mascara by this stage.

To my surprise, though, the woman doesn't even look up at me in response. She doesn't seem to hear me at all. Is she drunk? Or on something? I mean, she doesn't seem right, but I don't get the impression that she's under the influence of anything. And it's weird that she's all alone. Has she just lost her friends? Have they left her? Does she live around here?

I'm still a tentative fifteen feet away, but she's the only person around and I'm sure she should know that I'm talking to her. We're so alone, in fact, that it's definitely adding to the eeriness.

But the woman doesn't answer my question, continuing to stay hunched on the pavement. "I heard you scream," I try again. "I was just passing, but… I wanted to check that you were OK."

I don't know why I would have been passing; the biggest building on this street is the cinema, which is, of course, closed at this time. The other shops are clothes shops and more quiet newsagents; we're in an odd sort of limbo between the hospitality area of the town and the high street. I am glad, though, that we're away from the noisy partygoers and busy chippies. That would only make the situation more stressful, I'm sure.

For a moment, I think I'm getting a response – but instead, I realise that the woman is only fumbling with the strap of her high-heeled shoe. She just about manages to get the silvery contraption undone before she yanks off the shoe and flings it across the street. She's clearly frustrated. She doesn't say anything, staring down the side street; and I don't know what I'm supposed to do here. I have more pressing concerns, frankly, than a screaming woman who won't answer my questions… and yet again I'm involved now. Why am I always involved?

"I'm looking for my friend," I tell her, trying a different tack.

"She's called Maeve, she's fourteen. Blonde hair, a little bit bigger than me."

Most of me is sure that I'm not going to get a response, that I'm essentially talking to a brick wall; but then suddenly, the woman looks up at me. There's something oddly dull about her eyes, though I can see that she's in physical pain. She lets out a tiny groan before she speaks.

"That wasn't your friend," she says hollowly, grimacing in pain as she massages her ankle.

Hesitantly, I take a few steps closer. I'm not sure what she means, but any response has to be good. "Did you see someone?" I ask cautiously. "She might have been running – I mean, you might not have seen her that well…"

Before I even finish the sentence, though, the woman is shaking her head. For a minute I think it might be absentminded, that she might be thinking about something else entirely, but then she looks back up at me. "I fucking saw her properly, alright?" she says harshly, before her eyes are back down at her ankle.

I flinch back automatically at her aggression. I don't want to get attacked. Clearly, though, the woman's mind isn't on me. She's biting down on her lip, and I can see her ankle starting to bruise already. "Did you… did you go over on your ankle?" I ask tentatively.

She nods, once, sharply. I wait, hopeful that maybe this will get her talking – but, of course, it doesn't. I'm not sure what questions to ask. She's clearly seen *something* – she just doesn't seem interested in finding the right words, or in telling me what she's seen. Maybe it's down to the pain. I don't know how to help. And, frankly, I'm sick of feeling helpless.

I take another few steps closer, closing the gap between me and the woman. I can see, now that I'm close, that she's shaking. Whatever she's seen, it's upset her. I might not be able to understand what's happened here, but I know a good bit about feeling panicked. More than that, though, she's hurt, and I don't want to leave her, no matter how keen I am to find Maeve.

"Take a deep breath," I advise her hesitantly, feeling my head tilt sympathetically without really meaning it to.

She blinks, once, hard, like she's blinking away the ghost of a bright light from her vision. "That was…" she tries again, still seeming to be unable to get the sentence out. I wait, patiently, but she doesn't seem to be able to get any further.

"A girl? A teenage girl?" I prompt, hopefully. "It might have been my friend, I think she ran down here."

My words are becoming slightly gabbled as I simultaneously try to comfort this woman and find out if Maeve has been down here. It's too much. My brain feels like it's been in the sun too long and it's overheating. I wouldn't be surprised if I caught alight. I try to take my own advice and take a deep breath, but I'm frustrated and I want answers.

"Please," I plead, the words forcing themselves out of my mouth from nowhere. "I need to find her. If you saw which way she was going…"

Am I really still trying to find which way Maeve has gone? Because I could just try a road. I could leave this woman here and carry on towards the coast, as I had planned. Yet somehow I'm sucked in here. I need to know what that woman saw and why it's rendered her incapable of explaining it. Something tells me that it's important.

But the woman is shaking her head again. "No, no," she says listlessly. "That was… the bloody…" She screws her eyes shut again for a moment, cutting herself off. I wait patiently, hoping she will continue.

"Rose," she says finally.

I wish this could be a bombshell moment, an explanation of why I'm so interested and why this woman is so scared. But I don't know a Rose. The name means nothing to me. I feel like I've physically deflated a little at the lack of pay-off.

It's a start, though, I guess, so I jump on it. "Rose?" I repeat quickly. "Is that… your friend? Did she do something?"

The woman shakes her head quickly, frustrated. "I saw her," she says. "Running across the square."

At least she is using sentences now, the power of speech seeming to return to her. Still, it's not a massively helpful statement. Why has bumping into her friend left her like this?

Somehow, I find myself kneeling down across from her. "OK," I say, slowly, encouragingly, a reassuring smile on my face. "Did you not expect her?"

It's a weak question and I'm all too aware of it. Still, it's out of my mouth now and there's nothing I can do about it. I wait, hoping for a better response this time.

She shakes her head. "She's supposed to be at *home*," she says irritably, as if it's somehow my fault that Rose isn't where she's supposed to be. "I trusted her, and…"

She tails off again; and though I'm sure this woman is very worried about Rose, I feel myself draw away. I guess this is just another disappointment. I really thought that this woman had seen something that might help me find Maeve.

Or did I? What was she ever going to say that would help me find Maeve beyond 'she went that way'? Why did I think that she would have some nugget of wisdom that would help me get Maeve somewhere safe? What's *wrong* with me, tonight? I should have left Maeve in the fucking forest.

Still, it's not this woman's fault. "You should go to A&E if the pain gets worse," I tell her, like she's called 111 and I'm the operator.

The woman frowns, as if I'm a fly buzzing around her head, an irritation. "The pain…" she repeats, and to my surprise, she gives a short, breathy laugh. "You don't know what you're talking about." She shakes her head again, but then her eyes are back on me. "Do you know her? Were you with her?"

I sigh. "No, I don't know any Roses," I say tiredly. My back aches; still, there's one last avenue to try before I give up on this. "Are you *sure* it was Rose who ran this way?" I ask, and I can hear the desperation in my voice. "Are you *sure* it wasn't Maeve?"

She narrows her eyes at me, finally seeming to actually see me. "Rose is like my little sister," she says, almost accusingly. She doesn't seem to like my implication that she's unable to tell her friends from random strangers. "It wasn't anyone else. And if I hadn't gone over on my foot…"

She huffs in frustration. I can guess the end of that sentence; Rose would have been in deep shit. By this point, though, I have come to realise that this woman isn't moving from her story. She will go to her grave insisting that she saw Rose run across the square at 3am in a slightly dingy part of Weston-super-Mare. Hell, maybe she did. But she's sure as fuck that she didn't see Maeve.

I've wasted time on this, and more than anything, I'm frustrated and annoyed. I should have just kept walking. What good was talking to the woman ever going to do? I don't know what's wrong with me. Why can't I get anything right?

I go to rub the woman's shoulder gently but then think better of it. As much as I want to be helpful for this woman, she seems to feel quite strongly repelled by me. I'm not sure what I've done. I quickly withdraw my hand as I see her facial expression, her eyes still narrowed and her mouth set in a thin line. I put my hands on the pavement and push myself up to stand. I feel myself sway slightly. I've been awake a long time.

I don't offer the woman a goodbye; in truth, I'm not quite sure what to say to her. "Hope you're OK," I say eventually. And I do. I hope she goes to a doctor to sort out that foot; and I hope that she finds Rose. As for Rose – well, I hope she gets home safely too. I don't know what else I can say about it.

It feels wrong to leave this woman alone, in pain – but what else can I do? She has to want my help, I guess. As soon as that thought pops into my head, I feel myself scrunch my face up physically. I hate that saying. It's almost as contrived as when people say they hope someone gets the proper help they need.

But I've got the proper help and it seems to be doing fuck all. It's 3am, and I've climbed over the back fence only to chase a fourteen-year-old across the city. I'm not behaving like a stable person and God knows that they're going to extend my section now. I've got the proper help, and it's not helping me. I am so frustrated and worn down and I just want to *sleep*.

Part of me hopes that when I die, I'll see Zoe.

I need to find Maeve. I can't leave her. But once she's safe, I need to be too. Once she's safe, I'm gone.

20

The Christmas period rolls around way too quickly.

Usually, I like Christmas – I don't go overboard, but I like it. It's a good excuse to hibernate for a week or two and not have to go to school. Plus, my mum is marginally more relaxed about chocolate consumption at Christmas than she is the other eleven months of the year.

This year, though, of course, it's different. I'm locked up. I'm sectioned. I won't be decorating the tree with my mum and dad, or watching films with my friends in school because the teachers can't be bothered to teach anymore this term. I don't know what Christmas is like stuck in hospital, but I can't imagine that it's great.

Getting out of bed on 1st December takes even more effort than usual. I drag myself up and have a shower as I do every morning; I put clothes on and go through to the lounge. This morning, though, I can tell that everyone around me seems similarly slightly subdued. On the one hand, I suppose it is nice that we all feel in sync, that I'm around people who feel the same way that I do; however, it's when everyone is grumpy and pissed off that 'incidents' tend to happen.

I get the impression that the staff are picking up on this atmosphere too, because as soon as our daily morning meeting finishes, Zoe and the redheaded activity worker come into the dining room with armfuls of cardboard, paint and stickers. This has to be a distraction technique. For me, of course, just having Zoe nearby is a boost; but I can see why they've decided that this morning is the morning to start a project.

Zoe smiles at me as I approach, curious. "Hiya," she says cheerfully.

The warm feeling in my chest is there again. "Morning," I reply. "What are we doing?"

By this point, a few more patients have approached the table, as curious as me. Before Zoe can answer, Bronwen (the redhead) speaks. "We're going to make a Christmas tree," she announces proudly. "Out of all of this!"

"We're not allowed a proper Christmas tree?" asks Flick, my fellow patient, sounding a little put out.

Zoe and Bronwen exchange a look, and it's clear they don't want to dwell on this. "So, we were thinking, we could make it in three layers," continues Bronwen hastily. "And then slot it all together!"

I'm not sure that they've thought through exactly how we're going to build this thing, but I can't deny that I feel engaged in this activity anyway. There's something oddly fascinating about it. When Bronwen goes over to the TV and turns on the radio, and the room is filled with Christmas songs, I have to admit that I feel considerably lightened by the whole thing.

Over the course of the month, we spend a lot of mornings doing things like this – decorating the ward with paper chains and pictures of Santa, making cards for each other and our families, building a Christmas post box that someone gets to empty and distribute every day. On the one hand, I guess that Christmas offers up a new range of things to do; but even though all these activities are fun, I'm always aware that we are being distracted from the fact that we are apart from our families and friends.

As the day approaches, the topic on everyone's lips is Christmas leave. A few people, who are at a firmer stage of recovery, know long before the 25th that they have a week, or five nights, to spend at home with their family. Others, who are really struggling, are being forced to face the possibility that they might not get to leave the ward at all. It should be divisive, there should be jealousy and ill feeling over all of it; instead, however, everyone is being respectful. I guess everyone can see the fragility of the situation; it only takes one incident to lose your leave, and even those who are doing better have had that happen before. We might be in different boats in terms of how much leave we're getting, but we're in the same boat in that we have no real agency over our own Christmases.

In terms of Christmas leave, I lie somewhere in the middle. I know that I'm not going to get a week of leave – especially since the doctors know that I don't want to set foot in my parents' house, let alone spend the night there – but I'm hoping that I get something. I'm several hours from my parents' house on the ward, so my parents have decided to stay in a cottage or apartment nearby, and I can go and visit them there. A few months ago, I would have preferred to stay on the ward, but my relationship with my parents has actually improved.

I feel like a bit of a traitor, truth be told, for forgiving them, for letting what has happened slide; still, it's hard to be mad at them, when they have, in all fairness, stuck by me since the bridge incident. They've regularly made the long journey to see me, and brought me treats. Moreover, they haven't gotten angry about it like I thought they would. I think the shock of nearly losing me has put things into a rather harsh perspective.

I put to the back of my mind that, despite this, I'm scared to stay in their house. I'm not sure that thinking about that is especially helpful right now. I have tried a few times, tentatively, to mention things at home to the therapist that they've assigned for me here, but she doesn't seem to want to listen.

My mum cried the first time I saw her since coming into hospital. Not that this is especially unusual; she is the kind of woman who gets set off into tears by adverts. But seeing her face that day, I knew that this time, she meant it. It has been hard to be angry with her with that facial expression burned into my brain.

I do kind of feel, as well, that the distance has done us good. It's easier now that we don't have to have arguments about the mundane stuff. Besides, only seeing each other for a few hours a week, there isn't time to have a fight. There is barely time for my mum and me to snipe at each other, even if we did have the inclination. Overall, my relationship with my parents has gotten a lot better since I moved out.

(Since they haven't had to put up with me, I think, but I put that out of my mind.)

As the 25th approaches, the ward gets emptier and emptier. At first this doesn't really make the place much quieter; some of those are who are really struggling can be pretty loud by themselves. By the time Christmas Eve arrives, however, there are just three of us left on the ward. And, fortunately, none of us seem to feel like kicking off the day before Christmas.

The support workers and nurses seem appreciative of this. They let us use the ward money to buy snacks and let us sit in the lounge with our duvets and watch Elf. Two of my favourite staff members in particular seem to want to make things cheerful for those of us stuck here. Considering that they are spending their Christmas Eves here too, I actually find it quite touching. It isn't a bad Christmas Eve, but it's a weird one.

I am nervous for Christmas tomorrow; I am hoping that all goes smoothly, that I don't ruin Christmas for everyone. It is going to be odd waking up on the ward on Christmas morning, but I am lucky that I get to leave for a few hours, to see my parents in their holiday apartment. I'm doing the best of the three left here; one girl just has a few hours of time with her family in the visiting room, and the other isn't going to be able to leave the ward at all. I can't help but feel slightly guilty that I'm getting out at all.

Zoe has already gone on annual leave. It feels odd to know that I have to spend nine days without her. Usually I just don't see her at the weekends, and even that is long enough. I guess it's good that she gets to see her family, though. I have been spending a lot of time imagining her Christmas with her parents and siblings. Maybe it's weird, but it soothes me.

I'm very aware that one day I will see Zoe for the last time. If I'm struggling to manage nine days without her, how am I going to cope when she's gone forever? I put this out of my mind, purely out of necessity. I can't think about it. I know I won't be able to come up with a solution.

When I wake up on Christmas morning, I can hear a couple of staff members laughing not too far from my door. It's not a bad way to wake up. I sit up in bed and stretch, wondering what the time is. I smile as I see that a staff member has left a few presents from the ward by my door, which has been left ajar as it always is during the night. Everyone gets the same presents, of course, but it's still nice. I put them on my bed and go to have a shower.

When I come into the lounge, showered, dressed and appropriately made up, my fellow patients are both already in there. Keira is clearly anxious, anticipating her visit, and Saoirse looks like she's been crying in the night. I try to smile at her, to cheer her up; she manages only a weak smile in return. Today may be just about manageable for me, but it niggles at me how unpleasant it might be for her. Especially when I'm with my parents and Keira is on her visit.

There are staff around, though, of course, so she won't be alone. And I'm guessing they will let her have charge of the TV remote. I'm trying to find silver linings, but I'm aware that maybe today will just be shit for her.

Maybe she will feel better when it is over, when the rest of the patients start to return to the ward from their various homes. Of the three other people to return, I'm pretty sure at least two of them are due back tonight, and the other one will be back by the 28th at the latest. Then everything can return to normal, with fewer bothersome reminders that we are away from our homes and families.

It's about an hour later when my parents come and collect me from the ward as planned. I feel guilty, leaving. Now I feel like it's not just painful to be left on the ward; it's also kind of painful to leave people behind there. I have to promise myself that they will still be OK when I get back.

The six hours that I have with my parents pass largely uneventfully. That's not to say that they are unpleasant; I have fun, and I think my parents do too. I feel bad that they have to drive all the way home on Christmas Day. At least they seemed to like their presents; I haven't really been able to get to any shops to buy presents this year, so I've been knitting madly. A hat for my dad and mittens for my mum. I'm quite proud of them. I've had so much time to practice knitting that I've gotten quite good at it, I think.

I'm almost holding my breath when I come back on the ward. I don't want to come back on to find that someone's hurt or ended up in A&E. To my relief, everything seems to have stayed settled. Keira and Saoirse are occupied watching a film, and the staff are still in a good mood. My own mood is starting to dip, now I'm back here, but I know that I have to keep it together. And I do.

I'm going to see Zoe in three days.

Before that, though, the other patients start to return onto the ward. Again, I'm apprehensive about it – I know how low I felt coming back here tonight, however much I wanted to hide it. I worry that people are going to hurt themselves. In fairness, I am always apprehensive about this, especially when I'm away from the ward. You just never know what kind of situation you're going to walk back into.

This week, though, when Christmas Day is done with and we are on the weird week between Christmas and New Year, there seems to be something in the air, and it's not bad. Everyone seems, well, not calm, as such, but managing. In fact, scratch that – calm is most definitely the wrong word. Maybe it's just that everyone feels like pissing around and doing stupid things rather than kicking off. There's an odd sense of camaraderie in it.

Every day I expect this union to start to drift apart, but it doesn't. Then, we hear some news – that the 'unsettled' ward downstairs is being closed to new patients, because of safety concerns. Even though I was barely down there any time, this kind of doesn't surprise me. There was some dodgy stuff managing to happen down there.

What this means for us, though, is that, for the time being, no one is being admitted to our ward. Added to the fact that no one up here is particularly close to getting discharged, this means that the patient group isn't going to change for a little while. There is an odd stability to this that I've never felt before in here. Friendship groups in here, so I've seen so far, don't last. People come and go, and things change. Now, though? Now I almost feel part of a team.

We play Monopoly endlessly, not to mention Just Dance on the Wii. Our activities are limited, especially now Christmas crafts are no longer on the menu, but we still find ourselves doing things together. We also, for some reason, watch a lot of supernatural horror programmes (until they get banned when we try to conduct our own séance).

One night, we are sitting in the lounge, chatting and sharing jokes. There are no staff around – apparently they have decided that we are all settled enough to entertain each other for a while, while they get on with paperwork.

I have a blanket wrapped around me, and my feet tucked under me. I feel slightly indolent. We have already scrolled through the TV guide and found nothing; we have already looked through the DVD box and realised that we've watched all of them. It's good that the atmosphere is relatively relaxed, because I'm very aware of how situations like this can switch.

Flick's long legs dangle over the sofa across from me. I can tell from how she's sprawled that she's bored to tears. At least it's a lazy, lethargic kind of bored, though. Not a frustrated, kicking-off kind of bored – and I'm grateful for that. Flick is younger than me, athletic and energetic; she thrives on excitement and chaos, and staff tend to refer to her as an 'instigator'.

(I'm a 'follower', apparently; I try not to take offence about this.)

"They're watching us through the window," Flick says gloomily, stretching slowly. I turn around to look through the office window; and she's right. They have their eyes on us. In their defence, doing this is not necessarily without logic.

"We can't even play 'blackouts'," she adds, slightly indignant.

'Blackouts' has been our game of choice for the past few weeks, whenever we can get away from staff supervision. Truth be told, I play it in my bedroom alone sometimes. I'm not sure why we like it so much; all it involves, essentially, is making ourselves faint. The first time I played, I woke up highly confused and disorientated – and of course, everyone found this hilarious.

I suppose there is a thrill in the game that is hard to come by, when you are locked in three rooms all day. In any case, I've become just as addicted to it as the others have.

But right now, we are definitely being supervised. I suspect that if we try to move to the other lounge, the support workers will get suspicious and follow us. I'm not sure why they are so vigilant tonight; maybe because the staff here tonight are all staff who work here regularly, who know how boredom tends to end. On the other hand, maybe they have just caught on to 'blackouts'. It's not exactly a sanctioned activity, and probably one they'd like to avoid.

The atmosphere is decidedly flat. Somehow, we all seem to be brighter when we're not being babysat. I try to think of things that we are actually allowed to do. Monopoly doesn't exactly seem right, tonight. Besides, I think someone swallowed the little metal dog.

Before I can think of anything else, Saoirse lifts her head from her own lazy position next to Flick. "They can't hear us, though," she points out, and suddenly everyone is a little bit more alert.

I look around the room, a smile now playing around the edges of my lips as I see grins start to form on my friends' faces. Saoirse, ever observant, has made an excellent point. As long as we look like we're just chatting, we can talk about whatever we want.

Flick's eyes dart up to the support workers at the window, alternating between paperwork and glancing at us; presumably she does not see anything worrying, because her grin widens even further. She slides off the sofa cheerfully to sit cross-legged on the floor, her hand resting on her chin. I can tell that possibilities are racing through her mind, of all the things that we could talk about. I'm not apprehensive, though – Flick is bouncy and energetic and boisterous but she's totally harmless. Last time we went with one of her ideas, we ended up playing 'Never Have I Ever' with plastic mugs of squash.

"We could tell our stories," she suggests brightly.

I stiffen slightly. I keep the smile on my face – I don't want to be the wet blanket – but this time, I'm not sure Flick has thought this one through. My story – well, there are things that I've barely ever acknowledged out loud, let alone spilled to a room full of teenagers that, really, I don't know that well. Even the rest of my life, the less secret bits, aren't something that I generally like to broadcast. I'm not sure I can be part of this conversation.

Moreover, I'm not sure that it's a great idea for anyone else to be part of this conversation either. The mood on the ward feels somewhat changeable already; we don't need anyone to dip and have an incident that means they lose their leave.

Flick's smile falters for a minute. Maybe she can tell from the faces of the group that this might not be her best idea. There is a short, tense silence. Not for the first time, I'm a little worried about how tonight is going to go.

But before I can say anything, Saoirse sits up properly, and I see her take a deep breath. "I'll go first," she says, an unusual note of stubbornness in her voice.

There's something about Saoirse, who is usually so shy, taking control of the situation; for some reason, I feel totally unable to react, let alone speak. I'm still not sure that this is a good idea – but there's no way that I can stop Saoirse talking right now. And, in fairness, I'm not sure I want to.

The events that Saoirse calmly lays out to us... well, my chest hurts and I feel almost frozen. The fact that these things have happened to Saoirse is painful, is heart-breaking in itself; but the fact that I have known her for all this time and I have barely had a hint of an idea that she has been through these things... I feel so numb that I almost can't process what she is saying. When she finally stops – when she finally gets to the part of the story where she is admitted here, miles from her home – well, there is silence. I don't think I am the only one who feels unable to speak.

It is Flick who breaks the spell, as she reaches out and pats Saoirse's shoulder. This should be woefully inadequate, for what we have just heard. But Flick is not comforting her; she is not trying to make it OK. She is acknowledging it. And for some reason, this is exactly what is needed.

It is fitting that Flick goes next. I worry as she starts that there will be a sense of one-upmanship; but this concern is quickly banished. Her story is totally separate from Saoirse; and I think that it is this that makes this conversation somehow doable.

With each story, my heart breaks a little bit more. I have known these girls for mere weeks, but I feel like I know them inside out now. To hear the things that have been done to them... it's not right, and I grow more and more numb with each passing sentence. None of these things should have happened. Rape, abuse, bullying... the stories are all different, but none are without these factors.

Then it gets to me, last in the line. For the first time, there is a long pause, as I try to collect my thoughts. I'm still not sure that

I want to do this. Even if I were to tell them – would they believe me? Or will they hate me? It was all my fault. I can't get away from that fact. I'm the evil one, in my story. I don't want my friends here to hear the story and hate me, especially when they have all been done so badly to.

I open my mouth, my throat dry. I start with the easy bits – feeling like a weirdo at school, getting outed – and, at first, I tell the version that I have been telling the doctors and even the psychologist. I hover quickly over Mrs Fletcher finding me self-harming and briefly mention getting sectioned on the bridge. But with five pairs of eyes looking back at me, all of whom have just bared their souls, admitted to the worst things that have happened to them, I have to tell the truth. I'm not sure why, and yet I feel totally compelled. I talk about my mum, my dad. I admit that the crash happened. I bare my soul.

And before I know what's happening, I go further. I tell them why we crashed.

For a second, there is silence. But then conversation resumes. It is no worse, I guess, than what I have heard from all of them. There is something in this – something I can't describe. I feel safe. I feel accepted. I feel part of the team.

Yet this is almost scarier than knowing I'll have to leave Zoe; because I'm not kidding myself that I will see many, if any, of these girls again when I leave. We will fracture six ways, scattered across the country. I was sure this morning that I can't do without Zoe; now I feel part of a team, can I do without my teammates?

*

It's a week into January when the strange Christmas peace abruptly wears off.

Tensions have been rising between patients and staff all day, to such an extent that by teatime, I'm sure that something is going to kick off. For the first time, how close we are worries me – because

I strongly suspect that whatever is going to kick off isn't going involve just one person.

Tension like this is always worse when the more popular staff members aren't on shift, and today the ward is staffed almost exclusively with support workers who we don't know and agency nurses who, as usual, don't give a shit about any of us. It's not a good atmosphere. Patients are getting increasingly frustrated with being brushed aside by the staff for things like cups of squash or items that they have to be supervised with, and this isn't helped by the fact that no one has any staff they trust to talk to about the serious things. For my part, I have been up all night with nightmares, and not being able to escape my own head has meant that I have spent the day getting increasingly stir-crazy from being locked up in three rooms. I should be used to this, but today I'm not.

And I'm not the only one. This isn't going to end well.

I see Zoe briefly in the morning, which does soothe me slightly, but for the rest of the day, she is working on other wards and I don't get a chance to even have a casual conversation with her. I don't think this helps anyone else, either. Zoe is well liked, and her presence on the ward might have calmed things down a lot.

I'm sat at the table in the lounge, legs jiggling, trying to force myself to read, when I hear a commotion around the corner. I look up automatically; something quickly tells me that whatever is going on there is more pressing than the book in front of me. I realise quickly that I can hear arguing; and though I can't make out exactly what is being said, I can hear staff members' voices as well as patients'. Clearly, something is happening – and I'm not in the slightest bit surprised.

I fold down the corner of my page in my book as I get up from the table. It feels good to move. I'm suddenly charged with energy, and I'm already ready to become embroiled in the argument. I'm about to round the corner to see what is actually going on when the commotion abruptly comes to me, and most of the ward comes running around the corner into the lounge. A few staff members follow, stern faces on, but it's pretty clear already who is winning this argument.

To be honest, it doesn't really matter what the argument is all about. It's never about what actually starts up the argument. What's pertinent, though, is that today the staff and patients are well and truly on opposing teams.

I catch Flick's arm as she comes near me. "What's going on?" I ask, a note of urgency in my voice that I don't quite expect. "What's happened?"

Flick huffs, though I can tell that she's more keyed up than actually angry. "Ugh, they're just being ridiculous," she tells me, audible to every member of staff in the room. Clearly, this is entirely intentional and she even accompanies these words with a dirty look over the staff, just to make sure that they get the message.

I know that things aren't going to calm down anytime soon, but I'm still surprised when Flick turns to me and leans in, speaking only to me this time. "We're going to barricade," she says in a low voice, that I can hear the excitement in quite easily.

Of course, I am older than Flick; I should be more mature than she is. But I'm keyed up too. I'm struggling too. I'm irritated too. I'm irritated at the situation we're in, and I'm irritated at the agency staff who care so little that they refer to us by our initials and speak about us as though we're not there. If Zoe was here, or any of my favourite support workers, things would be different. To be honest, I'm willing to hazard a guess that if any of Flick's favourites were here either, then things would be different for her too.

Not tonight, though. Tonight, I don't feel like being mature and trying to calm the others down. Tonight, I am absolutely on board with the idea of a barricade.

Barricades are notorious on the ward, and even more so on the admissions ward. They are annoying enough for staff that we feel like we're getting our own back, and, if I'm being honest, there is an element of fun in them. They are rarely successful, but trying at least gets a bit of frustration out.

I need no encouragement from Flick, and as I look around at the gaggle of patients now around me, I can tell that once again, I've actually been accepted into the group. There's something heartening about this; there is always a niggling doubt that no one likes me, and being included in this campaign actually makes me a little warm and fuzzy. More than that, though, it makes me willing to do pretty much whatever. These girls know me – really know me – and I can't let them down.

There isn't much time to think about it, anyway – the words are barely out of Flick's mouth when a hand grabs my forearm, pulling me along with the group as we suddenly charge into the bedroom corridor and slam the door of the corridor behind us. Someone yells for a few of us to push hard against the door that we've just closed, while the others run to the opposite end of the corridor to push hard against the other door. With both of these doors firmly shut, there are no two ways about it – we are well and truly barricaded in.

The staff – understandably – are pissed. I can hear the screechy voice of Jeannette the nurse, who has been particularly horrible all day, on the other side of the door. I suppose it is hard to monitor us while we're all locked in a corridor, but I am finding it hard to muster up any sympathy for Jeannette. Well, for any of them, really. Maybe I'm being callous. But after another day of being brushed off and ignored, I don't really feel like doing the staff any favours. If they don't want to treat us like we matter, why should I feel sorry for them that their evening at work won't be as easy as they thought?

Inside the corridor, however, there is a real party atmosphere. This isn't an exaggeration – all five of us in here seem to have gone from stir-crazy and keyed up, to hyper and finding all of this thoroughly hilarious. It's not hard to fathom why – we're in control in here. The staff can huff and puff all they want. There's absolutely fuck all they can do about it.

Well, that's not quite true. It's not long at all before they press their emergency response buttons and back-up starts to come up from the other wards. Normally, this would mean that this little adventure would be at an end, but we're all so full of adrenaline that we are nowhere close to giving up.

So I plant my feet on the floor and push against the door with my back, a friend on either side of me doing the same. Somehow, we're actually winning, even with the built-up male support workers from the men's ward pushing on the door from the other size. They try to talk us out too, but I'm ill inclined to listen to staff who are using our actual names for the first time today. I wouldn't even be surprised if they had to look the names up. Why should we listen to anything they have to say?

It's a little bit of an anti-climax, though, when things very quickly become a stalemate. They give up trying to talk us round; they give up trying to push the doors down. I suspect that their new strategy is to just leave us to get bored and come out by ourselves. Clearly, they have misjudged the atmosphere in here. This isn't going to end anytime soon.

I sit with my back against the door, Flick on one side of me and Saoirse on the other. I have a huge grin over my face, and as I look at my two friends, I can see that they are feeling the same.

"I think we've fucking won," says Saoirse, out of breath and pink-cheeked, sounding frankly jubilant.

I'm not even sure why it's so funny, but I suddenly feel a wave of giggles come over me. Once I start, I can't stop. It feels kind of like a release, in some way, like at least I am getting some emotion out. It's contagious, though, because as I start to laugh, I hear Flick and Saoirse do the same. I even look up to my friends on the other end of the corridor and see that they are chuckling too. There's something oddly wholesome about this moment.

I try to ignore, though, that the other effect of this laughter is that it is heightening the euphoria that is coursing through my body. Once again, I suspect that this isn't just me.

As a few more minutes pass, it starts to feel a little safer, a little less likely that the staff are going to suddenly stampede in. Cautiously, we start to move away from the doors. Though we stay ready to defend the doors again if necessary, we now start to mess around in the corridor, laughing and joking. We can hear the staff milling around the door of the corridor, and for some reason, this is hilarious. It might be the adrenaline, or it might just be knowing that there is absolutely fuck all that they can do. It is nice that the shoe is finally on the other foot, as it were.

But while this adrenaline is nice, it soon starts to become apparent that things are not going to stay hilarious. For a group of people who have spent a lot of time feeling low and depressed and anxious, this sudden euphoria doesn't feel exactly... safe. Added to this, the feeling of being a caged bird that has wriggled free through the bars, well – this corridor isn't big enough to hold that amount of energy.

It starts when Hannah, the youngest of all of us, turns to Flick. "Give me your shoelaces," she urges her, out of the blue. She is grinning, bouncing, but it's immediately clear what she wants to do with the laces. There is a reason that the staff haven't been allowing her to have her own.

This would just about be fine, except, with all the energy ricocheting around this corridor, Flick actually leans down and starts to take them off. "Flick!" I exclaim, at the same time as Saoirse. Flick straightens up, to look at the two of us, and for a second there is something like panic in her eyes – but then Hannah is laughing, playing it off, and Flick starts to laugh too. It's funny, I guess. I exchange a look with Saoirse, but this is just as brief, and within a moment, she and I are laughing too. It's funny. We have to hold on to that.

Suddenly, there is a quiet thud from outside the corridor. Our heads snap up in unison, but it's not the door of the corridor; in fact, it's the office door locking shut. It's an everyday sound, one that we should all be used to. Why is it so panicking?

Everything suddenly seems to matter more than it did half an hour ago.

Hannah races down to the door of the corridor and peers through the small window to look at the office. "It's fucking Jeannette," she tells us, somewhere between a shout and a yelp. "She's phoning someone. The police! I bet it's the fucking police!"

This would usually seem like a stretch, but as soon as she utters the words, my mind immediately accepts them. From the looks on the faces of the others, their minds seem to have done the exact same thing.

"They're going to come with riot gear," Flick says darkly. "To drag us out."

Keira's eyes narrow. "The dicks!" she says furiously. The harsh sound of her voice bounces off the walls and I suddenly feel claustrophobic for a moment. It's almost too loud for the space. Everyone seems to be crowded in much closer than we were a moment ago.

"Would they... would they do that?" asks Saoirse, her voice quieter, her eyes wide.

She rubs at her chest agitatedly and I can tell that all of this is starting to make her anxious. Somehow, however, this just makes me angrier at the staff. Of course, I have no real idea if Jeannette is calling the police or not. But either way, it is their side that is causing the problems, and upsetting my friend.

Hannah seems to be thinking the same, because as I look over to her, she is giving Jeannette the middle finger through the window. I feel a sudden mad desire to laugh; and though a second ago, that would have seemed exactly in place, something right now makes the idea of laughing seem totally inappropriate. Maybe it is the fear on Saoirse's face; maybe it is the anger on Flick's. Somehow, now is no longer the time to laugh.

"We won't let them in," says Flick fiercely. "No matter what they do. We'll fight them – the police too, if we have to."

Hannah is nodding firmly. "Yeah," she agrees. "They think

they can do what they want with us. We can't give them an easy time."

It's starting to become unclear, now, whether we are talking about the police or the staff. Maybe it is starting not to matter. Maybe whoever tries to get us out of here is going to be on that opposite side.

I don't get the chance to reply, because suddenly Hannah is shouting out again. "Jeannette's coming," she yells. "Someone help me with the door!"

It's almost instinctively that I rush over to the door; I barely think about it until I am pushing up against the door again. I am still surrounded by friends, but the rush, the camaraderie, has become bitter, angry. This isn't an adventure anymore; this isn't a quest with my compadres. This is fearful, and angry, and I feel suddenly that everyone who has ever hurt me is on the other side of the door, clamouring to get into us.

I don't want to get hurt again.

Images swim in my mind that I'm trying desperately to remove. My eyes are shut as Hannah and Flick and I push hard on the door, just in case someone starts to come in again. I hear footsteps behind me as Keira rushes to the other door, to make sure they can't get in there. I can hear staff moving around on the other side of the door, though they don't sound like they are going to try and start to get through the door again...

Then I hear a heavy thump behind me. My eyes flick open automatically, surprised, and it only takes a second to see what has made the noise. Saoirse is flat on her back in the middle of the corridor. From the look of it, she's passed out cold.

Flick and I exchange a look – and it pains me, almost disgusts me, that we both glance out the window to check that there's no staff around to suddenly rush in before we go to Saoirse. In the three seconds since she fell, it has become abundantly clear to me that this has already gone too far. Why was this a good idea, again?

But we are all still buzzing. It's awful, but this isn't something that's just going to melt away amicably. There are too many feelings reverberating around this small corridor. What's more, it painfully hits me that the staff we have been fighting are people too. It's not actually unreasonable that there's probably feelings bouncing around out there, too.

I don't know what to do with Saoirse; it feels pretentious to start taking her pulse or putting her in the recovery position. I'm not a fucking doctor. To my relief, though, by the time Flick and I reach her, she is awake again, pushing herself up to sit, rubbing her forehead slightly.

"Are you OK?" Flick asks urgently.

I feel a rush of relief when Saoirse nods. "Yeah," she says quickly, and thankfully doesn't even sound too groggy. "Sorry, just when I get…"

She tails off, looking sheepishly down into her lap. I get an urge to hug her, but I don't. The fact that she feels like she has to apologise… I shake my head at her, hard. I don't know what else to say.

There is a little comfort in that Saoirse manages to get to her feet without any help and seems to be fine. Maybe she is fine – maybe it was just a nervous thing that we can ignore, and get back to rebellion – but no matter how many times I repeat that to myself, everything tastes different, and I'm scared.

For some of my fellow comrades, though, this seems to have only heightened things, to only have made the rebellion ever more important. I'm not sure of the logic of this, and I am becoming increasingly aware that this is out of my control now. I catch Saoirse's eye, once, and I discern from the look she gives me that she is the only other one in this corridor who understands how I feel.

But then Hannah is calling out, and Flick's head snaps around to her, and she runs back to the door to carry on our defence. In the other direction, Keira calls out – she sounds mildly panicked, alone at the door by herself. Saoirse quickly tears her eyes from mine and goes to join her, her socks sliding on the slippy lino. To my surprise, I hear my name too – Hannah and Flick want me to join them. Despite the worries that are starting to mount up in my chest, feeling included motivates me to go and join them at the main door. I'm not sure how I feel about myself, that I can't voice what I'm starting to think, just because I finally don't feel like everyone hates me.

Jeannette is still in the office, accompanied now by a few more support workers; so far, no police have appeared. Flick, Hannah and I peer through the small windows on the door, waiting. Part of me hopes that things will calm down, the longer we watch; but if anything, things just continue to build. The staff in the office are definitely planning something – because as we watch, more and more staff start to make their way into the office...

"They're going to try and barge in, again," Hannah warns us angrily – and this isn't an exaggeration, she has gone from irritation to full anger, now. "They're going to push against the door—"

"We took them last time!" Flick breaks in, her voice squeaky against Hannah's mutter but no less angry. "They won't get in—"

"What's going on?" yells Keira from the other end of the corridor. "I can't see – what are they doing?"

"They're gathering!" Hannah hollers back. "You bet – any moment, I'm sure—"

I can hear the panic in Keira's voice as she replies. "Should we come down?" she asks, her voice close to a shriek. "We could help—"

"They'll come down the other end if they see you've moved!" Flick bursts in. "We've got to keep going on both doors!"

Keira breathes out audibly. "Yeah, alright, alright," she agrees. "Just get ready, in case—"

But then, suddenly, they are gone.

It's not as mystical as it sounds, but when we turn back to the windows, having been distracted for only a moment, the office is now totally empty. They have filed out, apparently in a calm and orderly fashion, because we have completely missed them doing it. There is almost a sense of tinnitus – like their absence suddenly rings in our ears, like the quiet is louder than all the commotion was.

"Where have they...?" Flick manages.

"The police," says Hannah darkly. "They've gone to let the police in. They're getting out of the way. So they don't get hurt when the police come up with their riot gear."

I open my mouth to answer, a frown on my face – because surely this is ridiculous – but I don't get a chance to speak. From the other side of the corridor, I once again hear a loud thump. I look – and Saoirse is flat on her back again.

I hear Keira swear – whether from fear or anger, I can't tell – and this time, I don't stop to look for police approaching in riot gear. Keira crouches down beside Saoirse, and Flick and I skid down the corridor towards Saoirse's body. Only Hannah remains by the door, watching for the police.

This time, she doesn't sit up straight away. For a moment, she stirs almost feebly, wriggling back into consciousness. She's not dead, but the fact that I even have to tell myself that frightens me. This isn't just a nervous reaction; this can't be just her fainting out of nervousness. There's something really wrong. It's horribly ironic, but she needs a nurse.

"We need to get her out," I say at last, finally finding my voice. "We need to get her seen to."

Flick and Keira look up towards me as if they had forgotten that I could speak. I understand the reaction; I had almost forgotten, myself.

Before they can respond, I hear a voice behind me, at the door. "No," protests Hannah, once again angry. "No way."

Hannah starts to continue, but I've stopped listening; as I look back around, Saoirse is starting to sit up. "Are you OK?" Flick asks again.

Saoirse nods, quickly. "Yeah." It's almost like a repeat of earlier. But this time, Saoirse's face is considerably whiter.

"She's not right," Flick whispers. If it wasn't such a serious situation, I could almost laugh at Flick's marvellously unsubtle stage whisper. It's a relief, though, to have someone on my side.

Keira nods too. "Let's get her out," she says, a little more loudly.

"It's OK," Saoirse protests feebly, but no one is listening to her. It's not OK. I think all of us know that it's not OK.

When I hear Hannah's voice call out again, I expect it to be her own protest, even her own support of Saoirse's wobbly insistence that we don't need to get her out. Before I even hear her words, though, I hear her tone. It's something I can't quite characterise; it's angry, certainly, but I hear resentment and frustration too. It's the tone that my heart has been beating to all day.

"How are we going to get out?" says Hannah, heatedly, painfully, fearfully.

She's right. Actually, of course she's right. Ironically, all the doors to the corridor are designed to lock when they are closed, only able to be opened by one of the fobs that the staff carry. We've spent the last few hours trying to keep them out; but without one of those fobs, we are locked in here ourselves. Saoirse is ill, Saoirse might be hurt – and there's fuck all we can do to get her to medical attention.

There it is, the aspect of Hannah's tone that I couldn't quite grasp. Abandonment.

Hannah's words seem to ignite the intensity of the corridor all over again. As abandoned as we have felt by the staff all day, I at least have had a little stubborn part of me that is sure that, essentially, they wouldn't let anything happen to us. But now, we are alone, and without help. And that fact is like petrol to a flame.

Before I know what is happening, Hannah has turned back towards the window in the door, this time hammering at it angrily, trying to get any staff member's attention. Keira jumps up, runs to the other end and starts doing the same. Soon, Flick is at the door with Hannah. Saoirse is propped up against the wall, still looking a little woozy; and since I have never been great at making my voice heard, I sit next to her. This is all I can think of to do.

As the minutes pass, I hear the voices of Keira, Hannah and Flick grow ever more insistent. I feel anger and frustration bubble up in my chest myself. Why would they leave us like this? A tiny part of me reminds me that we were being little shits. Of course we were. But somehow this doesn't help. We didn't want to be left behind.

Finally – finally – we hear the beep of a fob being scanned, a few corridors over. All of our ears prick up at the sound, as footsteps start to echo in the first corridor of the ward. As much of a relief as the sound is at first, it quickly begins to multiply and multiply as more and more people start to enter the ward. For a moment, fear catches in my chest – has Hannah been right all along? Have they genuinely called the police to come in riot gear?

As the door to the lounge finally beeps open, for the first and last time in my life, I am relieved to see Jeannette leading the charge. As much of a dick as she is, she is better than police in riot gear.

My relief starts to wane very quickly, though, as more and more staff members start to enter the lounge. At first, I recognise them, all of the staff who have been working on the ward all day, but soon unfamiliar faces start to populate the room. It looks like Jeannette has gathered staff from all over the hospital to come and deal with us. They have heard us banging and have come to handle *us*.

I mean, this seems blatantly unsafe for the other wards, and frankly I don't trust Jeannette to run a village fete, let alone a psychiatric hospital – but the main thing that is starting to cause a burning in my chest is the look on Jeannette's face. This isn't them coming to help us; this isn't them coming to examine Saoirse, who is now looking distinctly green. This is them come to quash us. To flatten us. And, you know what? I'm quite sure that I'm not the only patient here who is tired of being bulldozed.

I feel the anger that pricks up in my chest, of course I do – but if I'm angry, it immediately becomes apparent that Hannah, Keira and even Flick are going to be apoplectic. Sure enough, I barely have time to register the entrance of these staff members before I hear Hannah start to scream.

"Just go quietly," I bleat, though I know that none of them can hear me. "Just go quietly and they'll have no excuse to restrain us!"

This is bullshit, of course, and I know it. They will do what they want, because they always do what they want. We have no power here. The rush of adrenaline that I felt earlier when I had the slightest bit of agency over my whole life – well, that's gone. We have fallen into their trap, and they are going to do whatever the fuck they want.

Jeannette's fob beeps against the door to our corridor and I feel Saoirse's hand grip mine in something like panic. I hold on to it, unsure what else to do, as staff start to march into the corridor. Of course, Hannah barely lets the door swing open before she is hitting and kicking, fighting the staff with everything she can muster. I close my eyes. I knew that she wasn't going to go quietly, but even staff who have been as dick-ish as they have been don't deserve to get beaten up in their workplace.

They are on her immediately, using their control and restraint techniques. They are efficient – this is the best I can say of them. This is their job, I suppose. They handle Hannah as efficiently as a postman sorting out his letters. Only Jeannette has a vindictive look on her face that I itch to slap off.

I don't – I stay with Saoirse – but unfortunately Keira seems to have had the same thought. She lurches towards the nurse, fists raised. She doesn't even get within two metres of Jeannette before she's being restrained off in another direction.

And Flick – well, it suddenly hits me just how young Flick is, as she starts to kick staff away as they get near her. I know what Flick has been through, so maybe I'm not exactly surprised at just how angry she is. She's hurting people, I know – but that doesn't mean that I think it's right that two six-foot-tall men have grabbed her by the arms and are restraining her away.

Then, the tinnitus is back, because all the staff are engaged in tackling Hannah, Keira and Flick, and Saoirse and I have somehow ended up alone in the corridor again. Anger floods through me – could they not have just kept their bloody tempers until Saoirse was safe? – but, really, I don't blame them. I'm not sure I blame either the staff or the patients. I think this is shit for everyone.

I'm barely even able to register it as I hear a slightly quieter thump beside me. I look around, the corridor swimming, and Saoirse has fallen unconscious again. And we're alone, again. This time, I don't even have my comrades to help. I'm totally alone. I jump to my feet, looking around – and there is no one. There is no one to help.

I feel totally overloaded, overwhelmed, overly put upon. This is too much. This is too much. This is too much. I don't know what to do. I don't know how to help. I've messed up everything. I should have held Flick back – I should have persuaded the others to come out of the corridor way earlier. I should have just pretended to push on the door and the staff could have gotten us out earlier...

Then, suddenly, I am not real. I register vaguely that I do not know any better way to explain this; in my panic, my mind has totally left my body. I don't feel like I have a body. I don't feel like I exist at all.

Saoirse is semi-conscious next to me, slumped against the wall, and there is nothing I can do. I am not here – how can I do anything if I'm not even here? I gaze around hazily but there is no one else here, either. It flicks across my mind that maybe no one else exists either. I don't know what I'm supposed to do.

If I didn't feel like I was floating, I think I would be feeling exhausted.

I think of falling asleep. I think of not feeling any of this anymore. It suddenly registers that I haven't been as alone as this *for a long time. Maybe – maybe in all this ridiculousness – maybe it's an opportunity. An opportunity that I won't get again for a long time.*

This is where my memory tapers off; I would like to say that the next thing I remember is waking up in a warm, quiet bed, with Saoirse sat up in the bed next to me, with Zoe or even one of my favourite support workers by my side. Instead, I wake up on the lino floor, shaking violently as Jeannette snips through the pair of tights that I have tied very tightly around my neck. My throat aches from the pressure, and my bare legs stick to the plasticky floor. Saoirse is gone; and I can still hear Hannah screaming all the way from whichever de-escalation room they've stuck her in.

"Fuck," I whisper hoarsely.

Jeannette looks at me like I am a speck of dust – like I am totally insignificant. I guess we can say with certainty that this hasn't been a professional learning experience for her. Anger flares up in me, but it's weaker now. Now, I just feel resigned.

"Stay in your bedroom," Jeannette says dismissively.

I find myself nodding; I don't have any fight left in me tonight.

"Is Saoirse alright?" I ask.

Jeannette's eyes flick back towards me for a moment. Even though we're still talking, she has clearly checked out of the conversation. "Yes," she says, with an impatient sigh, like she can't work out why I'm asking.

I nod quietly. I don't have the energy to fight.

"Stay in your bedroom," Jeannette repeats, and once again, I nod. I touch my sore neck tentatively, wincing slightly at the pain, as I collect myself up from the floor and walk, alone, into my bedroom. This isn't how tonight was supposed to end. We were supposed to be a team; we were supposed to be standing up for each other. Now we have been scattered across the hospital, scattered much sooner than any of us had expected. I don't feel part of a team anymore.

I know that when I wake up in the morning, everyone will be back on the ward – or at least safely in A&E, in Saoirse's case. It just breaks my heart that all of us, tonight, will be suffering alone. We have tried to push back against the system that has placed us all here; but equally, I'm aware that, mostly, we have been twats. I am the oldest; I should have known better. Being part of a team was nice; but being forcibly separated is the opposite. It was always going to end like this.

This, I think to myself, as I try to lie down on my bed and ignore the screams of Hannah, Keira and Flick, is what it is going to feel like when I leave. I should have known not to get attached. Clearly, getting attached was the worst thing I could have done. How have I been so stupid? It was always going to end like this.

21

My head is pounding as I rush straight through the square where I met the woman, down along the road that I think leads down to the coast. The fact that it is the side street that the woman apparently saw her friend go down is irrelevant to me. Finding Maeve is what matters now; I've got a job to do and I need to do it.

I can hear my footsteps echo as almost everything else lays quiet now. A part of me is relieved; I know Maeve hated the fighting and the shouting so hopefully she's feeling safer. But another part of me finds it eerie. It's literally never quiet on the ward. There's always something going on, even just nurses bustling around, checking on people.

I wonder where they think I am. I haven't seen any police since McDonald's; maybe they are looking in other places. Maybe they think I got on a train. Maybe they are checking the roof of the multi-storey car park.

I'm being morbid. I shouldn't joke. I suppose I won't be laughing soon.

I need to keep my mind focused on finding Maeve. If I get distracted, I'll miss her. And if I end up back at the hospital without even getting Maeve somewhere safe, then I don't know what I'll do. The police won't believe me if I try to explain the situation. And what can they do about it anyway? Maeve may be young, but she's entitled to walk the streets if she wants to, and I feel certain that she won't tell them the truth about whatever's happened to her. I don't know what she'll do, left alone in the streets. I only know that the outcome won't be good.

I keep striding down the streets until I'm hit with something significant – there, in front of me, glistening slightly in the moonlight, is the coast.

It's bittersweet. This is what I have been looking for; it will be easy to find Birnbeck Pier from here. All I have to do is follow the coast.

I walk past closed chip shops and ice-cream stands with the shutters pulled down. I can see the 'normal' pier, solid and flashy, but with its entrances as firmly shut as the rest of the seafront. It's probably getting close to dawn, now. Everything feels a little bit less grubby as I can finally anticipate the rising of the sun.

What happens if I'm still looking for Maeve when the sun does come up? It's going to be impossible to find her with the crowds of tourists that hang around here. The only positive I can see is that her school might report her missing if she doesn't turn up. Unless her parents lie to them. I don't even know enough about her situation to know if they would lie. Why am I fighting so hard for a kid I know nothing about? She could be the one lying.

She *could* be – but something in my chest senses that she isn't. For some reason, I trust Maeve. I trust that the little bits that I've got out of her are the truth. We're on the same wavelength, I'm sure.

I should be following the coast road, looking for the broken pier where I'm sure I'll find her; yet somehow I'm finding myself approaching the low wall dividing the pavement from the beach. I hop over it, swinging my legs over easily. My Doc Martens land heavily on the sand. They're not made for this. I quickly untie my laces and pull one shoe off, then the other, then my socks. I roll up my jeans, just enough for them to expose a few inches of ankle. My granny would roll her eyes that they're too tight to go any further.

It's still dark as I approach the coastline. I hope vaguely that no one will see me approaching the sea and assume that that's my destination – because it's definitely not. I'm not sure why, but I'm intensely sure that this isn't how I'm going to meet my end.

I feel peaceful, for the first time tonight. For the first time in a long while. I'm alone, and it's dark, but right now I feel… not quite like nothing can touch me, because I'm still very aware that it could do. Maybe instead I just feel like nothing will want to.

I keep walking towards the coastline, my feet sinking into lukewarm sand. I try not to look; I want it to surprise me when I reach the cold sea. I want to not know it's coming until it's here. A nice surprise.

I haven't really thought it through, though, because instead of cool water – even painfully cold water, as I know really it would be – instead, I reach mud. Thick, sinking mud. I almost laugh aloud. I'm not living the holiday dream; I'm sinking, slowly but surely, into the sticky reality. This has to be a metaphor, somehow.

As I pull one foot out of the grey mud, the other sinks further. I'm stupid, I should have remembered that most of the Weston-super-Mare coastline is sinking mud. I literally told Maeve this just a few hours ago.

I remember coming into the centre for the first time with my parents, in my dad's car. The seaside theme was clear immediately. The pier, the ice-cream stands, the sticks of rock… it all becomes highly ironic when you realise that the beach isn't, actually, a beach. It's sand, certainly – but then the mud takes over and paddling becomes not only unlikely but actually dangerous.

It tempts me, though, for a minute – I could just keep walking into the mud, let it draw me deeper and deeper. By the time I reach the sea, I'll be so deep in the mud that I won't be able to swim away from the freezing water...

Maybe it's the prospect of this, but I'm already turning around, back towards the sand. I can't put my shoes back on now; my feet are coated in thick, boggy mud, with sand sticking to it like sprinkles on a Mr Whippy. This is grim. But I guess it means that my only option is to keep walking along the beach, shoes in hand, until I reach Birnbeck.

Still, I can't say that it's unpleasant, walking along the sand with the cool night air blowing my hair out to one side. Especially once the mud dries and instead becomes crusty rather than sticky. I'm tired, admittedly; but I feel much calmer than I did when I was striding down dodgy side streets.

But... where's Maeve? As I get closer and closer to the old pier, I become more and more certain that I'm not going to be able to find her. Surely I should have seen her by now? That's the thought that keeps coming through my mind. If we're both heading to the same place, from the same place, surely we should have bumped into each other? How has she managed to get such a head start on me?

This wasn't how I pictured my last night. I thought I would buy some pills, buy a drink or two... then sit somewhere quiet as they lulled me into sleep. Of course, that was overconfident and probably sugar-coating it. In reality, an overdose would probably just have just left me puking at the side of the road until a stranger called an ambulance.

I think that is coming through to me, now. Something so awful is never going to be pretty, or poetic, or neat. I am so, so tired. But that doesn't mean that I can just slip into sleep forever. It's going to hurt. It's not going to be pleasant; it's going to hurt.

Of course, looking back, I can think of good days, and I can think of fun that I had. But it all seems so far away now; and for good reason. It has faded away because everyone involved has faded out of my life. I thought I was alone when I was younger; but now I really am alone. I sit in one room all day and I can't find one bit of fucking meaning in my isolated life.

Even as I think these things, I know that Katy would have a counter-argument, and I know that if I heard it, I would listen, just for a little while. But it's too *late* for that. Right now, looking out to sea, I am totally sure that tonight is my last night. That tonight I'm going to go.

I don't know how to reconcile myself with the fact that I am about to hurt everyone who has ever known me.

My sandy, muddy, crusty feet plod on, though, as if representing my still-beating heart. Is my heart betraying me by keeping on beating when that's not what I want anymore? Or am I betraying my heart by asking it to stop doing all it knows? My head is spinning and I can't think about that. Instead, I concentrate on the beating of my feet on the sand. I slip and I slide over soft sand, but my feet still beat, one step then two step then one step then two step…

Right now, I am sleepwalking. I am already gone. But before my heart agrees to stop beating, I have to do something good. I have to save Maeve. I don't want the last thing I ever do to be abandoning someone who I now call a friend.

In the sky there is the faintest hint of light starting to break. I don't have long. When people start to fill the streets again, I haven't got a chance of avoiding the police. They will find me and take me back to the hospital and tonight will have been a waste. Now the staff at the hospital know I am both willing and able to climb over the back fence, they will probably start locking the door like they're supposed to. And there's no way I can get away during the day without being seen. Going back now would mean making my life worse without any real possibility of my ending it on my terms.

So I keep walking, tired though I am. I know I'm doing the right thing, for myself, and for Maeve.

I wonder, not for the first time, why exactly Maeve decided to run away from home tonight. I wonder where she came from; how she ended up in Weston-super-Mare of all places. Almost everything about her being here just doesn't make any sense. Still, I push it out of my mind again. Sometimes it just doesn't pay to think about things. There's a part of me that's convinced that thinking too much about things is my problem. Maybe I should just stop caring that I have no future and no prospects; maybe I should stop caring that my head is too full of hurt to maintain a normal lifestyle like everyone else. I suppose if I stopped thinking altogether, then I would stop thinking about the hurt.

Katy told me once that putting something in the past wasn't the same thing as saying that it wasn't hurtful. I see her point; but the hurt in my head feels like it's ingrained, like it's written on the inside of my skull for the little woman in my head to read over and over again. I see it reflected on my thoughts and my behaviour and my relationships. Without it, I'm not Heather. I don't see how I can put it into the past when it's me.

I do know that Katy will be upset when she hears. She has put a lot of effort into me and I do appreciate it. I guess it's just unfortunate that I have always been a lost cause. I hope she doesn't blame herself.

One thing I know for certain, however – I know that Katy will be *furious* when she finds out. That the door was left unlocked; that no one had spoken to me all evening before I went; that I managed to miss my medication this evening without any of the nurses noticing. Katy will raise all hell, I have no doubt about that. Somehow, I feel the tiniest of smiles tug at the edges of my mouth when I think about it; but the rest of me hates the thought of her being so angry. The intensity of hurt that ends up being masked by anger isn't lost on me.

At least I matter to someone.

I'm feeling sorry for myself, and I mentally tell myself to snap out of it as soon as that thought drifts into my head. I shouldn't *want* people to be upset that I'm gone. If I'm as alone as I'm sure I am, then I will cause no pain. But somehow I can't seem to reconcile the two.

I have made a surprising amount of progress along the coastline while I've been thinking all of this through. My feet are still dirty, but the mud seems to be flaking off in large chunks now that it's dry. I debate trying to find somewhere to dip my feet into water to wash it off, until I realise that I would have to walk along the sea wall, and even then I'd be relying on the tide being in. I'm not actually sure how to tell if the tide is coming in or out.

So I keep walking, occasionally reaching down to try and brush off more lumps of mud. I should probably put my shoes back on now that I'm a bit cleaner, but I feel more attuned to my surroundings with my feet bare. I cringe at myself slightly for being sentimental. But right now, there isn't any real reason to put them back on.

I follow the coastline along as I had planned, until I reach the Marine Lake. Bloody hell. I have been so focused on my thoughts that I haven't been thinking about the unsentimental end to the beach that comes in the concrete Marine Lake. Still, I know which direction to go in. All I have to do is keep walking.

What I haven't counted on, though, is the fact that I'm now walking along a road. Although I walked along the road earlier, that was when I could hedge a bet that the hospital wouldn't have noticed I had gone yet. To walk along a road where police could drive by at any second – by this time, doing that feels downright risky.

The only alternative, though, is to walk along the sea wall, the plan which I discarded just a few moments ago. This time, I consider it properly, even stopping walking for a moment to look down the narrow wall that I would have to wobble along… Fuck that. I guess I'll have to take the road.

I would probably be less conspicuous with my shoes on, and again I consider it; but again, I decide not to. Instead, I lurk at the edge of the pavement, trying to blend into the wall so as not to draw attention to myself. I'm aware I look young for my years and I don't want some dodgy old guy to try and lure me into his Transit van. Similarly, I don't want any well-meaning adults trying to take me to the nearest police station.

The irony of that isn't lost on me either.

I feel *drawn*, now, to Birnbeck Pier. Where an hour or two ago, I thought it was just a silly idea cooked up by a kid, now I feel like I have to go there. I can't explain. Something is pulling me there. I try to convince myself that it's just the idea of saving Maeve before I go. I try to convince myself that it's just the idea of doing something good before I go to sleep.

I've got to stop sounding like a character from *The Fault in Our Stars*; there is no sleep. Before I die. Before I die die die die…

I repeat the word in my head until I'm desensitised to it. I don't want to believe that I'm just going to sleep; there's something about that idea that trivialises it, that trivialises everything I've gone through and all the pain that people around me will feel because they weren't able to stop me. As for the idea of Heaven and Hell… well, all I feel sure of is that there's nothing. Maybe that's why people say sleep, because it's the closest thing they can think of to a total oblivion. I'm convinced that that's what is waiting for me: oblivion.

Yet Birnbeck Pier draws me, and I keep walking. I force myself to stop thinking existentially, and instead I quickly stride along the road by the Marine Lake, keeping a lookout for cars. Luckily, it's late, and there's no one about.

All through this walk, I have avoided looking over in the direction where the derelict structure of Birnbeck Pier sits. If I don't look at it, I don't have to think about it; and yet simultaneously, I'm doing what I need to, and going to find

Maeve. I can assuage the fear that she's upset, or hurt, by focusing on the feel of the pavement on my feet and the cold night air against my cheek. Ironically, I think that might be a mindfulness technique that a well-meaning professional taught me.

I'm nearly back to the coast when I see something. I don't want to look at the pier; but as the pavement by the road runs out, I am forced to look up, back out to the sea. For a second, nothing registers. It's just the pier, dilapidated and forlorn-looking as it always is.

But then I blink – and something makes my heart drop in my chest. All through the walk, I have hoped that I will find Maeve waiting by the fencing that surrounds the pier, or maybe sitting in the old car park that leads to the ruins. Now, though, I see something that makes me sure that this prospect is long out of the window.

At the end of the barely standing wooden structure, there is a light glowing at the end of the pier.

22

EUPD. Emotionally Unstable Personality Disorder. That's what they label me with.

I'm not sure how I feel about it. On the one hand, I guess that having a name for whatever's wrong with me kind of makes it feel more genuine, like I'm not just making it up... but on the other hand, I'm not sure I like this particular name. 'Personality disorder' makes me sound like a serial killer. People are going to think I'm dangerous.

This is the main reason that I don't tell anyone. I know that the doctors have told my parents – very much against my will – but other than that, I keep quiet. I know deep down that none of the patients here would judge me on it; I just don't quite feel ready to claim that part of me.

There is one aspect of the disorder, though, that I have to admit makes perfect sense. That is my relationship with Zoe.

I adore her, most of the time. The warm feeling in my chest that I can't quite name – she is pretty much the only person who can make me feel like that. And when I feel like that, I feel on top of the world. Most of the time, she doesn't even have to do anything to make me feel like that. Most of the time, all she has to do is be in the room. Apparently this phenomenon is known as having a 'favourite person'.

Adoring her, though, means that I trust her more than I trust anyone else. When I'm sad, she is the only one I want to talk to. Hell, even when I'm happy, she's the only one I want to tell about it. I can feel myself rapidly becoming obsessed with talking to her. This makes things very difficult when she isn't around.

And this isn't the only thing; I read in the sheet of paper that they give me about my condition that people with EUPD sometimes do a thing called splitting, where their feelings about people flip suddenly at very small triggers. And, of course, I'm so besotted with Zoe that she is the first person I split on.

One day, she gives me an odd look. It barely takes a moment to sink in; and instantly I am hit with a wave of feeling like she hates me. Like she wants rid of me as soon as possible. I feel, in all honesty, like I am totally destroyed. That is the only way I can describe it. I genuinely don't want to exist anymore. I'm not just suicidal. I want to wipe my whole self from existence. What am I worth if Zoe doesn't want me?

And I'm not only totally despondent; I'm also furious. Why would she make me think that she wanted me, if she was just going to leave? Why did she let me feel like she was trustworthy, if she was going to drop me? I pace backwards and forwards in my bedroom, tears running down my face, but my fists are clenched. I want to smash my head into the wall, but I don't want to have to explain to the support workers why I'm upset. I hate feeling like this. I don't want to feel like this anymore.

When the time comes for the group activity that Zoe will be running, I force myself to shelve the tears. Luckily, several years of lying to everyone around me mean that I'm able to hold tears back quite effectively. I take a few deep breaths, like I'm supposed to – though I am only trying to hide my emotions, not actually calm myself down. As angry as I am at Zoe, my instincts tell me that it's best that she doesn't see it. I need the anger; it's too important to get rid of – but I don't need the staff to decide that I'm too attached to Zoe and not let me see her anymore. Right now, I just need to seem normal. Which is not the easiest thing I've ever done.

I sit through group with my fingers digging into my arm. It takes this physical act to keep me grounded enough to get through the hour. It also reminds me that as soon as this is over, I can go back to my bedroom and do another little cry, as well as probably hurt myself.

But as I'm walking out of the room when group is finished, I surprise myself by suddenly turning around where I stand. Zoe – who is walking right behind me – starts in shock, a little frown coming to her face.

"Is everything OK?" she asks, her voice as soft as it usually is. She even tilts her head at me, clearly clueless about what's going on in my head.

My shoulders are shaking. "Do you hate me?" I burst out, feeling tears come to my eyes.

Zoe's eyes widen slightly. She shakes her head quickly. "Of course not!" she tells me. I can tell from her face that she's confused, even as she tries to reassure me. "What made you think that?" she adds, her little frown now more pronounced.

I sigh, feeling tears start to spill. I don't want to full on sob at her, so I don't trust myself to open my mouth. Instead I shrug, looking down at the floor. Just talking to Zoe… my anger is starting to dissipate. I still feel broken, I still feel abandoned – but at least I don't feel mad at her anymore.

My urge is to throw my arms around her neck and hug her, but I know that's not allowed. I'm also very aware that another therapy worker is still in the room, watching the exchange with a little smile. I hadn't realised when I did my about-turn that Zoe and I weren't alone, and I think it would seem odd to ask this other therapy worker to go now.

Zoe reaches out and gently touches my shoulder. "You don't need to worry about that," she reassures me. "Ever. OK?"

"Zoe doesn't hate anyone," pipes up the other therapy worker, Priya, helpfully. Twenty minutes ago, I wouldn't have been able to laugh at this, but now that Zoe has reassured me herself, I manage a smile. Besides, I like Priya. I don't want to hurt her feelings by letting her know that her input in this situation isn't exactly invaluable.

In any case, I nod, though I know that I'll be worried about it again in a few days. I wipe my eyes on my jumper and head on to pretend to eat lunch.

Over the next few months, mine and Zoe's relationship follows this pattern over and over again. Everything is fine, then something happens, and I split on her. She reassures me, and everything is fine. It's fucking exhausting. I can only imagine that it must be for Zoe, too. Luckily, my fucked-up brain has managed to pick someone very patient to be stupidly attached to.

The thought of losing Zoe, when I leave the hospital, terrifies me. There's no way around it. Staff and ex-patients aren't allowed to keep in touch in any way. It's not considered appropriate. I don't know what I'm going to do without her. I don't know how I'm going to keep breathing, to keep above water.

And with the thought of being discharged – for me there is an extra element to the fear. I'm turning eighteen in a month. No one seems to think that it's possible for me to be discharged in that time – so, instead, I'm being sent to an adult ward.

(Not, actually, that I have anywhere to go even if I was discharged. Finally the staff here seem to have realised that the house with my parents isn't a good option. They don't know everything, of course, but I've trusted them with enough for them to know that I can't be well there.)

I've heard a lot of things about adult wards. Some staff members seem to think that the best way to turn round the older patients and get them well enough to be discharged is to tell horror stories about adult wards that they've worked in or heard about. This is all very well, but when it's a certain fact that you're going to one no matter what, it's not particularly helpful.

Even those who tell more balanced stories about adult wards still don't exactly make them sound pleasant. In all truth, I'm terrified. It's lucky I trust the therapists and (to a certain extent) my psychiatrist, because they are telling me that they're trying to find as suitable a place for me as they can. I get the impression that this task is somewhat of a mammoth one.

I do understand why it's hard to find a place for someone like me, I guess. My risk is still high enough that they can't send me anywhere without locked doors and restrictions on what items can be on the ward. But places like these for adults tend to be, well... hectic, I suppose. And not in the barricading/intentionally-pissing-off-the-staff kind of way that adolescent wards are. The unsettled ward downstairs is psychiatric intensive care, known as PICU; but PICU for adults is very different, apparently. As I understand it, it's full of people who are unwell in a different way that I am. So they are trying to step me down from something as intense as this. But an open ward, or somewhere similar, wouldn't be safe. I do understand the dilemma, but it's frustrating. Is there no one else like me who needs help beyond the age of eighteen?

I try, mostly, to keep it out of my mind. Wherever I get sent is totally out of my control. On the one hand, that makes it a little easier not to obsess; but I do start to feel like I'm in freefall. There is nothing for me to do but wait.

Also on my mind, of course, is the looming birthday itself. All my friends from school are having parties and going out to pubs to celebrate their eighteenth. When Amelie comes to visit, she invites me to her birthday party, but there's no way I can get the doctors to approve me going to that. I think Amelie knows that, too, though I do appreciate the gesture. Everyone else at school is forgetting all about me.

I'm very aware that the celebrations for my eighteenth involve a birthday cake made by the hospital kitchen and watching a film that I've seen maybe four or five times with the other girls. Usually on someone's birthday, we get petty cash to get some snacks, which is pleasant, I guess. It's not going to be a bad birthday, I suppose, but... it's not exactly how I pictured it. I'm not sure that it's how anyone pictures their eighteenth.

I'm lucky again, though, that I'm getting a visit. I'm being let off therapy groups for a few hours so I can go out and have lunch with my parents. I do feel lucky to get this; the hospital is quite a drive from my parents' house and it's nice of them to make the journey up here. I think if I could forget that this was such a big birthday, then I would be looking forward to the day.

The other association when I think of the day, though, is that of anxiety. Because as the day comes closer and closer, I become more and more hyper-aware that any day now, I'm going to leave this place, probably without any warning. I've seen other patients turn eighteen and get shipped off to a random ward at an hour's notice. I'm very aware that now this isn't just a possibility, but a definite prospect.

It makes me antsy, I will admit that. It's not the place that I'm worried about leaving, of course – I'm looking forward to stepping down to a slightly less secure setting, and I'm looking forward to maybe having Wi-Fi again, and having my own mobile phone. Besides, surely adult wards are less full of antics – I can't imagine barricading myself into a corridor with patients who are in their thirties.

No, what I'm worried about is the people that I'll never see again. The human psyche, surely, isn't meant to undergo this – to just lose everyone in your world one day and never see anyone again. That can't be right. People can't be expected to go through that.

It's late, a few nights before my birthday, when I walk out of my bedroom into the corridor. I should be sleeping soundly, aware that I still have a few days before I'm set to be shipped off like a last-minute parcel. I still have a few days of knowing that I'm going to go to sleep in the same place that I woke up.

For some reason, though, I can't quiet my mind. We're supposed to stay in our rooms after lights-out at 10:30pm, but

I can't stand staring at the same four walls anymore. Besides, I get along with most of the staff that are on shift tonight; they are usually quite relaxed about me sitting in the lounge when I'm anxious until I'm calm enough to go to sleep. Anyway, whoever is meant to be monitoring my corridor has left their chair and gone off to do something else. Really, I should make the most of this.

My feet are wrapped up in thick socks, even though it's nearly spring. There's something I find slightly gross about people walking around barefoot on the sticky lino of the ward. Even in the slightly eerie calm that settles over the ward when everyone is asleep, the woolly layer around my feet muffles my footsteps and I walk silently along the corridor and into the lounge. Sitting in there is Claudie, sat comfortably on one of the plastic sofas, her eyes on a clipboard with observation records on it. It's only when I step into her direct eyeline that she looks up.

I hover awkwardly for a second, but Claudie is smiling. Her eyes, though kind, look worried. "Are you alright?" she asks, her brow slightly furrowed.

I understand why she's worried; I rarely come out at night. Even if I'm really struggling, I tend to stay in my room and try to sort things out by myself. For me to be out of my room when I should be sleeping – well, I can understand why it's a red flag for her.

Quickly, though, I see Claudie's face relax a bit. She knows me well; I'm pretty sure she can tell from my face that, though I'm anxious and restless, I'm not going to hurt myself. It's a little depressing, but on such a busy ward, sometimes it comes down to firefighting, and stopping people from doing themselves lasting harm. A lot of staff would dismiss me once they realised that I'm not in danger, and tell me to go back to my room, but Claudie is one of the good ones. She wants me to be OK in all senses of the word.

I shrug slightly. I'm not sure how to answer her question.

Claudie gives me a little smile. "Come on," she says, gesturing to the space on the sofa next to her. "Sit down a minute."

A smile comes onto my own face, but I'm aware that it's a little sad. That's how I feel, tonight. Drained, even as I'm so preoccupied. I sit carefully down next to Claudie, drawing my knees up to my chest so that I'm curled up, and turn to face her. She has put the clipboard down, and her chin is now propped up on her hand, leaning on the top edge of the sofa.

"What's going on?" she asks, nudging me gently.

I sigh. "I don't know," I tell her, because I don't. "I'm just… I'm broken." Claudie frowns, but now I've started, I don't want to stop. "I'm so useless," I blurt out. "I hate being like this. I do, I hate it. I just want all this over." Something catches in my throat. "It's too much," I say finally.

For a beat, neither of us says anything. I should be upset, I guess – I should be crying or shouting. But as in pain as I am, I can't muster the energy to be passionate about it. I feel flat. I feel numb.

When I finally look up at Claudie, her face is sad. "Oh dear," she says heavily.

I nod – this seems like an appropriate reaction. I don't get the chance to speak, though, because Claudie isn't finished. "You have so much going for you," she tells me, holding my eye contact in a way that makes me sure that she means what she is feeling. "It just boggles me that you can't see that. Because you have so much to offer the world."

I go to shake my head, but with Claudie still holding my eye contact, I don't quite feel like I can. I wish I could believe her. This would be so much easier if I could believe her.

She sticks out a hand and touches my knee gently. "Honestly," she adds. "I can't promise you that things are going to get easier straight away, I know, but I just…"

She tails off, and I wonder what it is that she wants to express but can't find the words for. This is part of the reason that I like

Claudie; she doesn't bullshit. If she doesn't know how to say what she means, she doesn't try and fill it with platitudes. She knows, I'm sure, that I've been told nice things about myself – she has told me plenty of nice things herself – and it's nice to hear, sure, but I think Claudie knows that I need more than that.

"You're going to have so much fun, at uni," she tells me firmly.

Her words are loaded, and I think I understand her meaning. I mean, Claudie knows how much I love to write, she knows that I would love to study English at uni – but I know that this isn't just encouragement. This means something more than what she is saying.

I'm not quite right, here, now. I know this. Of course, I don't want to leave Zoe and I don't want to leave my friends – I don't even want to leave Claudie – but this isn't the place for me, anymore. I know this. And I hope that Claudie is right. I hope that I will get out of here and get out of the adult ward and go to uni and – you know what – bloody fit in, without having to lock myself in a corridor.

It's hard, to show Claudie that I understand what she means. Eventually I nod, giving her a small smile. And I think she understands me, like I understood her.

We talk a little longer, and Claudie slips in a few nice things about me, but my mind is elsewhere right now. It's weird, feeling like this. Is this how Amelie will feel, leaving school at last and going onto the next thing? It's not the same situation, at all, but somehow I feel better that maybe I am experiencing something a bit the same as someone my own age. In fairness, Claudie is barely a few years older than me, straight out of uni herself. Maybe I feel like Claudie did at my age.

Minus, I guess, the time I have to spend in a psychiatric hospital before I can get to uni. But I try and put that out of my mind. Think about uni. Think about normal.

After a little while, I feel less restless, and before I know it, I am pulling myself up from the sofa and walking back towards my bedroom. I'm a grown-up, nearly. I've got to be able to look after myself. It pains me – and I hate this – but Claudie isn't always going to be there.

I try not to think about how much I am going to miss everyone, as I once again settle down in bed. I'm sleepier, now, and it shouldn't be long before I get to go to sleep and stop thinking. I hate lying in bed and thinking. But I guess that right now, I don't like anything much that makes me consider my own life.

As I lie there, I try to rearrange things in my mind. I try to think adult; I try to think normal. Because I can't do all of this anymore. It's too much. I can't do the drama, and I can't do the heightened emotions. I need a rest; I need this to end. So you know what? I'm going to leave, and I'm going to go to uni. Like Amelie. Like everyone else my age.

I fall asleep quickly. There is no more I can do tonight.

23

As soon as it sinks into my head that there's someone at the end of the pier, I start to run as fast as I can, sprinting across the short bit of beach that leads to the fences which block off Birnbeck Pier from the public. Tourists don't come to this small, shabby bit of beach that doesn't even lead to the sea. No one wants to have a picnic by a building site.

I have barely taken three strides onto the beach, however, when I feel a sharp pain on the sole of my foot. For a moment, I continue to run; but whatever the pain is, it spikes each time I put my foot down. I reluctantly stop, yanking my foot up so I can see the sole. Sure enough, there is a chunk of broken glass sticking into my foot. I sigh and quickly pull it out, causing me to wince in pain. Maybe I need to be more careful. This isn't an ethereal walk along the coast. This is real life, now.

I quickly brush as much of the residual mud and sand off my feet as I can in a few seconds and pull my boots back on. My hands are smeared with blood from the cut on my foot and I feel a sharp pain where the glass was; but I wipe my hands on my jeans and try to ignore the sting.

As I approach the fencing, I can't see where Maeve has managed to climb over. Of course it is Maeve at the end of the pier.

I don't even entertain the thought that it could be a coincidence, that it could be someone else. Somehow, I just know.

I push away thoughts of 'how can I possibly know' as I walk around the fencing, looking for a way in. I make a frustrated mental note of the irony – that I climbed over a fence to get here and now I'm shut out by another. There has to be a way in.

I'm starting to despair when finally I spot an old shopping trolley lying a few feet away down a drop. Well, this is Weston-super-Mare, I suppose. I walk cautiously to the edge of the drop before crouching down to reach the handle of the shopping trolley. Maybe Maeve discarded it after she climbed over. I can't see any other way that she might have got in here.

It takes all my strength to pull the trolley from the bank up to the fence. It's not particularly heavy but it sticks to the mud on the bank and weeds seem to have grown over the wheels. I have to pull particularly hard to snap their stems or uproot them; it's still too dark to tell exactly which I'm doing. Something about this niggles at me, though; this trolley has been there, untouched, for a while. This isn't how Maeve got in.

But I can't dwell on that. I guess it doesn't matter anyway. She's young, potentially agile – maybe she's just very good at scaling fences.

I quickly scrape the trolley over the concrete (the wheels have long since given up the ghost) to the part of the fence that looks the most accessible. Luckily it holds my weight and gives me enough of a boost to be able to yank myself up and perch on the edge of the wooden fence.

Now I'm on the edge of the fence, though, I can see that the wood below me – the wood that I'm supposed to land on – looks dodgy as hell. I'm terrified that if I land too heavily then I'm going to plummet right through the surface and down to whatever's below. I can't even tell if that would mean landing on concrete below it, or sand, or deathly cold water. It's too dark. Am I willing to take the risk?

I try to take it slowly. I'm perched precariously as it is. Screwing up all my courage, I keep a firm hold on the top edge of the fence as I slowly lower myself down onto the wood, testing it with my tiptoes. Luckily it seems to just about be holding. I don't know why I'm acting like this is going to help; being able to take the weight of my toes is not going to be the same as it taking my full body weight. But now I have no choice; I don't think I can haul myself back up onto the fence, and there isn't any other way to get onto the pier anyway. I'm going to have to test the rotten wood somewhere. This is Russian Roulette. And I'm going to have to play.

I can see the light still on the edge of the pier. This is why I'm doing this.

I close my eyes as I lower myself further. First the ball of my foot makes contact with the wood, then my heel; and then slowly, cautiously, hesitantly, I peel my fingers off the edge of the fence. I almost cry aloud in relief as the wood holds my weight.

I'm celebrating prematurely, though, of course; I have to get all the way to the end of this rotting pier without falling. If I was worried about falling through wood that might be over concrete, or maybe over sand – how worried should I be about ending up plummeting down into the freezing-cold sea?

I've come this far, and I'm not going to go back. But this is the most daring thing I've ever had to do. I don't know that I'm going to actually make it.

I call out Maeve's name, but my voice is immediately lost in the wind. I can't see her, either – just the light, shining resolutely. I'm guessing it's a fire she's lit – as ridiculously dangerous as that would be – unless she's managed to hide a phone or a torch from me. Though, I don't see how she could. All she's been wearing all night is that thin sundress and hoodie. I don't know where she could have hidden any electronics.

I'm guessing (rather, I'm hoping) that she's just lit the fire to show me she's there. I can't think of any other reason why she would want to do it. We were supposed to be visiting the pier, having fun and messing around, not burning it to the ground. And anyway, Maeve isn't destructive. It wouldn't make sense for her to be setting fire to the pier.

But some of our earlier conversations are niggling in my mind. She did say that she wasn't going to kill herself, and I cling to that, but... well, what was it that she said when I asked where she was going to stay?

"*I don't know that I am.*"

I still don't understand what that was supposed to mean. The vague sense that Maeve knows more than she's letting on – that her situation isn't as simple as she's trying to make it seem – is becoming a certainty in my mind. I don't know what I'm meant to do.

So I do the only thing I think that I can. I start to walk down the derelict pier.

My heart is pounding as I cautiously reach out to grab a bit of railing around the pier entrance (where I think the entry booth would have been). It is metal and I very gently tug at it to test that it is secured on and can take some weight. To my relief, it can. I grip it tight and carefully move my left foot onto a piece of wood by the railing. I press down my foot, and once again it holds. Christ, this would be so much easier in the daytime.

I move my right foot over to my left, squeezing myself onto one plank of wood. It's reassuring to be able to the cling to the railing, and I manage to see in the gloom that it seems to run down the pier for at least another twenty-five metres. This has to be a good thing; I can guide myself along it.

I debate taking my phone out and using it as a torch, just to see where I'm going, but I need both hands and I don't want to drop it. I'm not precious about my electronics; I just feel like I'm safer having it with me. I'm not sure who I'm intending to call; it would just be nice to have the opportunity to call *someone* if needed.

The railing is a good shout; it definitely doesn't feel as scary making my way down this death trap with something to cling on to. I tentatively press down on each part of the wood before I let it take my weight. It's a lengthy process and I move slowly towards the island at the end of the pier. At least at the island, which is rooted to the ground with concrete, the footing will be a bit more secure. On the downside, though, if the wood of the walkway falls in while we're on the island, we're totally stranded. I think about the tides again – I think about clambering down from the island, back in the direction of the road – but even if the tide goes out far enough to let us walk back up to the road, it won't be sand we're walking over; it will be the dense, sticking mud that I walked into earlier. This time it won't be just my feet getting mucky; we will sink so far into the mud that we might actually suffocate.

Birnbeck Pier seemed like such a good adventure idea two hours ago. Now it's clear that Maeve has led me into an extremely dangerous situation.

I can't shake from my mind that she's planning to hurt herself. Why else would she pick somewhere like this to explore? I mean, I get the lure of old building sites – I think it's an actual thing, urban exploring or something – but to actually get all the down this precarious structure and set a fire on the island… well, Maeve is being much more reckless than any healthy person would.

I just need to get her back to the stability of the shore, and we can talk. I can persuade her to go somewhere safe. A&E, the police station, whatever. I don't want her to get sectioned, but I just don't know what to do. I'm starting to understand what my school friends went through, when I was putting myself in danger all over the place.

One more safe step forward, one more safe step forward, one more safe step forward…

I reach for the railing to take another step, but my hand grips thin air instead. My hand can't find anything to hold on to, even as I wave it frantically, trying to find *something*. There's nothing there. I'm going to have to walk along the wood alone.

I look up towards the island. The wind is definitely picking up now, and I know that calling Maeve's name will only disappear into the sea air again. I thought it was getting light but mostly all I can see is gloom, lit up only by the fire at the end of the pier. I don't want to do this. I could turn around, I could grab the railing and I could make my way back to shore. But what if the wind picks up again? What if the structure continues to sway? Maeve could end up stranded on the island. Her fire could spread. I wouldn't leave anyone alone in a situation like this, but especially not Maeve.

Why do I feel such a pull towards her?

I force myself to take a deep breath, pulling in cool, salty air to my lungs, trying to calm down. There's at least another twenty-five metres to get to the island structure. And even then, judging from the height of the light, I suspect that Maeve has climbed up onto a higher platform there, somehow. I'm going to have to work out how to get up there too.

I've got to do this. Let's rip off the plaster.

I stick out my left leg precariously and test the wood. Secure. I shift my weight forward onto it, then bring forward my right leg. I stand poker-straight, feet glued together on the smallest piece of wood possible. This is going to be terrifying.

The wind batters me now that I'm not protected on one side by the railing and the indoor walkway. I sway involuntarily on my tiny perch. I'm going to fall. Staying still like this, I'm going to fall.

I have to do it, and I try to mentally detach myself as I stick my left foot out again, test, shift my weight, bring forward my right leg. It's a process. Just focus on the process. Granted, I'm stealing this technique from overhearing staff members persuading eating disordered patients to eat. I'm not sure it's the most psychologically sound technique, but essentially you don't focus on what you're doing and the implications (good or bad). Instead, you just focus your mind on the physical process. Just moving some limbs. Casually moving some limbs. Not about to die in the sea without rescuing Maeve.

I walk stiffly and robotically along the rotting wood for several metres. I test the wood firmly; but I am not evaluating or contemplating. I don't allow myself to think about what I'm doing, even to congratulate myself for getting so far or to egg myself on further. I don't look down, focusing on the light ahead of me.

But now I'm getting closer – the light doesn't look like a fire. It's flickering, certainly, but it doesn't look… warm? I can't put this into words. It's… less like a fire, than a glow. It just has some sort of quality about it that doesn't look like a bonfire.

There's a brief relief, though, in that whatever the light is, it's contained. I really thought that a bonfire on a wooden pier would lead to disaster. If anything, though, it's fading. Not extinguishing by any means, but fading slowly…

It transfixes me a little.

And then I fall.

I lurch forward as my foot plummets straight through the rotten wood – but luckily the wood is durable enough that the hole doesn't widen too far and I manage to just about stay on the pier, wedged in the hole that I'm not quite skinny enough to slip right through. My left leg dangles through the hole as I fall flat on my front, and my other leg is awkwardly crouched, having by some miracle managed to stay where it was.

My heart is pounding and even more adrenaline rushes into my system. I try to take deep breaths but I can't concentrate as my whole body starts to shake. I could die here. I need to act now.

Luckily, my right leg is planted firmly enough that, with my hands pushing down hard on two more secure pieces of wood at each side, I can just about pull my left leg out of the hole. I lean to the side, so that when my leg comes out, I can roll sideways into a foetal position, my legs tucked up to my chest.

For a minute I stay there, shaking hard. I need this minute to calm down. I need this minute to remind myself that I didn't fall through. That I'm OK. Whatever's happened, I'm OK.

Or am I? I'm curled up on a derelict, rotting pier, next to a hole that I nearly plummeted through. I'm so scared that I wouldn't be surprised if I'd pissed myself. There's a part of me that wants to tell myself to breathe, to take deep breaths and count to ten… but what am I powering through for? *None* of tonight has gone how I planned. I never wanted any of this. Why am I preparing to keep going with this shit? Why am I about to talk myself into going further out to sea? And why – *why* – am I still following this creepy fucking fire?

I lie there for a good few minutes before I'm calm enough to consider my options. Most of me is crying out to run back to shore *(I don't take risks, I don't take risks, this is what happens when you take risks)*. I know that the wood leading back that way is safe. Surely if I just come back the way I came, I won't go through the wood again.

But I'm slap bang in the middle of a large expanse of exposed wood. The railing that I gripped on to so tightly earlier is at least twenty feet away from where I'm lying now. How am I going to navigate safely back to the railing? It's just as far as it would be to keep going to the island. How have I ended up in a situation where whichever way I turn, there is a high possibility of falling to my death?

I wonder briefly what Katy would think if she saw me now. I don't think this is what she meant by positive risk-taking. Or maybe, actually, it is. If I get caught and she gives me grief about tonight… well, claiming that I pushed myself out of my comfort zone definitely wouldn't be a lie.

I laugh, crazily, madly, at the thought. I can't cope with this. I can't make it to the island. I don't think that I have the physical ability to. This is too much.

My heartbeat, to my relief, finally starts to slow. My body

temperature cools down, and the shaking in my hands starts to settle. I'm in the eye of the storm.

I know what I have to do. I have to keep pushing through.

I pull myself up to kneeling first, being extremely careful that the wood I shift myself awkwardly onto is solid and safe. When this works, I plant my hands either side of my knees, and push. I rock forward awkwardly, my eyes squeezed shut – but somehow, I manage to get to my feet. I'm shaking like a leaf, but I'm on my feet.

It's slowly approaching daybreak, but the light at the end of the pier burns brightly as if it was pitch black. This time, I don't try to force myself to move like a robot, focusing on the light – this time, I look down at my own feet. This time, I trust in myself.

I watch my feet as they take steps forward. I feel like I'm in a trance again, but this time I'm checking properly, determined to keep myself safe. Only twenty feet. Only twenty feet to go.

I count the steps as I take them, moving forwards slowly and steadily, forcing myself not to rush. To my relief, most of the wood at this part of the pier seems to be more stable. I'm not sure if I'm relieved when I realise from a large hole in the wood to my side, that I'm no longer walking over the open sea. I'm nearly at the island, with sand or rock beneath me.

Finally I take the last step off the wood, and reach concrete. I am shaking, but this time I'm shaking with relief and pride that I've managed to reach the end. I gulp in cold air, feeling slightly sick. I'm still full of adrenaline and I can feel it as I grin in relief. God, I understand why people do extreme sports now.

Then I remember the whole reason I've scaled that bloody death trap. The light. Maeve. My head snaps up to look. What I see almost makes me take a step back, back onto the uncertainty of the wood.

Maeve is standing at the end of the pier. And the source of the light? The source of the light is Maeve.

24

The morning after I speak to Claudie, I finally start my leaving book.

This is something that every patient here does; when they get their leaving date, they start a notebook where all the staff and patients can have a page to write them a goodbye note. I don't get a leaving date, as such, of course, but I know it's going to be soon and I want more than anything to be ready.

I let a few patients write the first few messages; whether this is somewhat cursory or not is debatable. I do genuinely care what these patients think of me, and I appreciate their messages; but the message that I really want is one from Zoe, and I think everyone knows it. Luckily, no one seems to mind. I'm not the only one here with a favourite person.

Zoe is writing up the word puzzle for the day on the whiteboard one morning when I approach her. She turns, a smile on her face. "What's up?" she asks lightly, pen still in hand.

I hesitate (Zoe always makes me nervous) before, instead of speaking, I stick out my leaving book towards her. She looks down at the red book, and I can tell that she instantly recognises it as one of the ward notebooks. To my relief, when she looks back up at me, she's still smiling.

"Will you write in it?" I blurt out, feeling that my cheeks are a little bit pink. I don't like asking anyone for anything, especially Zoe – but this is something I feel like I need. I don't know if I'm hoping for closure, or just a piece of proof that Zoe existed. Any device that can take photos is banned on the ward, so I will never have a photo of Zoe and me. I will never have a photo of her at all. I know that as soon as I have my own computer, I will be Googling her name to try and find a photo of her that I can save, but I imagine she has a fairly difficult-to-access online presence. These words, written with a shit biro in a flimsy notebook, might be the only proof I can ever hold that Zoe wasn't just a figment of my imagination.

Zoe tucks one of the loose strands of hair that she always has behind her ear, still smiling as she meets my eyes. "Of course I will!" she says brightly, though there is a slight frown on her face. I get the impression that she is a little confused as to why this is as important to me as it clearly is.

I don't think the confusion is helped by the fact that I can't make myself stay and watch her as she writes. Instead, I wait for her to take the red notebook in her hands before I turn and walk straight out of the dining room, and back to my bedroom. My fingers dig in to the tops of my arms as I hug myself, trying not to feel the searing physical pain in my chest as I think about leaving Zoe.

I sit cross-legged on the lino of my bedroom floor, trying to focus my mind on a book. There isn't much in my bedroom that I can distract myself with – even though staff constantly tell us to distract ourselves from what we're feeling. Whether this is helpful advice or not is a different issue altogether. Right now, I just want something to stop me thinking about Zoe.

It's maybe fifteen minutes later when I hear a soft knock on my door. I put down my book and get to my feet, making for the door. My chest still hurts. I'm not surprised, though, when I open the door to see Zoe, holding my book.

She stretches it out to me, a little tentatively. When I go to take it, however, she keeps hold of it herself.

"Can we talk?" she asks, her voice gentle if uncertain.

My eyes widen slightly and my heart is hammering. No matter how much time I spend with her, she always provokes this reaction in me. I don't know if it's panic, or just a desperate desire to do the right thing. I never want to do anything wrong with Zoe.

I nod, of course. The fact that she wants to talk to me... the pain in my chest feels like it's easing, the warmth spreading back in. Where Zoe is concerned, I go from zero to a hundred in seconds. Sometimes I feel like I'm at zero and a hundred at the same time. It's the most I feel about anyone, about anything. If she wants to talk, I know that I'm not going to say no.

She relinquishes her grip on the notebook, letting me take it and hold it close to my chest as she gestures to the Quiet Room just across the corridor from my bedroom. I know what she's asking. I nod again.

My heart suddenly twinges with a physical pain. This might be the last time I get to speak to her properly. How am I supposed to give this up? Nothing *makes me feel so intensely as Zoe does*. Why do people not understand this? Why do people not understand why I wouldn't want to lose the only thing that stops me feeling numb?

I sit in one of the plasticky, wipe-clean armchairs and Zoe takes the similarly upholstered sofa opposite me. I automatically tuck my feet up, feeling a tiny bit of comfort in being so tightly curled up. Zoe, on the other hand, sits on the edge of the sofa, leaning forward on her knees, her head tilted sympathetically already.

"I just wanted to..." she begins, before trailing off. I get the impression that she hasn't fully thought through how she's going to word whatever she's trying to say. I wait.

"I know this transition is going to be difficult for you," she tries again at last. "Turning eighteen is hard enough already. And I know leaving everyone you know here..."

She trails off again, but this time she holds my gaze. For a few seconds, we stare at each other and I feel like my chest might explode.

But then her eyes move, and she's smiling, and she starts to talk again. She's encouraging me; she's telling me it's going to be alright. That I'll adjust. That I'll get out of hospital if I just keep working.

I have heard all these things before, from many people, and it has never been particularly helpful. Somehow it doesn't surprise me that even from Zoe, this still doesn't help. But I still don't want her to stop talking. If I had the choice to stay in this room forever, I would stay. Even if I had to listen to this encouraging bullshit for the entire time, I would stay.

I just don't want Zoe to go.

And then suddenly she is frowning at me, looking a little heartbroken; and I realise that I've said that out loud.

"I'm sorry," I add quickly. "I didn't mean... I just..."

Now, suddenly, I don't know what to say either. It's true. I don't want Zoe to go.

For a second, there's silence. Then she seems to dredge up a smile from somewhere. It must be right from the depths, because it looks like one of the saddest smiles I think I've ever seen. I want to talk – I want to reach over to her and hold her hand. But that's not allowed. All I can do is sit quietly and look at her.

"I hope I haven't made things harder for you," she finally says at last.

I feel the tears running down my face before I even realise they are coming. I can't look at Zoe, now. I can't believe I've made her feel like that could even be an option. How could she ever make things harder for me?

"Oh, sweet..." she begins when she sees the tears, but I'm shaking my head.

"Don't think that," I blurt out, my voice shaking. "Please don't think that. You've helped me so much."

I finally find the strength from somewhere to look up at Zoe, wiping my eyes with my sleeve. Her big blue eyes look back at me. Somehow it feels like something has changed, though I can't identify exactly what that is. For another long moment, we look at each other, silent.

Then Zoe is smiling again, nodding. "I'm glad," she tells me very gently, very softly. "That's all I ever..." She shakes her head firmly to herself. "You've got such a future ahead of you," she continues after a moment. "You can do this. You're going to get yourself out of hospital and in ten years I'll be reading your column in The Sunday Times."

A genuine smile flicks around my lips, though my stomach hurts at the thought of a life where I can talk to Zoe, but she can't talk back to me. I know I have to live without her but I'm not sure I know how. I want to tell her I love her; I want to tell her not to be upset when ten years go by and I'm long gone. Right now, that's the only future I can see for me. Dead and buried before I'm twenty-eight.

But I hold on tight to the smile and try to act like I'm OK. I nod quickly. "You're going to be such a good psychologist," I tell her reciprocally (because of course I've interrogated her about her career plan before). I mean it, though. She's going to be the best. I have no doubt about that.

I'm still holding my leaving book as she stands and I do the same. I am about to cling it to my chest again when Zoe holds out her arms to me. "Come on," she says, more lightly now, more brightly. "Leaving hug."

I don't need telling twice. I put the book down on the edge of the armchair and I throw my arms around Zoe's neck, holding her tight. I hear her laugh quietly as I cling to her. "That's OK," she says gently, and she holds me back. For the final time, I feel like Zoe cares about me.

25

I don't know if it's my fight-or-flight response kicking in, but, looking at the glowing teenager ahead of me, I freeze.

What am I looking at? I don't understand how I could have mistaken it for a fire, even from so far away. My mind lurches back to the forest, to finding Maeve lying there. It's the only point of reference that I have; the only time I've ever seen anything like what I'm looking at now. How have I not thought about that all evening? It's not like the thought has been stolen exactly – but it's like the thought has been sat there in disguise. How can I have forgotten how important it was?

I'm shaking as I try to keep my eyes focused on Maeve herself, but the light is distracting. I'm not sure quite how it makes me feel – there's something unsettling about it. Whatever the feeling is, it isn't good. There's something about it that just makes me want it to stop. I feel a wave of anger run over me and I almost think of hitting her; I have to quickly remind myself that it's Maeve stood in front of me. This isn't someone that I want to hurt.

But the feeling unlocks something that I couldn't explain earlier. "Those men – the ones who threw bottles at you…"

It's as much as I can get out at the moment and Maeve seems to realise this. She looks down at her feet and nods. "They were coming towards me and I got scared," she says quietly. "I thought turning it on would help, but…"

I clear my throat, force myself to shut my eyes for a minute. "It's unsettling," I admit. "Can you turn it off now? Please?"

She looks back up at me, sadness on her face. "It unsettles you too?"

I sigh. "I'm sorry," I say, though I'm not sure what I'm apologising for. "Yes, it does."

Maeve holds my gaze almost fiercely. "I had to turn it on to get you down here," she tells me, a note of urgency in her voice. "I didn't know how else…"

She trails off. For my part, my head is reeling, my thoughts out of control. None of this makes any sense. However, I feel myself relax a fraction as Maeve finally turns the glow off, as suddenly as if she has flicked a switch inside her head.

Now she looks like herself, at least, and my anger dissipates quickly. As she wraps her arms around herself and sits on the floor, curled up, I struggle to remember why I thought she was a threat a few seconds ago. I swallow, hard. Something deep within me, instinctive, still tells me not to go too close to her – but my executive function overrides that. I take a few steps closer to her and sit down.

Still, there's something in my core that tells me not to touch her. I stay about a metre away, shifting around slightly until I settle for kneeling, my hands clasped in my lap. It's not a natural way for me to sit, but I guess this isn't a normal situation.

For a moment, there's silence.

"What *is* that light, Maeve?" I ask eventually.

She shakes her head. "I don't know," she tells me, and somehow I believe her. "I never had it, until…"

Until what? Tonight has been exhausting; I'm tired and impatient and I want answers. A huff of breath escapes me, and I have to bite at my lip to stop myself snapping at her. She's young and she's frightened; I shouldn't push, I know, but…

And then I realise how ridiculous that is. Because normal fourteen-year-olds can't make themselves glow like that.

"What happened?" I ask, persistent even as I try to keep my voice calm. I have to be the grown-up here. Hell, I actually am the grown-up here. This is the first time I've really thought that with any certainty.

Maeve shakes her head fervently, pulling me out of my thoughts. "I just woke up with it," she tells me, distress eating at the edge of her answer. "In the forest. When we met."

I frown. "OK," I reply slowly. "But when I met you there… you didn't seem… confused? You knew where you were."

I see Maeve scratch hard at her arm as she grimaces at my words, and my automatic response is to take her hand, to move it away, to stop her hurting herself. But again something stops me. I keep my hands to myself.

"Yeah," she admits, a little high-pitched. "I don't even know how, though. I chose—"

She breaks off abruptly and stares down at her lap. But she's said it now, and I'm not about to let her take it back. I feel my eyes narrow as I watch her discomfort. "You chose?" I prompt doggedly. "What did you choose?"

To my surprise, Maeve makes a wounded noise. "*It doesn't matter,*" she says, her voice suddenly piercing. "I just need to… I need to keep you safe…"

"I'm the adult, Maeve," I remind her, but she barely lets me finish my sentence.

"It's not about that," she insists. "It doesn't matter how old I am, or why I'm here…"

I hear myself breathe out angrily as if it's someone else doing it. Somehow, the trust I had in her is running out of my grip like sand. "Of course it matters," I say sharply. "You need to tell me the truth, Maeve."

She sighs deeply. For a moment, there's silence. I have a million questions but I sense that she will be more likely to speak if I give her some space to phrase things her way.

"Do you remember that car accident you were in?" she asks at last.

A sharp pain stabs in my chest. I know what she's talking about – of course I know what she's talking about – but I don't want to let my mind go there. "When I was fourteen?" I say, my voice high-pitched and sharp. "How do you know about that?"

I feel, for what feels like the millionth time, the urge to tear deep gashes in the skin of my arms. Any time anyone mentions... I shake my head. The rush of emotion that courses through me is hard to ignore, but I know I need to stay present in this conversation. Now isn't the time to hurt myself.

My eyes are keenly trained on Maeve as she bites her lip. I get the impression that whatever answer she has to my question, I'm not going to like it. "And you remember how... things got more difficult after that?"

I breathe out heavily. "Don't talk about it like that," I say, my voice harsh. I don't let anyone talk about this. "I don't know what you think you know..."

Even as I say it, the rush of emotion that I felt before doubles. I am so furious with Maeve – for her to bring up these things, for her to know about these things – but I'm just as angry with myself. How do I still let all of this affect me so much?

A flash of images run through my mind, images that I spend a lot of my time trying to keep in little boxes in my head. This part of my past is the only thing that Katy has never been able to make me feel better about. I try to hold the images back, but the floodgates are open now, and I'm vaguely aware that I've started to cry, staring down at my lap as I sit uncomfortably on a derelict pier. I don't know how my life has gotten to this point.

"I'm sorry," I hear a voice say, somewhere in front of me, meek or even scared. "I didn't mean..."

I shake my head hard. Am I reassuring Maeve, or telling her

to stop? Telling her to back up and explain why she's lured me here without using my past as some kind of excuse?

There's a long pause before I force myself to take a deep breath. "I know," I say shortly, gruffly. "I know you're not trying to upset me. Just tell me how you found out."

I finally look back up at her. I'm aware that the way I'm responding to this already isn't particularly conducive to her sharing the rest of her story. But suddenly anger is coursing through my body and I am finding it hard to worry about her feelings at the moment.

None of this makes any sense. I honestly can't think of a single way that she could have found out about the accident, apart from everything else. There was a news article in the local newspaper at the time, I think; but that was four years ago, when it happened. Why would she have been reading four-year-old newspapers?

And even if for some reason she had been, how would she know how to find me? Even if somehow she had found out which hospital I was in, how would she have known I would be in the forest? *I didn't even know that I was going to run away tonight.* How can she have known that I was going to do it before I did?

And, of course, the other thing I can't explain – how is she *glowing*?

I shake my head hard as my thoughts start to go around and around in circles. I can't make sense of this, and the only person who is able to explain is staring at me without speaking.

"Maeve, you can't just leave it there," I say, and I can still hear the sharp note in my voice. "You need to explain."

Maeve closes her eyes. "I'm trying," she says, softly, though I can hear the frustration in her voice. I get the impression that whatever her endgame was meant to be, she didn't expect to have to explain all of this.

I stay silent, hoping that there will be something oppressive about the silence; maybe if I stop talking, she will start explaining just to fill the gap.

My eyes stay firmly on Maeve as she swallows, hard. "I was there," she says at last.

What?

I feel my hands start to shake. That isn't possible. She can't have been. All the witnesses came forward to the police – just a young couple and a middle-aged man. All three of them testified that they never saw anyone else there. And I met them, the witnesses, at the police station. She's lying. She can't have been there.

There's more than a note of sharpness in my voice, now. "Don't lie to me," I say acridly. I realise that I'm glaring at her. I only get hostile when I'm frustrated like this. And I'm tired of being lied to.

Maeve shakes her head. "I'm not lying," she says in a small voice. "It's… more complicated than that. Look, just let me finish."

I breathe out angrily. "All I've asked for you to do is give me answers."

She nods quickly. "I know, I know. So that's what I'm going to try and do."

I can't tell if I'm slightly mollified by being listened to, or just really keen to hear what Maeve has to say for herself, but I manage to bite my tongue and give her a short, curt nod. I know I need to give her a bit of space for her to be able to explain; if I keep jumping down her throat, she's going to clam up and I'll never get a proper answer.

And I *want* a proper answer. I trusted Maeve; she's the first person I've trusted in ages. I don't want to have put my faith in the wrong person again. I really want to be able to help her, like I had planned. But at this moment, I don't see how she is going to dig herself out of this hole.

I dig my nails into my arm as I look down at the muddy island we're sitting on. I'm sure there must be rats everywhere around here. I try not to think about it. Whatever happens, I shouldn't be here much longer.

Finally Maeve takes a deep breath. "Just let me finish," she says again. "I promise it will make sense at the end."

I nod curtly. I will do what she wants and listen.

"Imagine," she says tentatively, "if – when you were unconscious after the crash – and you suddenly knew you had a chance, to live or die, but to live, you had to convince someone else to live…"

She trails off, and I'm just as frustrated. I'm not sure what she means. And even if what she's saying is true – well, I'm not sure it makes any sense.

I sigh. "Maeve, that doesn't explain anything."

She closes her eyes again. "Things weren't great already," she tells me quietly. "At home. You know that. You know what…"

Maeve looks up at the sky, and it's my turn to close my eyes. Though I no longer feel like I can trust everything she has told me tonight, the one thing I do trust is that she's scared of aggression. Just like me. Somehow the fact that she is so reluctant for me to know about what is going on for her at home, makes me trust more that her reactions are genuine. It sits uncomfortably with me that half the reason I trust in this, is because I recognise it.

I force myself back to the present and give Maeve a cursory nod. "Alright," I say, a bit more gently, a bit more conciliatory. "I do know that."

She nods eagerly. "You do!" she says, quickly jumping on the slight gap in my anger. "But I didn't know… I didn't know what the next few years were going to be like – I knew we'd be struggling, I guess, but…"

Maeve breaks off, perhaps at the look on my face. "We?" I question tiredly.

But before I can ask any more questions, Maeve quickly continues. "The point is, I thought that… that things would be better. And then it came to me… that I had the chance… to stop it happening… to stop you dying tonight…"

She looks up at me almost pleadingly. But I almost feel like, the more Maeve speaks, the less things make sense. Maybe she can tell what I'm thinking, because she sighs.

"I know it doesn't make much sense," she says sadly. "I wish I had more information to give you, or something to make this seem – well, possible, I guess."

She sighs again. "Look, I've got weird, fuzzy memories of… maybe a tunnel, or something – but the next thing I really remember is waking up in that forest with you standing over me," she tells me at last. "What happened, like, technically… I can't answer you. But it all started with being in that car crash."

None of this makes any sense. I mean, talking of tunnels and all that, I can see what she's hinting at. I don't believe in things like this – reincarnation, or ghosts, or whatever category this comes under. Maeve is in front of me, and she's solid, and I'm sorry, but I don't believe she can be *dead*.

I bluster for a second, searching for a logical explanation. "Well, you must have amnesia, or something," I say bluntly. "From whatever happened to get you to the forest. I don't know, maybe lack of oxygen to your brain…"

Suddenly, though, she doesn't look afraid anymore. She's smiling a little smile now that saps my confidence, and I fall silent, looking at her and feeling a bit gormless. In the heavy silence, Maeve takes a deep breath and snakes out a hand without moving her gaze off my face for even a second. Her hand lands on my knee and this time, I allow it. My eyes shut almost automatically – and I can't explain it, but I feel reassured. Safe.

I don't look at Maeve as I reach out to her hand and cover it gently with my own.

"Heather," she almost breathes. "Heather. The paramedics pulled you out of the wreckage – but I got stuck. You lost a little part of you. And now, well… I'm here. To save you."

My head is reeling now; because what Maeve is saying doesn't make any sense. Why would the universe care about me staying alive? Why would anyone?

I don't want her to stop me. That's the easiest way to sum up what I'm thinking. Even with all of this nonsense aside – with Maeve being some kind of ghost angel thing – with some kind of tear in the time-space continuum – with *any* of this aside, my feelings haven't changed. I want to rest. I want to sleep. I want to stop feeling like this.

If anything, this makes me want to go more. If Maeve is telling the truth, and there's life after death – I'm not sure I want to take theological advice from a fourteen-year-old, despite how frustratingly right her explanation seems to feel – then if I die tonight, I get to see everyone I love again. I can watch over Zoe and make sure she's safe; I can make everyone's lives easier without me to deal with. Really, all Maeve has done is bring me to a suicide spot. Because if I jump off the edge of this island, I'm definitely not going to be here tomorrow.

I don't have the heart to say any of this to Maeve. Instead I sigh and try to tell her the truth.

"I don't want you to stop me," I tell her simply.

Maeve sighs herself. "I know," she says, sounding downcast. "I mean, I thought… I thought you would want to be saved. Like I could just jump in the sea and drag you out to stop you from drowning. I didn't realise…"

She tails off once again, but I know what she's getting at. She didn't realise that, right now, I want to drown.

I sigh. "You know how hard things have been," I remind her. "Up to where you are. Allegedly. Whatever. And after that, things have just gotten worse. Mate – you'd be better telling whoever sent you to save me that we should have died in the crash. That would be a better outcome."

Maeve looks at me sadly, but I just shrug. "If you miss out on our next few years, Maeve… you're not missing much, I promise."

There is a long silence. The sea is calm, albeit still loud. I look outwards for the first time. I have been so focused on Maeve, and getting safely down here, that I haven't really noticed my surroundings before. If this situation weren't so dangerous, I'm sure I would find being out here kind of calming.

"There must be something," Maeve presses eventually, almost desperately. I don't look around at her. I suppose it must be hard to hear that you have nothing good coming up in your life.

As I continue to look out to sea, I wonder if the scenery is calming me after all. For some reason, Maeve no longer feels like a pressing issue. But I force my mind to get back in gear. Have there been any good parts of the last few years? Of course, I'm biased; any stretch of time that starts with a car accident and ends with suicide isn't going to seem like a good period. Especially as everything got worse in between. Everything at home, then everything school falling to shit, then so much time in hospital… At first glance, there is nothing positive to relay back to Maeve.

But then something hits me. I find myself thinking of a moment where my hand was in Zoe's, and I was safe.

Before I can say anything, I feel one hot tear slide down my face. I look away from the sea and down into my own lap. Zoe made me feel safe, and she has to be a good part of the last few years, but… now she's gone. I'm never going to see her again. Does it count as a positive if it's over as certainly as if she had died?

"There's very little," I answer at last.

Maeve continues to look at me with big eyes. "Look, I'm sorry, but you can't kill yourself tonight."

I close my eyes for a second. This is too big of a subject to be discussed right now. And in all honesty – I don't *want* to kill myself tonight. I don't want to hurt the few people who care about me. I don't want to forever be known as the dead girl. But – and I always come back to this – I haven't got a choice. I can't keep living like this. Nothing's making me better, and I just want to *sleep*…

"Why not, Maeve?" I ask eventually, exhausted. "I know this isn't what you want, but…"

But to my surprise, Maeve's gaze hardens. "No," she answers, suddenly. "It isn't. But that's not why you can't do it." She takes a deep breath, and I find my eyes narrowing again. What is this big bombshell that she wants to drop?

She stands up, digging into her pocket, and pulls out a business card. A business card, from the policewoman that I hid from. A business card, that could send me instantly straight back to hospital.

"You can't," Maeve continues, "because I have this."

26

The next few days form the most drawn-out goodbye that I have ever known. I know, throughout all of them, that I have only a few days of security before I'm going to be moving any day. I worry every time I see a staff member that I like leave, and every time one of my friends goes on home leave for a few days; is this going to be the last time I ever see them?

I give more hugs than I've ever given in my life. I'm well aware, even as I give them, that none of them will make me feel as safe as it did to hold on to Zoe. But I'm also well aware that I have to put that in the past.

I wake on the morning of my birthday to the sound of knocking on my bedroom door. I stretch out sleepily but I'm sat up in bed when the door opens. I have no idea what the time is. It must be early. The ward is quiet. It doesn't sound like anyone else is awake yet.

As the door is pushed slowly open, I see Claudie and two more of my favourite support workers peeking in to check if I'm awake. I smile tentatively, though I'm a little confused as to why they are there. In truth, I'm still half asleep. But once they see me, they grin. I don't get a chance to ask what they're doing before they burst into a spontaneous (albeit whispered) rendition of 'Happy Birthday'.

A proper smile comes onto my face. This is a nice way to be woken up.

Claudie beams especially brightly at me, and I notice that she is holding something behind her back. I tilt my head, but I don't have to even ask. She is so excited as she takes a small parcel out from behind her back and sticks it out towards me to take.

This is a surprise to me, actually – usually staff don't get presents for patients' birthdays. I must frown ever so slightly as I take the parcel, because suddenly she's explaining herself. "It's from all of us," she tells me quickly. "We just thought… as it's your eighteenth…"

She doesn't have to finish her sentence; I know what she means. I'm smiling again. "Thank you," I say to the three of them, and mean it. I rip off the paper; it's a book. Perfect. Something tells me that I'm going to be keeping this book for a long time. It's the gesture, more than anything.

I keep smiling, and from the looks I get back from the support workers, they get what this means for me.

This is the overriding memory that I have of this birthday. As I expected, the best word to describe the day, is 'pleasant'. I get out for a few hours, and I get nice presents and cake. I should be over the moon, frankly. Compared to some of the days I've had recently…

But I don't want to go down that rabbit hole. I know that everyone has tried really hard, as well, to make today bearable. Staff and patients and my parents. It's really kind of them. I'm not sure I deserve the effort, but I certainly appreciate it.

I get two days' warning, in the end, of where I'm going. It's a mental health rehab facility, they tell me, for people trying to adjust back to community living while recovering from serious mental health problems. That sounds like me, I guess. And it's much closer to my parents and my hometown, which has to be a good thing. I've even met the head nurse from the ward, when she came to assess me a week before. She seemed nice enough. Still, I can't help but be concerned. I don't want to be going somewhere new; I don't want to be going somewhere where I don't know anyone. And all the awful things I've been told about adult wards still ring in my ears. This is a move that, truth be told, I don't want. Unfortunately, however, I don't have a choice.

Packing takes a surprisingly long amount of time considering I don't have many possessions. I don't have a suitcase or a big bag so everything has to be put into tote bags for the most part. I also have a box of letters and special things – birthday cards, bracelets that have been made for me by other patients, origami swans that get progressively less wonky – and, of course, my leaving book with Zoe's message inside.

It feels odd watching my bags of stuff being loaded into the wheeled cage to be taken down to the car. It's not like this was my bedroom the entire time that I was here, I suppose, though it's certainly been the bedroom I've been in longest. And after all, this is the bedroom where every patient in the ward once hid in the shower in my ensuite to scare the staff into thinking they had lost them. So many stupid memories.

Leaving the ward goes as well as it can do. I don't cry, at least, though I do feel a bit like I might. I give last hugs to my friends and exhort last hugs from the staff, who tell me they're not supposed to hug patients. Then I make my way through the warren of corridors that I was led down when I arrived. I know my way perfectly, now. How did I once think that I would never find my way out?

Luckily, the nurse who is coming with me in the car to the new hospital is one of my favourites. Hope isn't the gentlest nurse by any means, but she's direct. I like direct. Direct is what I need right now. I take a deep breath while the security guy is loading my bags into the boot, though I keep my box of letters on my lap. It's the last thing I want to leave behind.

When I leave the building, they give me a bag with all my contraband in. This is exciting; obviously, they've binned the razor blades that I smuggled in through various methods, but everything else is there. Most excitingly, my mobile is in there. The thing I'm looking forward to most in the adult ward is being allowed my mobile phone, and a laptop when I get one. Closely followed, of course, by the unescorted leave that the staff have assured me everyone gets on adult wards.

Hope looks at me as I finish strapping on my seatbelt. "Ready?" she asks with a grin.

It's a two-hour car ride, and we are not allowed to stop – probably in case I do a runner at the motorway services. I feel so discombobulated that I can't even promise that I wouldn't do that. I don't feel bad, by any stretch, and I feel positive about the move – but I know that crazy times make me do crazy things. It's not just me, either. This seems to apply to quite a lot of people I've met in the past two years.

Hope falls asleep about an hour into the journey. I don't usually envy mental health nurses their jobs, but it does amuse me that Hope is getting paid to nap in a car for an hour. I consider taking a selfie with her in the background (I'm sure my friends from the ward would find it hilarious) but I don't want to get her in trouble. Besides, I'm an adult now. I need to do less stupid shit just because it's funny.

I look out the window instead. Last time I came this way, I was being driven to the hospital in the pitch black, so I don't recognise any of the roads we travel along. In an odd sort of way, it helps to feel like this is an adventure.

I'm definitely comforted, however, when I start to see place names that I recognise on the road signs. However this ward turns out to be – even if it's the nightmare that some of the nurses have described – I'm back home. I'm near my parents, and Amelie, and I won't be so isolated. If my extended family come down to visit my mum then I'll be able to see them. The location has to be a bonus.

As we advance further, I realise something else exciting. I haven't been able to Google Weston-super-Mare, so I only know that it's near Bristol; but as we start to get closer, I realise that I can see the sea. I'm going to live at the seaside. I don't know why that excites me as much as it does, but the idea of walking along the beach of an afternoon sounds really appealing. And if I've never heard of it – it has to be a quiet place, right?

(This reasoning, I'm well aware, is born from the panic that is currently coursing through me. But I need to focus on it – because otherwise I'm going to start sobbing.)

When we turn into the road that leads up to the hospital, though, my resolve does shake a little bit. The building is massive, and legitimately looks like it's been a psychiatric hospital since the Victorian times. It's nice that there is a big garden (big enough to even be called grounds) but I do slightly feel like I'm being committed, in the Victorian sense of the word. Like someone is going to strap me down and perform electroconvulsive therapy on me.

I'm worried enough that I reach over to Hope automatically, and shake her shoulder anxiously. She starts awake, looking around herself in what looks like confusion at first, but then she registers me and seems to realise.

"Crap," she says, a little blearily still. "I fell asleep. Are we here?"

I nod wordlessly, gesturing to the building with the big sign as we get closer and closer.

"Oh," says Hope, looking as surprised as I feel. "It's big."

I swallow hard. "Yeah," I agree. I'm not quite sure what else to say. If even Hope is surprised, this can't be normal.

I get a slight bit of relief, though, when we drive straight past the huge white building. For a minute, I think the satnav has made a mistake, that it's leading the driver to somewhere else entirely; but then I see a small house at the top of the hill ahead. Luckily, the small house has a sign – and the sign announces that this is the ward that we're looking for.

On my other side, Hope is visibly relieved. I suspect that the thought of leaving me in the asylum building made her feel a little bit guilty. But this house – this house will be friendlier, won't it?

I hold tight to my box as the driver parks and we get out of the car. He opens the boot, and Hope and I grab a few bags each; but because everything is in small, separate bags, it's going to take a few trips. I intentionally linger on the driveway, adjusting a bag onto my shoulder as I cling to my box, so that Hope has to go ahead of me. I hesitate, slightly behind her, as she rings the doorbell.

The woman who answers the door actually looks friendly. I don't know why I'm surprised; maybe it's all the horror stories that I've heard about adult services. Maybe I half-expected a Miss Trunchbull, holding out a straitjacket ready for me.

But this nurse looks OK, and she's obviously expecting us because she quickly steps aside, beckoning us in. "Nice to meet you, nice to meet you," she says with a small smile. "Let's get all your things inside, and I'll show you around. We've put you in bedroom eleven, up at the top of the house."

I try to smile back, nodding. The idea of trying to speak seems out of reach at the moment. I want to hide behind Hope like I'm a child and I have to remind myself that I'm an adult. I'm an adult now, and I need to act like one.

I'm almost disappointed when it only takes us one more trip to bring my things inside. Ferrying bags inside would at least keep Hope around for a little bit longer. Truth be told, I don't want her to leave me here alone. I can't deny it – I'm scared.

A tall woman approaches me, watching me in a way that makes me drop my gaze down to the floor. "We're making lunch," she tells me, her voice quiet enough but somehow also a little intense. "Do you want a sandwich?"

The question, although not particularly odd in itself, wrong-foots me for some reason. I nod. "Thank you," I add quickly.

The woman isn't wearing a badge or a lanyard like the nurse is, so I deduce that she must be a patient. It's a little reassuring that patients get to help with meal prep, just like the nurse who came to assess me said. At least I know she was being honest. In any case, the patient lopes off to start making the sandwich, and I'm left standing with the new nurse and Hope.

"Well, that's all your things," says Hope, and I notice that her voice has a note of uncertainty in it that I haven't heard before. Maybe she feels bad about leaving me here alone. But I notice that she keeps a smile on her face nonetheless.

"You're going to be fine, here," she adds quickly. "Alright? You've done so well."

I take a deep breath and dredge up a smile from somewhere. I don't want Hope to think I'm scared. I'm an adult. I can take it. Tears catch in my throat, but I force them down. I don't want Hope's last memory of me to be me bawling my eyes out, scared of the adult ward. Besides, I need to show everyone here that I'm big and strong enough to handle things. I'm a fucking grown-up, damn it. I have to do this.

Hope opens her arms towards me and I lurch towards her and hold on to her tight. I know she has to leave. I just don't want her to.

"We're so proud of you, OK?" she adds into my hair. "You got this."

I don't want to let go, but as I feel her pull away from me, I let her and step back myself. I don't want her to think that I can't manage. I cling on to the last remnants of my smile and look up at Hope's face. She looks a little teary herself.

Then, though, she's leaving. Before I can even collect myself, suddenly she's out of the door, the last little bit of me not-quite-being-an-adult gone with her. I have thought I feel adrift before, but as it turns out, I've never felt quite so adrift as I do now.

Various people introduce themselves to me, some nurses and some patients. I force down a cheese sandwich and play half of an unenthusiastic game of Monopoly with a support worker. The most eventful thing that happens is when a patient cautiously asks how old I am. When I tell her that I've just turned eighteen, it is like a lightbulb appears above her head. It makes sense. Why I'm here when I look so young.

My room, as it turns out, is in the attic. To my surprise, there's a TV in it. It's nice, actually quite cosy. I hope that once I've unpacked my things, it will feel like home. After I've taken my medication for the night, I decide not to force myself to stay in communal areas anymore that night. I know I have to get used to the place, but maybe unpacking will help me feel more settled here too.

It's maybe 9pm when I retreat back to my room. All my things are strewn around the room in tote bags. My box of letters is safe on the bookcase – which, in contrast to the adolescent ward, isn't nailed to the floor. I can't look at the box right now, though it continues to draw my eye. I want to think that I'll wake up tomorrow and all the people in there won't just be memories. That they won't be people that I'll never see again.

And, of course, who is on my mind the most but Zoe? The feeling that I felt at Christmas when I wasn't going to see her for six days is now amplified a hundred times. I'm never going to see Zoe again. How can that be possible? How can such a big part of my heart just be ripped out like that?

My breathing is shaky as I sit down on the bed. I don't want to be here. I want to be safe with my friends and the staff members who looked after me. Maybe things will be alright here, maybe not everything is weird and scary – but I want to go back to what I know.

My heart hurts as I sit hunched up on the bed, and tears start to come. I didn't want it to be like this – I wanted to be an adult who can cope maturely – but then I think, could an adult even cope with losing their entire support system in one fell blow? It's too much. It's too much for anyone.

I'm sobbing before long. And all I can think? That I wish Zoe was outside my door, hearing that I really needed someone.

27

I stare at Maeve, who is holding the business card aloft. Is it still a business card if it's for a police officer?

Temporarily struck dumb, all I can do is jump to my feet. My eyes are level with Maeve's now. When I find my voice again, it's scratchy and sharp. "What are you going to do with that?" I ask, my voice steady but poisonous. I can't believe, after we've been through all of this…

She holds my gaze steadily, without speaking.

Suddenly I'm filled with anger. "Great, so you can send me back to hospital," I say bitterly. One of my fists even clenches. "Where I'll be locked up even more for jumping the fence. Maybe they'll transfer me to a different hospital where I'm not even allowed outside. Then your little plan will work right out, yes?"

Maeve looks down at her feet. "That's not…" she blurts out, before she breaks off. "I want you to get better," she adds, a blunt note of pain in her voice.

"Not going to happen," I spit. I hate the way that I'm reacting, but a huge wave of anger has hit me straight on, and I'm tired of trusting the wrong people. I'm tired of being told what's best for me by people who don't even know me. I'm tired of not having control of my own life. This time, I'm fighting.

I don't give her a chance to rebut. "Look, if you try and call her, I'll just run. There's nothing stopping me. Hell, I'll run into the sea if I have to."

She looks at me painfully. "I thought you wanted to get me safe before you died."

I scoff, though she has a point and the idea of leaving her still doesn't exactly sit right with me. "Five minutes ago you were claiming we were the same person," I remind her harshly. "So I'm guessing if I die, then you do too."

Another wave of anger hits me hard. I force myself to look away; I can't keep looking at her. I'm furious. Should I be feeling like this? Should I not be grateful that someone wants me still alive? Somehow I can't see it like that. After everything that's happened tonight – after all of it, Maeve wants to force me back to being *committed*. I feel a sharp urge to kick something. Still, I have to let that urge pass. I can't guarantee that a swift kick to the wood wouldn't send both of us careering into the sea below.

I dig my fingers into my arm to try and get a hold of myself. I'm furious, but I'm not sure that taking out that anger on Maeve is going to be the most helpful thing I can do right now.

As I look up at her again, though, I realise that she is still thinking about my last response. Her face is hard; yet she doesn't glare back at me. Instead, she tilts her head. "I mean, yeah, *I will...*" she begins, a little awkwardly. I can't shake the feeling that she has a bomb to drop. "But I don't know what will happen to whoever this body belongs to," she says eventually.

Is she teasing me? Because she seems to have a slight smile on her face. Is this funny to her?

"You're not making sense," I snap. "Now you're telling me that this isn't your body?"

Maeve shrugs. "Well, yeah," she confirms, a little awkwardly, but still with the air of someone who knows that they have the upper hand. "I don't know whose it is, I just woke up in it. But it's not ours."

Ours.

I'm frustrated to the back teeth with all the complexities of this, but something about that word hits me hard. *Ours.* Whatever I do, now, I'm linked to Maeve and Maeve is linked to me. I have to concede that she does have somewhat of a point. Whoever the body I'm looking at belongs to, it's not me. By extension, it's not Maeve either.

My head is starting to hurt. "So if I go back to the hospital, what happens to you?" I ask, eyes narrowed.

Maeve swallows. "I think I go on with my light," she says simply.

I grit my teeth. "And... *that* body?" I can barely frame my thought aloud, I feel so ludicrous discussing this.

To my surprise, Maeve bites her lip. "I don't know," she admits. "But I think if I leave it, its original owner should come back."

I sigh. I'm so frustrated, and let's be honest, I'm so angry. I didn't want any of this.

"Fine!" The word is out of my mouth before I realise that I'm yelling. I don't really even know where the sudden volume comes from. Maybe it's just that, once again, the course of my own life is being decided by someone else. "You know what – fine! Call her – call the police, tell them where I am, send me back there. Do whatever you fucking want, Maeve!"

I'm tired of being kind. I'm tired of being understanding. I can't believe that I've been lured out here like this. I feel like an animal caught in a hidden trap. Why does everyone always end up letting me down?

Maeve's face is set and determined, and to my surprise she shakes her head. "I'm not going to call her," she tells me quietly. I almost scoff aloud. Who does she think she's kidding? Why would she be brandishing the number aloft if she wasn't going to call it?

But somehow – I don't know how the fuck she's done it – somehow I believe her. Where my voice was loud and brash, hers is small, secure and calm; where I have just been poking holes, she seems to know exactly what she's doing. I don't believe she's lying to me. For some reason, this time, I'm sure that she means exactly what she's saying.

"I'm not going to call her," she repeats, a steely look in her eye. "You are."

What?

It takes a few seconds before my brain computes exactly what she's said. I feel my face furrow into a frown. What is she talking about? Why would I ever agree to ring a police officer? As soon as the police know where I am, I have to go straight back to the hospital. Why would I turn myself in? Even if I *was* going to keep myself safe tonight, calling the police officer would only shorten my run of freedom.

"No way," I answer instantly. "Of course I'm not."

Maeve smiles again. "Yes," she says firmly. "You are."

She folds her arms stubbornly. "Look," she says, watching me carefully. "You're right. I could call her and tell her where you are, and she'll take you back to the hospital. If she even catches you before you hurt yourself somehow. What would be the point?"

I nod, a little surprised that she seems to be on the same wavelength as me. "Exactly," I say slowly.

Maeve fixes me with a determined look. "But this body hasn't done anything wrong. I know you, Heather. You don't want me to hurt this body, either."

She's speaking with the air of a poker player holding an ace. I sigh. I'm too tired to do anything but follow whatever she's laying down in front of me. "No, I don't," I admit exhaustedly.

"So we're at a stalemate," she continues. "If I call them, you run; if you run from me, then I'll call them. We're trapped here together."

"Along with some random girl's body," I mutter to myself.

To my surprise, Maeve smirks. "Exactly."

I bristle. "I'm glad this is funny to you, Maeve—" I begin, but she is shaking her head.

"I don't think it's funny," she replies, in a voice that I think is meant to mollify me. All it achieves is to remind me just how young she actually is. "I was just... well, now you see why you have to call them."

The exhaustion that has been creeping up on me finally hits. I don't know why it's taken this long, but I suddenly feel like I can't stand any longer. I half-collapse back down to sitting, leaning my head back so I'm looking at the stars. For a minute I feel slightly calmer, until I quickly force myself back to reality, looking back at Maeve. I didn't realise someone could look so sad whilst being absolutely sure that they had the upper hand.

"Explain, then," I say tiredly. "Tell me why I have to call them."

I'm not surprised when she drops down too, kneeling in front of me and watching me with keen eyes. She once again looks earnest. For a moment I try and remember if I cared so much when I was Maeve's age. Well – when I was Maeve *full stop*, I suppose.

That's a scary thought. I'm almost glad when she speaks and I have to focus back on that. "You can call them and tell them the truth," she says earnestly. "Most of it, anyway. Tell her you saw a light up here so you followed it. But then when you got down here, it was me and I'd started a fire. So you put it out but now you're out here and I'm threatening to jump and you find the card in my pocket—"

I can't listen to this. "What does that solve?" I ask heavily.

Maeve holds my eye contact intensely. "Because you're ending tonight by saving my life, not by ending yours."

This hits home.

"I'm not sure I even want to put you through the last few years, Maeve," I begin, but Maeve cuts in again.

"But you know I'll survive it," she bursts out earnestly. "You *know* I will. You did."

I sigh. "Maeve, I just…" I trail off. "I know you're trying to help. I know you are. But what's to stop me climbing the fence again tomorrow?"

She smiles sadly. "You said it yourself. They're going to be supporting you more, now that this has happened. And you're going to take the help. Because this time, you're taking the help for me."

"That's a technicality," I protest, but I know before she speaks again that she's right.

"Heather, you've spent the whole of tonight putting me first," she points out, her voice gentle. "You've tried to help me, and you've protected me. Keep doing that. Please. Keep doing it for me."

Of course, she's right. The part of me that has been so determined to stop Maeve getting hurt… that's the part of me I need to harness. Christ, I don't know how I'm going to explain any of this to Katy without coming across as even more of a nutter, but for some reason, Maeve is painfully right.

There's a long silence as she continues to watch me, and I try my best to keep myself together. Finally, I nod silently.

"Thank you," she says in a tiny, soft voice. "Thank you, Heather."

I turn away from her, looking out to sea again. The sun is starting to rise. Everything is bathed in light now, and I can't decide if I'm more or less afraid from being able to see my surroundings properly. I'm sure it makes our position less dangerous, granted, but it's more that I no longer feel like I'm somewhere isolated. I feel more part of the world, now.

"Does it stop?" Maeve asks suddenly.

I frown, surprised, shaken out of my reverie. "Does *what* stop?" I reply reluctantly.

Maeve looks down at her lap. "You know," she says quietly.

For a brief second, I'm not sure what to say, or what to think; why would I be asking if I already knew? But as soon as I think about it, I realise that Maeve is right. I know. I've known all along. All these suspicions, that I've had all night, about Maeve being hurt... I know why I've been having them. And I know what's happened to Maeve.

I take a deep breath in. I think, after everything that's happened, I need to talk about this with her. "Kind of," I tell her, hesitantly but honestly. "It's not necessarily better, but... yes. It stops."

Maeve nods quickly. I can tell that this is a relief to her. Maybe she was expecting that, when she got to ask me, I would be able to tell her that everything gets better; I haven't been able to do that, but at least I'm able to tell her that some things die down. For want of a better word.

There's a question I need to ask her too, though – because she's the only one who I think will be able to answer me. "Maeve?" I ask, after a minute.

She looks up at me expectantly. Is it my imagination that I feel like I suddenly recognise her expression from younger photos of me?

My breath catches in my throat and I force myself to take a breath. "Your neck – well, her neck...?" I say at last. I'm aware it's not a sentence, but it's the best I can muster.

"I don't know," she says sadly. "I didn't even know about it before you pointed it out."

I sigh. Maybe the person really in danger tonight was the girl in the forest.

I know that's going to weigh on my mind, but right now I haven't worked out how I'm going to fix that situation. It's taken all night just to work out me and Maeve. I guess I'll have to carry on thinking about the girl. Granted, I might never come up with anything – I guess I just have to try.

I look outwards again, towards the sea. It really is a nice view from here. I hope this pier opens again one day. Right now, though, it is kind of emphasising just how much I don't want to go back to staring at four walls yet.

"Do you think…" I begin, not turning to look at Maeve. "Do you think she… like what happened to us?"

She sighs. "Yeah. I think. I mean, I don't know. But I think so. I think it would be too much of a coincidence, for her to have bruises like these…"

I can't look at her. "Occam's razor," I summarise, looking out towards the sea instead. "If it seems like someone's dad is hitting them…"

"And their mum is trying to cover it up?" finishes Maeve hollowly. "Yeah. It's probably true."

I don't know what to say to that. Maeve has summed it up better than I could. Part of me wants to tell Maeve to tell Mrs Fletcher the truth when she asks – yet I can't even be sure that doing that would make things any better for either of us. What's happened to get us up to this point hasn't been great, I know, but I'm not about to start messing with it. It's happened now. I don't know what good it would do to start messing with it.

I'm still looking out to sea. I don't want to leave things like this. With a deep breath, I look back over at Maeve. This is the last time I'm going to see her; I know that.

"Can we sit here a while?" I ask quietly.

Maeve nods. "Yeah," she says calmly, though her small smile looks forced. "We can sit a while."

I'm not surprised when her hand snakes out towards mine and rests on top of it. For a moment, we sit in silence, clutching on to each other. It's picturesque, here. If this is my last moment of freedom for a while, at least it's a quiet one. I sit with Maeve, and I rest.

28

At first on the adult ward, I try to force myself out of my bedroom for a little bit of time each day.

I tell myself firmly that I'm never going to settle in if I stay in my bedroom all the time. Yes, most of the patients are far older than me (I think the lady closest in age to me is thirty-two years old), but they are probably nice people. Is it that different, talking to them, than it was talking to patients on the adolescent ward? Some of them were only thirteen or fourteen – there must have been a maturity gap there. It's going to be fine eventually; it's just going to take some work on my side.

I am convinced of this, so I watch films with others in the lounge and I join in games of bingo (could there be more ironic of a cliché?). On days that feel harder, I bring bits of my art stuff downstairs and work on it at the dining-room table. At least I'm staring at four different walls, I tell myself. But, honestly, I'm not sure it's helping. My total friend count is still resolutely zero.

The only time out of my room that I genuinely enjoy is time with the therapists. Not the psychology, look-into-your-childhood therapists, but rather the activity therapists, who let me participate in cooking meals and help me get my A-level work underway and take me to the library to pick up reading material to pass the time. These few hours doing things like this are definitely the best hours I spend outside of my bedroom. Without these, I'm not sure how I'd be.

In fairness to the psychology therapists, though, I do also like the lady who's been assigned to me. Her name is Katy. She's pretty young, which has to make it easier to talk to her. And she's definitely got the proper qualifications to be a psychologist; I know this because I Googled her and read some of her doctorate thesis. For some reason, she seemed to think it was slightly hilarious that I had done this. More than anything, I think she just hadn't expected it.

I'm not sure if I trust her yet. She seems nice, and friendly, and like she is the kind to listen; but I don't know her yet. I am adopting a drip-feeding approach; I'm telling her a few small things first, as a test. If she reacts helpfully to these small things, maybe I'll tell her some bigger ones.

Maybe I'll tell her why we crashed.

I don't need to adopt this approach with the nursing staff, though – primarily because our relationship quickly becomes one of a mutual intense dislike. They are not like Claudie here. I'm 'difficult' in their books – and I find them patronising and kind of snarky. There is literally not one of them that I get along with enough to trust them properly.

This does not make it easier to force myself out of my room, admittedly, and I start to retreat more and more. I speak to Katy on an appointment basis, and the activity therapists will generally pop up to see me if there's something I can join in with. The rest of the time, I find myself occupying myself in my room. I'm not sure how this sneaks up on me in the way that it does; it just one day becomes apparent that I can't physically force myself to play any more bingo. It isn't even working. I don't feel more comfortable, I'm not making friends. Why the fuck am I bothering?

When I hit this thought, the art at the dining-room table stops pretty quickly too, because that's helping even less. No one wants to talk to me. Not, I think, because of any malice; probably not even consciously. I think it's my fault. I panic so much when someone does talk to me that it's probably easier for everyone when they stay silent with me.

And, besides – what do we have in common? Fuck all, that's what. The age gap is a massive part of it, but even with that aside, there isn't anyone here that I feel could be a friend given a bit of time. I'm alone here.

And I'm isolated, too – because that unescorted leave, that I was promised all adults get, is nowhere in sight. I'm not even self-harming, as far as they know; obviously, I'm still doing it in secret, but the doctors don't know this. They are just refusing me unescorted leave because apparently I'm not 'engaging' and talking with the nursing staff. This frustrates me. I don't want to talk to the nursing staff. I don't get on with the nursing staff. How is that anything to do with my mental state?

I do point this out to them but it doesn't really seem to convince anyone. Even Katy, who I believe is advocating for me in her own way in staff meetings, doesn't seem to think that I'm doing as I should.

It's hard, though, because I'm aware that the more time I spend in my room on my own, no matter what I'm doing – well, the more depressed I get. It's probably visible to them, and that's why they're worried to let me out. I should give them some credit, there, I suppose; but I don't know what they're expecting to change by just keeping me here.

I see my parents, twice a week. Aside from cooking and going to the library with the activity coordinators, that is the extent of my social schedule.

I don't understand how anyone is supposed to feel well when this is their life.

I'm angry, and I'm frustrated, and I'm sad. Amelie has left for uni; she phones me once to ask me how to use a washing machine. We laugh, and I miss her. I'm not sure if she misses me. After a while, she stops calling.

I video chat with Flick, even to the point of getting quite close with her, which does alleviate the loneliness a bit. But it's the same as with Amelie. As close as we all were at Christmas... well, six months later, and we continue to drift apart exponentially. When I first arrived here, all of us from the adolescent ward were still all embroiled in each other's dramas. Now? For everyone else, at least, real life starts to overtake hospital life.

It must be me. Right? It must be me. That's why no one wants anything to do with me anymore. That's why no one wants to stay. It's because there's something wrong with me.

Zoe never made me feel like there was something wrong with me.

I can't keep going over this.

Every time I meet a new staff member, I hope that my EUPD will do its thing and make them my new favourite person. That's all it was, with Zoe, right? Imbalanced brain chemicals and shit? They can't have been real, all those things that I felt for her. It must just be chemicals. I didn't know her. My chest shouldn't be hurting like I've been stabbed with a rusty fucking screwdriver.

For whatever reason, though, my EUPD won't oblige and just pick someone else. Maybe it's just being contrary, but for whatever reason, it just won't do it. I can't understand why. I need it to pick someone else. I need to feel the highs! I can't keep feeling all the lows for the rest of my life, without Zoe. That's the only thing that I can be sure of. That Zoe isn't coming back. Ever. I'm never going to see Zoe again.

This affects me so profoundly that I end up mentioning it to Katy. I can't not mention it – when Katy and I start to do a timeline of my life, and we reach the hospital section, it wouldn't be right to not mention Zoe. She has been such a big part of my life since I was sixteen.

I'm not a hundred per cent sure that Katy fully understands what my feelings for Zoe are. But I think she understands how sad it makes me that she's not with me anymore.

I guess that is something, but without anything else to grip onto, I can feel myself quickly slipping. I am getting sadder and sadder. How I felt on the bridge, how I felt at first in hospital, how I felt for all that time in school... it's all coming back. This time, though, I don't know how anyone is going to save me. I'm already on a locked ward. What can anyone do?

I sleep a lot. I'm napping in the day and crawling into bed before 10pm, the TV still on just in case my brain wants to think about anything that isn't 8 Out of 10 Cats Does Countdown *as I fall asleep. I can't think about everything that's happened to get to this point. It's not even self-preservation as it might have been in the past. Now, it's just... all I can do. I physically don't know what will happen if I think about it.*

It's probably ironic that they think I can't be trusted to go out alone in case I hurt myself, but they leave me alone in my room all day to hurt myself instead. I should be angrier about this, I think. Right now, it doesn't feel like I've got the energy to care about anything at all.

The one thing that I do have the energy to think about, though, is getting out. Not in a positive, let's-beat-my-mental-health way – in a what's-the-best-way-to-jump-the-fence kind of way. I can't keep doing this. I'm so tired. And even though I complain that the staff haven't got a fucking clue what I do in my room all day, I do know that there isn't anything here that I can actually end my life with. There's nothing high enough to hang myself off, nothing sharp enough to slit my wrists deep enough. This is purgatory.

I hate that I'm back to this. I thought I had done my time. I thought... I thought that missing my eighteenth birthday, being at least a year behind my friends in getting to uni – I thought that all of that was an exchange for me being better. *For me being* recovered. *Now it feels like I went through it all just to end up back at square one.*

There are no patients here who would miss me. The staff don't like me. Amelie has made new friends at uni. My hospital friends are back in their proper lives. And my parents? My parents can do without driving to Weston-super-Mare twice a week. If now's not the time, I don't know when is.

Katy knocks on my door one afternoon as I'm lying sleeplessly on my bed, pretending to read. I do this a lot. It satisfies the nursing staff because they can look through the window in my door and see I'm not dead without having to interact with me in any way at all.

(I'm being unfair, I know. But right now, I don't feel like being very fair to the people keeping me here.)

I sit up properly on my bed as Katy slowly pushes my door open, carrying a stack of print-outs that I suspect she wants me to read. As always, she looks immaculate, straightened hair swishing over her shoulder and nails perfectly manicured. She is smiling at me as she comes in; but it isn't long before the smile falters. She tilts her head, frowning at me.

"Are you OK?" she asks, clearly concerned. "You look..."

She doesn't finish the sentence but I'm already shaking my head. "I'm fine, I'm fine," I tell her quickly. It's easier this way. It's easier that I just lie.

She's still frowning a bit, though, as she looks at me. I can tell that she knows there is something I'm not telling her. She tilts her head slightly as she sits down on the edge of the bed. I can tell that she wants to ask more questions; but maybe she's not sure what kind of response she's going to get. Her eyes flick around my room instead; it's not exactly tidy. Still, she doesn't mention the mess as her eyes land instead on the half-finished piece of art on my bedroom floor.

"How's your homework going?" Katy asks, her tone light.

She's allowed to ask, I guess – the artwork was a therapy assignment from her. Last session, she brought me this huge piece of paper and told me to draw how I see things. Like the model student I am, I have already made a dent in it, two days later.

"Good," I tell her, relieved I don't have to lie. "I like doing things like this."

Katy smiles. "I'm glad," she says mildly. For a minute, we stay quiet as she continues to look at the picture. Suddenly, her eye lands on something, and she glances back at me, a little hesitantly.

"Is that the crash?" she asks, her voice still gentle but much more tentative.

I look away, breaking eye contact. I don't really know why I put that part of the drawing on. I am just spending so much of my time frustrated, and upset – and I don't know how to deal with it. I know, though, that I can't talk to her. Not about this.

"Yes," I answer shortly, still looking at the carpet.

I hear a small breath huff out from Katy. Clearly, she's trying to think of the best way to coax what I'm feeling out of me. And, clearly, she knows that she's going to have to do it very delicately.

Her head is still tilted at me. "I know... you mentioned... that there was a reason for the crash," she asks softly. "Is it... have you drawn it here?"

I feel her eyes on my face as I continue to stare down at the carpet. This is the last thing I want to have a discussion about. I don't know how to have a discussion about it. Every time I think about it – my stomach lurches as I remember the few minutes before the crash. The conversation that was meant to be light-hearted, suddenly taking a turn...

I shake my head at Katy, my eyes dropping to my lap. "No," I say quietly.

I sound oddly calm considering the fact that even the thought of what happened is making my heart pound in my chest. I don't want to talk about it. I don't want to admit that I nearly annihilated my own family, just because I was selfish enough to want to...

Katy is watching me closely. "You know you can tell me anything," she says, her own voice quiet.

I shake my head again. I can't tell her. I don't want to tell her.

That day, I had it all mapped out. It had taken so many hours of research to actually come up with a viable option; as bad as

I felt at home, I knew running away just to end up sleeping on the streets wasn't the right thing to do. What would that have even achieved? In any case, I had started Googling. At first, it was almost casual – just to see, just to imagine – but then I had realised that maybe I had options after all. I felt fucking miserable, and something had to give.

When my parents were out, I started to practice for the exercise test that I would need to pass to get into the army. I knew I was so unathletic that a sudden interest in running and endurance would be highly suspicious. I didn't want anyone to suspect what I was going to do. I didn't want to give anyone a chance to stop me.

The application form was filled in and ready to send. I'd never had a job before so I couldn't provide a reference, but I hoped that when it came to it, I could persuade one of my teachers to write me something. Not that they would understand why I was doing this. They hadn't heard me screaming and I could see why this move of mine would be hard to understand.

We had been to the cinema, the night of the crash. At this point, I was avoiding going anywhere with my parents, since it tended to end in an argument. Besides, there were few places that they wanted to go that I would want to go to as well. The cinema was one of the very few neutral-ish grounds that we could go to together. Our relationship wasn't great, but to be fair, we did have similar tastes in media.

And it had gone OK, actually. Maybe it was because you're not allowed to talk in the cinema, but we hadn't gotten into an argument. My overriding memory of the night isn't the film – I can't even remember which film we'd been to see – and I barely even remember sitting in the cinema. I don't really remember walking back to the car, or getting into it, or discussing what we were having for tea. All of that is foggy.

What I do remember… well, once we were in the car and there wasn't a film playing, the conversation turned very sour, very quickly. It was a depressingly familiar situation. If my parents weren't shouting at each other, they would generally be shouting at me. This was... well, just one of the reasons that I wanted to leave. I hated living on eggshells.

It was at each other, that particular night. I can't remember what the problem was. But finally I reached boiling point. I was tired of not mattering; I was tired of being an afterthought. I was fucking tired of always being wrong. Having to keep everything that was happening silent was too exhausting; though they said it was for my sake, it was just too much effort. For once, I just wanted to let something out.

And when I burst out with the fact that I had been hiding from them so carefully – when I told them that they had lost me – when I told them I was leaving...

"No," my dad said harshly. "You're not doing that."

I steeled myself, forcing myself not to look away. This was my choice. For the first time, I was determined to stand up for myself. "It's all organised," I told him, firmly, making sure that my voice was no softer than his. As an adult, he had to be able to handle it.

"That's ridiculous," my mum cut in. "Your dad's right."

I narrowed my eyes. "Now – now – my dad's right? When was the last time you agreed on anything?!"

Ironically, they both huffed in unison.

This was not going how I planned. "I've got to get away," I said sharply, my temper piqued even though I had promised myself that I would stay calm. "I can't take this!"

I was being honest, more so than I had been in a very long time. It was frustrating that the anger coursing through me was making it hard to make strong, well-backed-up, salient points. All I wanted was to make them listen.

"I'm not safe, like this," I carried on – quickly, to my own frustration, becoming hysterical. "I'm done!"

And I was panicking – but I was telling the truth. I was done. I had officially checked out.

I reached out my arm to open the car door onto the road...

My mum saw, and cried out...
My dad automatically spun around in the driver's seat...
Then he lost control of the car.

Even now, even thinking of it now, I can't shake the solid guilt that rests on my chest. It was my fault. It was my fault. As we rolled down that bank, the car colliding with earth and trees, and I screamed – I knew from that moment that the crash was my fault. If anyone had been hurt...

And since no one was, since somehow we all survived – well, I knew that I had to drop the idea. I had to do what they wanted. The universe wanted me to do what they wanted. I didn't want anyone else to get hurt because of me.

It is from this that I know I deserve to suffer.

I deleted the application. I let my newfound fitness melt away by staying in and eating Oreos every weekend. My dad has never mentioned it since. I don't even know if my mum remembers, since she got so concussed in the accident. I think the fact that the subject has been so taboo has made it even harder to admit to anyone.

They knew why I wanted to leave. Even if they wouldn't admit it – even if we never spoke about it again – they knew why. I suppose it acted like a reset button, in some ways. Things started to slowly taper off after that. Not exactly better, but calmer. Maybe because I finally realised that it was my fault – maybe because I knew that they had won.

We don't fight, now. I stay quiet. It must have been my fault all along.

I suppose this should have made me feel less like I was drowning; less like I needed to scream. But even though I wasn't being hurt anymore, somehow my head just didn't want to remember that I wasn't supposed to be miserable.

I'm roused from my thoughts about this when I realise that Katy is still watching me, even as I stare at the carpet. Her gaze is sympathetic, but I'm not ready to talk to her. I don't think that I ever will be. It's too late, now. All I want to do is sleep.

I don't say anything; I just shake my head. There's no point in explaining, now.

"Right," says Katy eventually, looking unsatisfied and perhaps a little worried. "Well, I just came up here to drop off these handouts. Can you have a read before our next session?"

I'm relieved that we've changed the subject, so much so that I even manage to look up at Katy properly. I nod. It's hard whenever Katy brings up our next session; recently, I feel like I can't promise her that I'm going to be still here for it. But I can't tell Katy that without really worrying her, and I don't want her to be upset.

"I'll read them," I add, able to hear the listlessness in my own voice. If I don't want to worry Katy, then I need to avoid talking as much as I can.

Unsurprisingly, there's a little frown on Katy's face, now. "Right," she says again. "Thank you. We'll talk in a few days, then. Yeah?"

I nod again. Katy has tried her best. I'm sorry that I keep letting her down.

29

I sit with PC Baker in a cubicle at A&E. I'm plonked on the bed, with the police officer sat in the visitor's chair. Maeve's body – I still don't know her name – is in Resus, being worked on by the doctors. Since I've come from a psychiatric hospital, they don't believe that I'm not hurt, and they've taken my bloods to make sure I haven't overdosed or anything else that I haven't told them about.

"Is she going to be OK?" I ask quietly.

PC Baker turns to look at me. She regards me steadily for a moment before she answers. "Well, it looks like she's taken something," she tells me with a frown. "So if you can tell us what that was…"

I look down at my lap. "I told you," I say firmly. "I literally only just met her. I found her about to jump and I called you guys."

"Hmm." I can tell immediately that PC Baker doesn't believe me. She thinks we've been sat on the end of Birnbeck Pier all night doing coke or something. Even though they've already tested my urine and I'm negative for everything.

They had to get a boat out to us from the Coast Guard, in the end; apparently it wouldn't have been safe for someone to walk down the pier to get to us. In fairness, that made sense. The fact that I made it down there can only be attributed to pure luck. I can't quite forget the moment when my foot went straight through the rotten wood.

The Coast Guard guy did have to climb up onto the island to carry Maeve down to the boat, though. Well, I say Maeve; I feel quite convinced that there was nothing of Maeve in that body by that point. She had lit up and gone.

PC Baker leans forwards. "What I'm struggling with," she says, in a calm voice, her eyes resting on mine, "is why you climbed all the way down a rotten pier to save someone who you'd never met, and who you didn't know needed saving."

This is a very good point, but I try not to be fazed. "I thought it would be a good place to hide," I lie quickly. "I saw the light down there so I thought I would just go along and see who it was and then I could just stay there. And the hospital wouldn't find me."

She looks at me impassively. "But when you got to the island, the young lady was about to jump."

"*Yes*," I say emphatically. We've been over this part of the story before; and with the amount of true crime documentaries I've fallen asleep to in the last few months, I know that the thing that makes you look guiltiest is changing your story.

"Hmm," says PC Baker again. "And she wouldn't tell you her name, or anything? How she got there?"

I shake my head. "I told you," I say stubbornly. "I grabbed her and pulled her back and she passed out."

Admittedly, neither Maeve nor I have thought out this part of the story very well. It's hard to explain why someone would randomly pass out cold just from being dragged away from the edge of a wooden pier. Maybe it's not such a bad thing that the police think drugs are involved. I don't know what on Earth is going to show up on the girl's toxicology screen, but maybe it wouldn't be so bad if it showed something. Oddly enough, I don't think there's a test they can do to check if someone else's soul has been inhabiting your body.

"Your card was in her pocket," I add, for good measure. "I didn't know who else to call."

PC Baker sighs, but I suspect she is running out of questions. None of this makes any sense, but is there actually anything she can ask to prove I'm lying?

"They should have your bloods back soon," she says instead. "Then we can think about transporting you back home."

I huff slightly before I can stop myself. "It's not home," I say quietly.

PC Baker tilts her head. "No, I'm sure it isn't," she says, a little surprised, a little more gently. "But running away isn't going to help that."

"I didn't hurt myself," I point out, finally looking back up at the police officer. I feel like this is a point that has gotten slightly lost in the drama of tonight.

She shrugs her shoulders as a way of agreeing with me. "That's true," she says slowly. "But… if you hadn't found the young lady…?"

It's almost ironic – PC Baker definitely doesn't realise exactly what she's asking. It's hard to know how to answer. "I don't know," I say finally, though I do.

"Alright," she says, clearly deciding not to push the point. I guess she can't prove anything either way. "Well, I'm sure the hospital will be glad to have you safely back."

I shrug with a little sigh. "Maybe."

I can tell that she knows I'm not convinced. She shifts in the chair, stretching. "How you've managed to get involved of all of this in an hour, I don't know," she half-mutters, but there's a small smile on her face. I think she likes the real person Heather more than the mentally-ill-troublemaker Heather that I'm sure the hospital has described to her.

There's one part of her sentence that just doesn't make sense, though. "In an hour?" I ask with a frown.

PC Baker frowns right back at me. "Yeah," she says, looking

confused as to what I'm asking. "It's what, 4am, now? Your hospital rang about ten to three. Said you'd been gone fifteen minutes."

It's a physical effort not to roll my eyes. It really took that long for them to notice. It's frustrating – if tonight was meant to matter, if tonight was meant to be a point of change, why am I now finding out that it took five hours for the nursing staff to even notice I was gone? If I'm meant to be getting better, shouldn't the hospital be looking like a good place to go back to right now? Maybe – I guess it was never going to be perfect.

For a moment, I waver over whether or not to tell PC Baker how long I've really been gone. But then I decide that if I'm making a new start, it has to be made on honesty. I shake my head. "I climbed over the fence about half nine," I correct her, a little hesitantly, with my tone one of admission. I can't help but feel guilty that I might be dropping the staff in it (even if my head is incredulously repeating – *five bloody hours?! What were they doing?!*).

PC Baker stares at me for a minute before she leans her head back against the wall. She mouths something that looks like a swear word, and sighs deeply. "Are you serious?" she asks in a low voice, clearly deeply frustrated.

I nod, a small apologetic smile on my face. "Sorry," I add helplessly.

She sighs again. "It's not your fault, love," she replies, more gently.

But then something seems to occur to her. She turns to me, still frowning. "What did you do for the first four hours?"

I shift around on the bed to avoid answering for a minute. "Walked around," I say evasively at last. "Had a cider. Sat on the beach."

I notice her glance down at the sand all over my jeans, the remnants of my walk on the beach earlier. At least that confirms my story. And, of course, why would I lie?

She stays silent for a minute. "Why did you run away in the first place?" she asks at last.

I swallow. This is a question I really didn't want to have to answer. There's no adventure, no crazy night with Maeve, to lie for in this. There's just a lot of pain, that in truth I don't want to look at just yet.

But PC Baker is sitting, waiting for an answer. Maybe I'm never going to want to address this. But right now, I have someone's attention, and she isn't going anywhere. This is supposed to be a new start, after all.

I look down at my lap. "I wanted to die," I tell her honestly, even as I feel tears start to threaten to fall. For a second, the sentence hangs heavily in the air between us. When I finally look up, PC Baker is watching me with an expression that I can't quite read.

"I'd like to come and see you," she says suddenly. "In a week or two. To make sure the hospital is… acting more professionally."

This isn't the reaction I expected, and I can't think what to say, so I nod quickly. In all honesty, I'm touched, and my heart hurts a little bit.

"Thank you," I reply quietly, but I hold her gaze in an attempt to try and make it clear exactly what I mean. She smiles, a little sadly, and nods again. She gets me.

The next few moments pass in silence, with PC Baker looking down at her boots, maybe a little self-conscious. When my own eyes stray down to her feet, I suddenly remember that I sat under a table earlier, looking at those boots for what felt like an age. I'm not sure whether to smile or cry. Tonight has been weird.

Finally, a doctor pokes his head around the curtain. "Hello, Heather," he says. I cringe for a second that I've given them my real name. When I met PC Baker after coming out of the Coast Guard boat, I briefly considered giving a fake name, just to be able to stay away longer – if I was just a random passer-by, surely I would be free to just leave? – but in the end I was just too tired.

I smile politely and nod. I feel drained.

He returns the smile, looking between myself and PC Baker. "We've just had your blood results back," he says, calm doctor voice on. "Luckily they're all normal. I think your ward are on the way to collect you."

I sigh, deeply. I knew that this moment was coming, but that doesn't make it any easier. For most of tonight, the worst possible outcome has been going back to the hospital with nothing changed. Going back to being locked up and isolated in my room.

If the doctor doesn't notice the weariness in the sigh, PC Baker definitely does. Out of the corner of my eye, I see her expression soften slightly, and to my surprise, she leans over and pats my hand. Clearly this is not the part of her job that comes easiest to her, but it's touching that she's trying.

"Are you allowed to tell me what happens to that girl?" I ask quickly, not wanting to think about how depressed I feel right now.

She hesitates. "I don't think so," she says apologetically, and I'm not surprised. I have to remind myself that the girl is a stranger; she's not Maeve and she never was. How she ended up with Maeve inside her is anyone's guess. I highly doubt that anyone will be able to give me a satisfactory answer as to how tonight even happened. I have to just remember it, and know it was important.

I think of Maeve, and I think of Zoe, and I think of PC Baker. I think of Amelie and Mrs Fletcher. These moments with them are the things that are important; these moments are the reasons that I need to hold on to. Just because something is gone doesn't mean that it never mattered at all.

It occurs to me that in a few hours, Katy will come onto the ward to start her day at work and will hear about tonight. How on Earth am I going to explain all of this to her? I'm going to need to decide just how far my new honesty policy stretches.

But right now, I nod, and I give PC Baker the most genuine smile I can muster. It's not her fault. I've probably been a right headache for her the past hour, and she's responded very kindly, considering.

"Thank you, anyway," I tell her, and mean it.

PC Baker clears her throat. Have I embarrassed her a little bit? "That's alright," she adds quickly, maybe fronting it a bit. "I'm just glad we're getting you safely back to your ward."

I'm tempted to snort but I know that won't help. "I guess," I say tiredly.

She gives me a rueful smile. "I'll see you in a few weeks, yeah?"

I nod. When I speak, my voice is a little stronger. "Yeah," I confirm, holding her gaze. It can't hurt, I suppose, to have one more person truly fighting my corner.

*

I'm waiting in reception for a support worker from the ward to come and pick me up when my phone buzzes in my pocket.

I frown, surprised. It's barely gone 5am; who is going to be texting me right now? I assume quickly that it must be spam. But I still take my phone out of my pocket to check.

Unfortunately, at first I'm not particularly surprised; it's just a notification telling me that my phone has connected to the hospital Wi-Fi. Why it's suddenly done this now is beyond me, but so is most technology. I'm about to slide my phone back into my pocket when an idea pops into my head.

I tap in my passcode and open my phone. I haven't got long before the taxi arrives. My eyes scan over my collection of apps, the usual mix of Facebook and Instagram and Minion Rush. Then my eyes land on Pokémon Go.

I look to my other side – where, to my relief, I see a door for Resus. Where the girl is still being worked on. This is a long shot, a massive long shot – but as I open the little list at the side of the screen, that lists people nearby, I feel a rush of delight when I see that a few metres from me, there is a player called EmilyRose01. I click on the user profile; and, when I look at the profile picture, it's a picture of the girl whose body Maeve was in. PC Baker may not be able to give me updates on how this girl is, but…

I smile slightly down at my phone as I press 'add friend'.

30

Even when Katy leaves my bedroom, I still feel wired, thinking about the crash. Granted, I managed to shut down her questions pretty quickly – and as always, I don't think she wanted to push me for answers. I'm glad of it. Still, the topic of the conversation doesn't leave my mind.

I sit on my bed, holding my book half-heartedly, until I'm sure that Katy is back downstairs. When everything is perfectly still, I jump up to my feet, pacing agitatedly across the small space of my bedroom. I don't feel right. I don't know how I'm meant to settle.

I feel like I did on the day of the bridge. I feel adrift. If I could leave my books in my locker and waltz out of school again right now, I'd do it in a heartbeat.

It is clear to me what else I would do in a heartbeat right now.

Finally I force myself to sit down. I can't quite face the bed or even the uncomfortable desk chair, so I flop down on the floor, the side of my head resting on the wall. I didn't think I could be wired and exhausted at the same time, but somehow I've managed it. My feet twitch in agitation even as I can't face standing up from the floor.

I sit in silence for a long time, because I know the choice I'm about to make is a big one. It's a bigger choice even than the one I made to leave school and go to the bridge. Since then, I have lost people along the way. Too many people. I know how it feels to lose someone. And it's not good. The conviction that I had then, that I would just be forgotten, that I would just fade away... I know now that that's not true.

But, frankly – I don't know what else I'm supposed to do.

Therapy hasn't worked, being pumped full of pills hasn't worked. I don't know what else there is to try.

And the hope that I've been clinging on to, that the reason I'm so miserable right now is because of the isolation and loneliness and aimlessness, seems to be fading fast, too. Even if that's true, even if I would feel better with friends around – when is that ever going to happen? No one wants me. It's me that's the problem, not the place I'm in.

I can't say that I haven't been thinking about the best way to do this. And, I've concluded, the best time to jump the fence is in the night. All I have to do in the meantime is wait.

I kind of feel like I should be doing something meaningful. A note, maybe? Or just trying to feel something, anything that means something. Should I be re-reading all my letters? Looking at photos? But I'm not sure I can put myself through that. Even my leaving book, with Zoe's handwriting in, stays in its place. I don't want to touch it. I can't take anything else, right now.

Eventually, my twitching feet persuade my heavy body to move and I slowly stand up. Unsure what to do with myself, I pick up the TV remote and turn on the most mindless TV programme that I can find.

I don't bother to go down to dinner when the time comes. I stay put in my room and snack half-heartedly on the biscuits that my Nana sent me. I'd rather my last meal be custard creams than dodgy-smelling veggie stew.

I almost wish it was winter and that night would fall about 5pm – then I could get this over with and fucking run. But it's August, and the days are long right now. I am watching mindless

TV for hours before it's finally getting on 9pm, and the sky is dark.

I creep down the stairs, my phone in one pocket and a wodge of cash stuffed in the other, along with a few other things I might need. I don't know why I'm creeping; I'm allowed to go downstairs. Nay, I'm supposed to be going downstairs right now, to take my medication from the nurse. Often I come down at this time to have toast as well. What I'm doing right now is totally normal.

I smile dutifully at the few patients who I pass on the stairs and as I go along the hallway to the dining room. This is where the door to the garden is – and, thus, my gateway to freedom.

I'm hesitant, though, as I step into the dining room. To give myself a little time, I pour a splash of squash into a plastic cup and fill it up from the sink. I don't feel like I can't make the decision; that isn't what's making me hesitant. I'm not sure if it's anxiety that something will go wrong, or simply hesitancy because I know it's against the rules. Even if I get caught, what I'm about to do is going to change how things are now.

I think that thought is what finally propels me out of the dining room and into the garden. I can't stand things staying like this anymore.

Still, though, I'm not out of bounds, or even very far out of my usual routine. I can't deny that over the past few weeks, I have paced in the garden a lot. Sometimes just to not be indoors, but sometimes staking the place out. In the day, because of the big glass doors, I know that someone is bound to see you climbing over. In the dark, though? This shouldn't be a problem at all. Besides, all my stake-outs have highlighted for me the exact place where I will be the least visible.

I wait until there are no smokers around before I slip behind the summerhouse where the staff hold meetings. Most of it backs straight onto the fence, but there is a small corner where the edge of the building is angled in a way that means you can't see behind it in the kitchen or dining room. So it's here that I squeeze myself into.

I know I haven't got time to dawdle now, if I want to get away before any smokers come out – or worse, a staff member. This pushes me to act. I can't afford to wait. So, quickly, I grab the top of the fence and hoick myself up so that the upper edge of the fence digs into my belly. Here, my staking-out has been helpful again – because in this exact piece of fence, I know there is a little crack in the wood which is just big enough to wedge my foot in and act as a leg up.

Then finally I'm high enough that my hips come over the top edge of the fence and I can swing one leg over, and then the other, and I'm sat on the fence. For a brief second, I look back at the illuminated façade of the hospital. But I know, again, that there's no time for hesitation. Instead, I turn back towards the road, jump off the fence and begin to run.

31

When I see Katy the next morning, she immediately envelopes me in a tight hug.

I start slightly, taken a little bit by surprise. It's not unpleasant, though. I didn't think I would feel safe here again – being looked after by people who took five and a half hours to notice I had gone missing – yet still I find myself relaxing into Katy's hug. I feel a little awkward as I squeeze her back slightly, but I find that I don't want her to let go. It's not Katy's fault that things are shit.

Eventually, she releases me. For a moment, her hands stay on my shoulders, holding me at arm's length.

"I'm so glad you're OK," she says quickly, seriously. "I heard what happened last night."

I bite my lip. I can only hold her stare for a few seconds before I drop my gaze down to the floor. "I'm sorry," I say quietly. This time, I do mean it. Worrying Katy was never my intention. In truth, I hadn't imagined that she would care so much.

She shakes her head. "I'm not mad at you," she says, her eyes darting over to the nursing office. I think I can guess who Katy *is* mad at.

"But… you're mad at them?" I prompt, grimacing slightly. I wouldn't want to be on the other end of Katy's wrath, truth be told.

She huffs. When her eyes flick back to me, though, they are gentle again. I have to say, I'm relieved that she seems to know I haven't done this just to be a twat.

Still, I want to know what she's thinking. "Because of the five hours thing?" I venture a little cautiously.

A flash of anger passes over Katy's face. Clearly, I have hit the nail on the head. "Yes," she says firmly, a bite in her voice. Although I've seen Katy pissed off before, I've never seen her angry like this. "They failed you, Heather," she adds vehemently.

It's my turn to shake my head. "It's alright," I say with a little shrug. "I shouldn't have jumped the fence."

Katy sighs. "Well... it's not something I'd like you to do again," she admits. "But we're here to protect you while you're still having these thoughts of harming yourself. It shouldn't have happened."

Maybe Katy's right, but I have difficulty feeling too upset about the situation. I mean, I'm frustrated, and it hasn't exactly helped me place trust in the staff members here, but I'm not angry. If anything, I feel a little guilty. I overheard a staff member say this morning that the nurse who was in charge last night has been suspended now. I guess that's kind of my fault.

But I do have to acknowledge – last night could have gone very differently. If Maeve hadn't appeared... I would probably be dead by now. At the very least, I would be badly hurt. Maybe I did need protecting.

I can tell from Katy's expression that she's thinking the same thing. That she nearly lost me. There's a weighty feeling in my chest that I've made her feel like this. I really thought... I really thought that it would just be losing another patient. But as I'm looking at her now... I know that she genuinely doesn't want to lose me.

"Yeah, it shouldn't have," I concede, feeling slightly choked. I have to quickly shut myself up and look away; I don't want to start crying in the corridor right now.

Katy lets go of my shoulders, looking at me with a sad expression. "Shall we go and talk properly?" she says, her voice more gentle now. "About what's going on?"

I find myself nodding, and with a small smile, Katy leads me into the Quiet Room to talk.

About the Author

Born in Bath, I have been writing creatively for most of my life, beginning with a fanfiction novel that I started at age eleven. I continued to be passionate about writing throughout school, then going on to complete a creative writing course with the National Extension College and a CertHE in Film and Literature with the University of the West of England. I have been published in Rife magazine, where I wrote an article describing my transition back to the community after several years in psychiatric hospital. Like Heather, I was first admitted to hospital at a young age and at eighteen moved from adolescent services to an adult ward. Although *When The Lonely Walk* is largely fictional, some of my real life experiences have made it into the novel and informed the feelings that Heather has about her own experience. This element, I feel, gives the novel a veracity that might not be found were it to have been written from a fully fictional standpoint.

Currently, I am working in a call centre for a healthcare charity whilst finishing my degree in Health and Social Care at the University of the West of England. I live in a village within Bristol with my fiancée.